WAR GOLEM

J. A. Giunta

Brick Cave Media
brickcavebooks.com
2019

Cover Illustration by Kyna Tek www.kyteki.com
Interior Illustrations by Kyna Tek www.kyteki.com

Brick Cave Media
brickcavebooks.com
2019

FOR CLIFF FARACI

I HOPE THE ANTICS WITHIN THESE PAGES GIVE YOU A
CHUCKLE OR TWO AND REMIND YOU OF ALL THE TIMES WHEN
WE ADVENTURED WITH PEN AND PAPER.

--J.A. GIUNTA

War Golem

J. A. Giunta

Brick Cave Media
brickcavebooks.com

Grizzletongue stood upon the stone platform, waving his staff over the cauldron. Fire blazed from beneath it, bubbling its contents into a steaming black morass. The smell was nearly perfect, a touch short of troll bile with the bite of a wyvern's liver. He studied the brew with his good eye, took note of each bubble's size before it burst across the surface.

"Another," he rasped to the red beside him.

The red goblin snatched up a nearby gray and tossed it in the mix. The screech of dying was short lived, and a plume of essence wafted upward. The lumpy bits of flesh and bones melted into the concoction, became one with the tarry liquid and left its surface like the skin of a newborn gnoll.

"Excellent!" Griz laughed, and the goblin host joined in. Their cackles echoed throughout the halls of the dark and broken castle, shook its crumbling stones until a shower of dust rained down from the shattered rafters. "The spell is all but complete."

He glanced at the war golem towering behind him, a massive iron body bound by enchantment and the skill of a hundred goblin craftsmen. It was the peak of their ingenuity, colossal proof of their expertise, a monument for the clans and a beacon for all to follow. For the moment, it was but a shell. Soon it would march forth and every kingdom tremble at its approach.

"Bring him," the shaman ordered.

With poles at each limb, the boy was lifted over the cauldron by four reds in war regalia. He had slumbered through the summoning. His clothing was strange and marked in a foreign language no magic could divine. He was pink and fleshy, typical of his people. It disappointed Grizzletongue to think that a human spirit would inhabit their greatest weapon, but he took comfort in knowing it was no ordinary soul.

"The most evil," Griz began, and the host cheered on with glee, "vile, heinous creature that ever lived! With a bloodthirst to rival the greatest Arch Demon! A soul so black its only joy is in murder and destruction! This," Griz shouted and raised his staff high, "is what we shall unleash upon the world!"

Rocks shook loose from the raucous cheering and crushed grays into paste. Still the laughter ensued, the thumping of iron boots, the clashing of sword and shield, until Grizzletongue ended it all with a swift flick of his dirty nail at the boy's neck. Silence fell over them, as the human body was drained of its blood and essence. When it was pale and empty, the reds tossed it aside and stood with their brethren in hushed anticipation.

Grizzletongue faced the war golem, searching for any sign the spell had worked. Whispers erupted from behind when no movement could be detected. The shuffling feet and murmurs of dissatisfaction began to grow louder.

The golem's eyes lit up and glowed, red as a bloody sunset.

Its hand twitched, the slightest of movements, but it was enough. Grizzletongue knew. His spell was a success. The golem turned its head, looked out over the gathered host, down at the shaman who gave it life, and opened its mouth to speak. Its voice echoed with hollow dread, as if death itself had spoken—three simple words that rang throughout the hall.

"What. The. Fuck."

* * *

Eric looked down at the iron hands and flexed them. Strange symbols were etched in perfect rows across every surface, wrapped around each finger, wrist and arm. No space was left unmarked. They gave off a silver light and thrummed like a heartbeat.

Unable to close his eyes, he looked out at the mass of tiny creatures staring back. Tapered ears, scarred from battle, wide eyes and sharp teeth, they varied in color but all looked like exaggerated gremlins from a movie. They wore armor, carried weapons, and beyond the crisp physicality of their presence, Eric saw their lives as a crimson glow with argent charges all throughout.

The one in front of him was old, much more so than the others. His life glow paled in comparison and the little bolts far less frequent. It spoke, but the words were distant, muffled by distraction.

Eric fought with the strangeness that enveloped his senses. He felt an overwhelming hunger, as if his body was completely empty. The urge to sate it filled his mind, clouded every thought, and clawed at his insides with a growing pain that would not relent. He more sensed than heard the wind outside the stone walls, as if the sound echoed through him from all sides. Insects scrabbling over dirt, moisture dripping from a cracked shutter, dust falling from the rafters, but most of all the scrape of coursing blood through veins and squishy organs resonated in the air like a cacophony of sounds.

He saw it then, at the corner of his vision, his own body lying still. It made no sound, had no glow. It was no more alive than the stones, without warmth or subtle movement. Eric snatched up the old creature and felt bones splinter beneath his touch.

"You dick!" he bellowed, and the walls rumbled at the force of his voice. "You killed me!"

"Please," it rasped and fumbled with a potion. "Let me explain!"

The others looked to each other with uncertainty. In unspoken agreement, they began to shuffle backward.

"What the fuck did you do to me?" Eric was so angry, he considered crushing the old dude and eating all the rest. *Eating them?* he thought, puzzled by the urge. *It's the glow.* He knew instinctively it was their life force he craved. "And why am I so fucking hungry?"

The old goblin tossed back the potion, draining the red liquid, and his glow for a moment grew stronger. It had somehow healed him, like a health pot from a video game.

Goblins. He knew what they were, as if he'd known all along but only now remembered. *Fucking goblins. You've got to be kidding me.*

"We brought you here," the shaman explained. What else could he be, his robes covered in bones and skin marked with dried blood? "To fuse your spirit with our war golem. But you shouldn't be able to speak! Or feel anything, not anger or hunger." He looked down at the floor, no doubt wondering if he'd survive the drop. "I don't understand. Something must have gone wrong."

"You saying I'm supposed to be like some mindless vegetable?" Eric brought him closer to eye level. "Is that supposed to make me feel better?!"

Eric wasn't breathing. He spoke fine, even shouted, but the old goblin's hair remained still. A tap against his chest caused a hollow echo to ring out. How was he even alive?

"I know this must be confusing—"

A shake interrupted the lame excuse. "You better start explaining, or I'll tear this place apart and kill every one of you."

Eric grabbed a nearby gray goblin with his other hand and ate him in one swallow. He felt the goblin die instantly, burst warm blood against his insides and come to rest in his right foot. The taste was god awful! Eric had no teeth or tongue, might not have been meant to eat, but it seemed like his entire body from within was a giant taste bud. The goblin was like sour milk over rotted chicken, topped with black licorice and doused in bile. The worst part was it persisted! It wasn't like taking a bite, enduring its foulness and moving on once it had passed. The taste stayed with him, lingering for too long, like heartburn from toe to head.

What *did* taste good, or at least felt good, however brief the sensation, was the moment he had absorbed the goblin's essence. It was like candy and an orgasm, a rush that tingled his brain—even if he didn't have one.

"Blech!" Eric wanted to cough, to hack up the remains. "Tastes like shit!"

"What you hunger for," the shaman said, "you'll find in small quantity here. I can show you much better prey, creatures strong enough to trigger a transformation."

That caught his attention. "You mean I can turn into shit, like a transformer?"

The goblin squinted one eye. "When you've consumed enough essence, you...evolve. You're meant to become stronger the more you kill. The transformation is fueled by the lives you take. Your body will grow, allowing more room for the glyph, and you'll be able to choose ways to improve yourself."

"Like upgrades?" Eric asked. "Wait a minute. Are you saying I can level up?"

He liked the sound of that! To say he was addicted to

leveling was like saying crackheads enjoyed a rock now and then.

"Of course," the shaman agreed, his voice nervous. "Destroy anything you like! It's why we chose you. Our plan was to set you loose upon the world and gather any treasure in your wake."

Eric laughed. The other goblins laughed with him, though half-hearted and afraid.

"That's the stupidest thing I ever heard!" He laughed again. "Seriously, though. You make this giant killing machine, stick me in it and don't think to put a geas on it or some way to control me? What's to stop me from killing you?"

"As I said," the shaman replied, "you're not supposed to be this intelligent. As for a geas, there simply wasn't enough room. We'd hoped control wouldn't be necessary, that we'd point you east and follow along as you wrought destruction."

"Yeah, well, like my dad always says, 'Hold out both hands. Put hope in one, and shit in the other. See which one fills up first.' Looks like things didn't work out like you planned." Eric put the shaman down and stared out over the others. "Now what?"

The shaman cleared his throat, as if surprised he was still alive.

"We...pledge fealty to you, Master!" Every goblin in the chamber dropped to their knees with him, hundreds of them. "We will serve you well, as you conquer all the world!" In unison, they said, "Master!"

"First things first." Eric pointed to his dead body. "You're going to preserve that somehow and find a way to put me back. Eh, eh—" he cut off any protest— "just do what I tell you."

Two red goblins held up the body, as the shaman got to his feet. He waved his staff, a feathered stick with a skull on its top, and mumbled a few words. Yellow crystal like amber began to grow at the body's feet and spread upward. The two reds let go, and soon the crystal fully engulfed his former body in a solid block.

"It is done."

"Put it somewhere safe," Eric commanded, his voice edged with warning. "Now, about this better prey."

"Oh, yes!" The shaman led him to a broken wall. "Look there."

It was a castle in the distance, ebon stone with thin towers that stretched up into a swirling storm of magical energy. The land between was in ruin, trees twisted and black, the ground orange and broken. Even the sky, an amalgam of blood and gold across an ocean of sickly blue, looked poisoned by enchantment.

"What is it?" Eric asked, intrigued by its power.

"It is the castle Thrallen. It stands at the very center of Faradim." Lightning crackled across its parapets and highlighted winged creatures circling the towers. "It is patrolled by undead, protected by wyverns in the air, necromancers on the ground and ruled by a lich with an iron grip upon the land."

Eric watched for a long moment, studying its every feature. He nodded and smiled, happy at the prospect.

"That *would be* a lot of xp."

* * *

Eric looked for a door, some way to leave the broken castle. Light shone through holes in the ceiling, pale rays strewn with dust that fell upon the sea of goblins. They were quiet, waiting, still on their knees. At the far end of the chamber, wooden double doors were cracked open and blocked by stones and fallen timber. It would take some doing to clear the way. Even then, he wasn't sure he could make it through.

He turned and punched the wall.

The new body was cumbersome, but it hit like a freight train. Rock and mortar exploded outward beneath his fist. The castle trembled in protest, rained down wood and rubble that bounced off his shoulders. A few goblins were not as fortunate. He looked back with a grin and shrugged—omelets and all that.

"Check me out," Eric said, "makin' doors like a boss!"

"Master, please!" The shaman coughed and wiped dust from his good eye. He barely opened the other, but when he did it looked milky. "There is no need to bring the castle down about our heads. I can make a portal when you wish to leave."

Eric would've rolled his eyes if he had any.

"Alright," he said. "So do it. Let's get with the killin' already." As an afterthought, he asked, "What's your name, anyway?"

"Grizzletongue, Master," the shaman said and bowed his head.

Eric's laugh brought down more debris. "Serious? Your parents hate you or something?"

"All goblins hate their offspring."

The shaman began waving his staff and uttering words Eric couldn't make out. Now that he noticed, the goblin's tongue was chalk white and covered in bumps like giant warts. Eric didn't know if he should feel sorry for him or be disgusted. Both, he supposed.

"You yankin' my chain?"

"A bit, Master, yes," Griz replied and smiled, then rapped the butt end of his staff against the floor. Its echo was more like a knock in the distance. Charred stones began to rise, upending earth and floor alike. "Before we engage Tragona's army, I thought you might like to choose a weapon from our foundry."

The stones became an arch, with a red afterglow and hissing smoke as if freshly heated by an inferno. In its center was a sheet of emerald light he couldn't see through.

The occasional ripple appeared, but they were rings of pale green rather than drops against water.

"Yeah?" Eric's gaze followed the ripples. "Waddya got for me, a sword of undead bane? An axe of lich slaying?"

"Nothing so grand," Griz said, "but they are of a size that should suit you. We have a tentative peace with the demons of Inexium. They allowed us to build our foundry in their realm, and in exchange we provide weapons for their war against the fey." He looked up at Eric, proud. "Their lava flows have magical properties. It is where you were forged."

"I wasn't forged," Eric said, his voice grating like rocks tumbling down a passage. "I'm just wearing this thing for now." The shaman nodded and looked away. "So, you make weapons. Are they as good as dwarven stuff?" Goblins looked to one another as if insulted then spat dark spittle on the ground. One's aim was off and coated a neighbor's arm. A scuffle ensued. They rolled away, punching and cursing. "I take it you don't like dwarves."

More spitting and curses.

Griz silenced them with a look. "The portal is ready, Master."

"I can't fit through that."

"You just need to touch the center," Griz explained.

Eric touched his fingertips to the light, and the world around him went dark. It flashed back into view with a dizzying speed, but his surroundings had drastically changed. The portal was still there, as was the shaman. Everything else was an entirely different matter.

They were underground now, with crimson and black rock that stretched upward for miles. Massive columns dotted the volcanic landscape, where stalagmites and stalactites had joined together. Lava flowed from a great lake, in streams and over an oozing fall. It swept around islands of unyielding rock and the scorched bones of giant monsters. Far off was an ebon structure, connected to smaller parts by a wall of obsidian. Liquid fire raged against it from the other side, but the creatures loping passed ignored its torrent. Sulfur filled the air, a burning stench like rotted eggs in the sun.

The foundry was a collection of anvils and molds, steaming troughs of boiling water, bright orange lines of channeled lava, smelters and hanging tools. The air was hot but not scalding. With dozens of goblin smiths hammering and shaping, sweating but still alive, Eric assumed some sort of magic kept them safe.

"Dwarves," Griz said, and two nearby goblins spat without missing a hammer beat, "are too concerned with the look of a weapon, waste their magic on longevity. We goblins use enchantment to strengthen our weapons, so the blade bends but never breaks, its edge nicks but never dulls. It is the lava," he continued and pointed out its vibrant glow. "Hottest in all the realms, infused by a thousand ley lines. It is here they all converge, why we chose this place to build our foundry."

Weapon racks were filled with swords and axes as tall as Eric, with more stacked neatly on the ground.

"If your weapons are so strong," he asked, "then why haven't the demons won their war? Why do you need a freakin' robot to rule the world?"

The goblins worked in silence. Either Eric had hit a sore point, or they didn't know the answer either. Griz only nodded, as if he'd pondered the same questions many times before.

"Weapons do not win wars."

Eric snorted. "Tell that to Japan."

Across one of the larger flows, a demon took notice and began making its way across the lava. It had thick limbs and a wide torso, with dark plates for a carapace across its thighs and midsection. Fire ran between its scales and dripped back into the river, which even at the center only rose as high as the demon's chest. All the while it watched Eric, as if gauging his strength. Its eyes were blood red, with vertical black gashes, and the spines on its head swept back like braids of hair. Unlike the paltry glow of a goblin's life, this one seethed with crimson light. Its essence was palpable, so strong it tugged at Eric's senses with an urgency to devour.

"Ho, this guy wants a piece of me," Eric said, fists clenched. "Come at me, bro!"

"Master, you must not!" Griz warned. "He is an ally."

It approached the foundry and stopped, looked up as if studying something in the air. It ran a claw across the surface of what must have been a magical barrier, sparking flashes of blue like deadly fireworks. Saliva fell from its mouth and burned the rock between its feet. It grinned at Eric in challenge.

"Can it get in here?"

"No, Master. The area is protected." Griz must have known what Eric was thinking. "You cannot kill him. Demons are incredibly powerful—"

Eric rushed forward and grabbed the demon by its neck with a grip that would have crushed a tree. Startled by the attack, eyes bulging in alarm, it tried to claw at Eric but couldn't penetrate the barrier.

"Dumbass! Thanks for the free xp!"

Griz pleaded for him to stop, but Eric couldn't hear over the sound of his own laughter.

The demon tried to cry out, but its voice was choked off. It fought to break free, to pull Eric outside the barrier, but their strength was too evenly matched. It took hold of his arm with both claws and slashed down, marring the runes across his forearm.

Eric screamed in pain but refused to let go. Surprise at being hurt was far outweighed by anger. He tightened his grip and punched the demon with his other fist. Two more times and bones broke. Again, the demon slashed him, gouging the iron as if it were flesh, undoing the runes that kept him alive. With both hands, Eric pulled the demon against the barrier by the neck. Magic exploded all around them in a shower of sparks, shrieking as loud as the demon's pain-filled cries.

A final pull, and its neck broke.

The glow of life essence fled its body and rushed Eric, filled him with power and the overwhelming abundance of possibilities. His body was afire with the glow. It filled every crevice, blinded him to all but the coursing flow of ley lines far below, deafened him to the world but for the thrum of life shaking his core. The shaman was an ashen haze, waving his arms in the blur, speaking words Eric no longer understood.

"Something's wrong."

He looked down at his ruined arm and realized the ward had been damaged. His hand still flexed, but he was incomplete, flawed. The pain came to him then, a grim reminder he could've died. His iron body could have died. What would happen to him then?

Griz still waved his arms for attention and when he got it mimicked putting his hand in the lava. Eric lost his balance and fell to his knees. The excess life made him dizzy, drunk with power and pleasure, railing against the pain. He shook his head and focused. The shaman was insistent, even took Eric by the hand and tried to pull him toward the lava.

"Stop talking," Eric said. Every sound echoed inside him, like a headache for his whole body. The goblin smiths had stopped working and watched. "If my arm melts off..."

He plunged it deep into the lava. The pain instantly subsided, doused in liquid fire. He expected the heat to hurt worse than any wound, but instead it was a warmth that soothed and made him whole. When he pulled his arm out, the iron was molten orange but intact. Even the runes had been healed, as if they'd never been clawed.

"Do you understand me now?" Griz asked.

Eric nodded. He wondered how the lava had healed him, how the runes were put right. Did his metal body have a mind of its own? A memory separate from his? He wasn't even sure how he knew or remembered anything, since technically he no longer had a brain.

His mind still swam with possibilities, the multitude of ways he could transform his body, evolve how he saw fit. It angered him how easily he was damaged, even if it was by a demon he shouldn't have been able to kill—or so Griz had told him.

"You must choose," the shaman said, "or the essence will consume you."

"I already have."

The glow faded away, expended in transformation. He held out both arms and watched as the runes turned and disappeared. The same occurred across his body, every rune, every ward, the entire glyph gone from sight. By Griz's tone, he wasn't sure if the shaman was amazed or worried.

"What have you done?" Griz asked, his words a mere whisper.

Eric got to his feet. "I turned them inward. That's the last time some asshat claws off my runes."

"About that." The shaman sighed and looked up with his one eye. "That was a foot soldier in Karron's army. You may have just caused a war between the demons and goblins."

"Wow, sucks to be you."

2

Eric walked toward Castle Thrallen. Rain began to fall in a steady patter of icy drops against his back. It left rivulets in the ground like orange blood, pooled into shallow puddles between the cracks of dried earth and clay. Trees were sparse, leafless and black. Their trunks leaned as if burdened by a great weight, with branches that clawed at the fouled skies in desperation or a thirst for vengeance.

Griz had opened a portal north of the goblins' ruined castle. It looked even worse from the outside. All of its four towers were toppled like giants and had smashed through other buildings on their way down. Boulders the size of small cars lay strewn about the courtyard, had made holes in the wall and the castle itself. Even from this distance, Eric could smell the stains of war upon its stones.

It had the taste of old pennies.

I'm gonna rust, he thought, with images of the tin man in his mind. He carried a wide steel sword over a shoulder. It was taller than him by a foot, though he had no trouble swinging it about—to the dismay of the poor few who couldn't move aside fast enough. He didn't care much for the goblins, even hated them for what they'd done. As for their offer of fealty? *I need an army of level ones like I need a second asshole.* Well, technically...He supposed they could be of use, but the only one that really mattered was the shaman. Without him, there was no chance of being human again.

He followed beside Eric as best he could, leaning heavily on his staff. The rest of them trailed behind, a mass of armored fools bungling into one another and dragging their weapons through the mud. Griz had ordered them to bring the demon's corpse and bury it, in the hopes no other demons had seen it fall. The smiths left behind had no choice but to keep working. A failed quota could just as easily result in war.

The ground shook with each step. Eric liked being strong enough to crush a demon with his hands, but the lumbering pace grated on his nerves, almost as much as the intermittent cackling and fighting from behind. They laughed like hyenas and at the stupidest things. A fart would set them off for minutes on end, let alone dwarf jokes about bearded women or the men's preference for sheep. There would be no surprise attacks or stealthy approach. The lich king would hear them long before they came into sight, not that it would be easy to miss an entire army of goblins marching on the castle.

More steps, still no patrols. He hated to think how slow he'd run or even if he could manage it. He had a long stride, but that didn't equate to moving quickly. It seemed for every advantage he could think of with this new body, there were twice as many downsides and not a thing to be done for it. He didn't seem to get tired, but the driving urge to feed was always with him. If he didn't need sleep, did that mean he could never dream again? What if he went too long without taking a life, would he power down like a toy with a dead battery?

"I didn't have to eat that demon to take its essence," Eric said to Griz. "Is that normal? Normal." He gave a short laugh. "I mean, is it how this thing is supposed to work?"

The shaman struggled to keep pace and breathed heavy as he spoke. "You were never meant to absorb life in that manner," he replied, "by physically eating. It is curious, though."

Eric wondered what the demon might have tasted like. He doubted it would be any worse than the goblin. He shook his right foot but couldn't feel anything move. If the creature was still rotting away down there, he'd have to find a way to get rid of it before the rot gave him bad breath. Robot halitosis. The goblins would laugh for hours if he told them.

"You screwed me," he said instead, plodding on, eyes ahead. "I'll never taste real food again, like pizza or a burger."

"Not necessarily, since you can eat and taste." Griz considered and added, "Perhaps the humans have this food in Westorval. We could conquer it and make them cook for you."

Eric didn't hear. His mind swam with all he'd lost.

"I'll never listen to music," he said, "and I just got a new phone!"

Griz huffed. "We have music, Master."

"Real music! Not lutes and shit." Eric looked up at the storm, gray clouds set alight by purple flashes. "I'll never play another game. That kills me the most." He was quiet for a time, as the wind picked up. Thunder rang out to the north. "Never get high," he continued, "or laid." He knew he no longer had genitals, but he looked down at the bare spot all the same. "I'm not even a person anymore. I'm a fucking monster."

"Even monsters take joy in living. Besides," Griz said and stopped to catch his breath, "if you are truly unhappy, there might be a way to return you to your body."

"It's dead," Eric said without stopping. "You killed it. What's the point?"

The shaman called after, "With the proper items and energies, death would not be an obstacle."

Eric stopped and turned, angry that this was the first he was hearing of it.

"You talking about a quest?"

"Unfortunately," Griz replied and straightened, "a monumental undertaking, which is why I was reluctant to mention it before."

"Oh, even better," Eric said, his voice heavy with sarcasm, "an epic quest! Why can't anything be easy for once?"

A patrol crested the rise of a hill just ahead and charged without hesitation. Four skeletons with swords, their eyes tiny orbs of crimson light, covered the distance much faster than he expected. Tendons and bits of muscle still clung to their yellowed bones, which made a clacking sound as they ran. Not far behind them came a shambling mass of decayed flesh and torn clothes. Its eyes were black ice, and rot oozed from every opening.

"These things are batshit crazy!" Eric laughed and knocked two aside. "Charging into me like that? The hell are they thinking?"

Griz dodged a sword swipe. "Undead follow orders, Master. They do little thinking."

A goblin asked in a trembling voice, "Is that one a zombie?"

Eric snatched it up in one hand and shook it like a rag doll. "This?" It snarled and clawed, left behind little gouges. "Does it look like a zombie?" He shook it in front of the goblin, spraying green and black ooze over his armor. "This is a freakin' ghoul! Zombies are brainless eaters. This thing will suck the life out of you. Huh, kinda like me."

He held it up for a closer look. Like the skeletons, it was surrounded by a haze of black energy. They had no life force he could sense.

"I can't absorb these, can I?" he asked Griz, unmindful of

the goblins fighting to stay alive—and doing a poor job of it. "Why even bother killing them?"

A guard was skewered through the chest, splashing blood across Griz's cheek.

"Dude, gross!" Eric sent the skeleton flying with a kick.

"They have magic, Master." The shaman seemed to be pleading. "Death magic. You can store it and use it another time."

With little effort, Eric clenched his fist and squished the ghoul into splintered bones and jelly. He tossed it away in disgust, knocking over a skeleton and three goblins. The rain helped wash the slime from his hand, but the smell of it lingered. The ghoul's magic became a pulse of black static around his body. The small claw marks it'd left behind smoothed over and were gone. It wasn't nearly as satisfying or filling as life essence, but there was a surge of power he found...pleasant.

"Looks like magic lava isn't the only thing that heals me," he said to Griz. "Good thing, too, what with the war and all."

"Indeed, Master." The shaman dodged another sword and sent a bolt of electricity from his staff. Ribs shattered from the blast. "Magic has many other uses, as well."

Eric smashed all four skeletons with his sword, one by one, only once accidentally chopping a few goblins in half. He did feel bad about it, though.

"Sorry. I'm not used to swinging this thing yet."

They all cheered in victory.

Death magic rushed toward him in a dark cloud and coursed over his body. It buzzed at the back of his head, like the tingle of a whisper too close in his ear. His aura of black static became a crackle of dark energy, the carpet charge of an angry god just waiting to be unleashed. He grinned like a madman, but the iron mask of his face remained unchanged.

Griz asked, "Cut a path to the front gate?"

"No." Eric watched his fist in amusement as lightning danced along its edge. "I want to circle around and kill all the patrols."

"Is that necessary to take the castle?"

The storm intensified as Eric turned and resumed heading north.

"Nope. That's just how I roll."

* * *

The storm worsened. Its clouds grew darker, choked off all light and brought an early nightfall. Rain became a downpour interspersed with hail, pebbles of ice battering armor and flesh alike. It made little difference to Eric. He felt the cold but not its effects. While the goblins frosted the air with their grumbling, he trudged on through the orange muck, glad he couldn't smell the patrol's remains anymore.

Visibility was a problem, in that there was none. He could barely see the ground a dozen steps in front, let alone castle Thrallen and its massive towers. The golem body enhanced his senses, vision especially, but ahead lay nothing but darkness and lightning. He saw no life essence or body heat, enchantment or movement. It was as if the storm itself was a magical construct, but he couldn't see its energy from inside.

Grizzletongue looked particularly miserable, his gray hair matted over warty skin, wet clothes weighing him down and bony hands clinging to his staff. It was hard to imagine something so small and frail could wield any power, but Eric had seen it in the fight—was even living proof. Or animated proof. He wasn't sure what he was anymore, with his soul trapped in the golem. He only knew how he felt, pissed at Griz and the goblins for what they'd done and torn by the strength and pleasure the iron body provided.

It felt *good* to kill!

He knew it shouldn't, that it was wrong to take a life, but

what choice did he have? Without life essence to sustain the golem, it would wither and die, taking his spirit with it. To where, he didn't know. He was as much a prisoner to his instinct for survival as he was to the magic that bound him. Besides, it wasn't as if he'd killed innocent children. He wasn't a murderer. If anything, he'd made the world a safer place by ending that demon and destroying the undead patrol. He'd do it again, too, when he reached the castle. It was a win-win. The world gets rids of a lich and an undead army, and he gets a little stronger in the process.

That's the kind of hero shit they give medals for, he told himself and held his sword with a tighter grip. *And if the lich has a bunch of gold we can use to buy whatever Griz needs to put me back in my body, all the better!*

Eric looked down at his iron hand, at the joints and grooves so unlike one of flesh and bone. His body still tingled with death magic and the black flashes of static across its surface. Glad the magic could heal him, since acquiring magic lava from the demon realm might not be possible anymore, he was still angered at how easily his body—the golem—was damaged. If a ghoul could gouge marks in the iron, what could a wyvern do?

"Why did you make me...the golem, I mean, out of iron?" he asked Griz. "Steel is stronger."

While Eric's voice easily cut through the storm, the shaman's sounded weak in the face of its wind.

"Iron holds an enchantment better, Master" he replied. "It would have been extremely difficult to weave a glyph into steel, and the outcome might not have been the same."

"I look like a fucking cauldron." Eric swung his sword in the air. At least he was growing used to its feel in his hand. "I suppose I should be grateful I have arms and legs."

"And a head, Master!"

Eric looked to see if he was joking. He wasn't. "Yeah. Well, now that the spell is done, can I evolve the metal into steel? Or something stronger?"

"That was our hope, Master," Griz said. Eric gave him a blank look that stated clearly how he felt about hope. "I am not certain if the transformation will require large quantities of steel or if the essence you consumed will suffice. If material is not required, perhaps a better choice might be star metal. It is very rare, far more pliable than steel and nearly indestructible."

"What, like adamantium or some shit?" Eric laughed at the idea of turning himself into a robot wolverine. "Ya know, for someone who can just snatch anyone from anywhere and stuff 'em in a golem, you seem to know fuck all about how the spell works."

Eric could see blood flush the shaman's face as heat, but Griz walked on in silence for a long moment before replying.

"It is never an easy thing," he said as if embarrassed, "weaving a spell with others. And you, Master, were an unforeseen circumstance."

"I'll take that as a compliment."

The sound of patrols on either side came rushing toward them, and a horn sounded from ahead in the distance.

Goblins rushed into position, and Griz said, "I think it is safe to say the lich king knows we are coming."

"Thanks, Captain Obvious." Eric held his sword in both hands, ready to strike. "By the way, was there a reason we brought an entire army? Seems all they're good for is dyin'."

Griz blasted a skeleton apart with his staff as it emerged from the darkness. "Some are more useful than others, Master!"

Dark energy rose from the shattered bones, and Eric pulled it to him with an open palm.

"Nice!" he admitted and cleaved a ghoul in half as it charged him. "Well, tell the crappy ones to hang back or start suckin' less!"

Goblins tried to flee but were pushed into the dozens of undead, died outright or ducked in time to let those behind suffer the brunt. Skeletal swordsmen, oozing ghouls, even a broken knight in full plate atop a long dead steed, the two patrols crashed into the goblin army without hesitation. Eric let loose a bolt of ebon energy into the face of a half-decayed dog. Its yellow eyes melted beneath the shock before its head burst apart. Crushing more with his sword, he absorbed their magic and used it against those who remained. Even the goblins helped kill a few, by sheer force of numbers and lack of choice.

The sound of horns grew closer, as he slew the last ghoul. He felt the vibrations of heavy footsteps coming toward them from all around. The attack had been a diversion. They were flanked and outnumbered. He even heard the pounding beats of winged creatures in air.

"Son of a bitch," Eric said. "They're gonna zerg us."

3

Eric's mind raced for a plan, some cunning bit of war strategy he might have gleaned from countless games. The storm had reduced visibility to a short distance, or he would've asked Griz to make a portal far to the north, behind the incoming patrols. They'd still be outnumbered but not surrounded, at least for a short time. He shook his head at the idea. There simply wasn't enough time to summon the portal for the goblins to pass through. And what was to stop the undead from following them? No, he needed another plan, and he needed it fast.

"Could you make a barrier," he asked Griz, "like the one at the foundry?"

Goblins spread farther out, weapons ready, as the shaman shook his head. "Not one that size and not without significant time or help."

A glance out across the clan showed the truth. Griz was their only shaman, and he had no apprentices. Eric cursed their stupidity, not for the first time that day. He had to keep the shaman alive, was about to order Griz to make a portal to the ruined castle and go through, when the patrols came into sight. Undead charged them from all around with unearthly howls and glowing eyes, and goblins began to die beneath the onslaught.

Half a dozen steps put him a good distance ahead of Griz. Eric figured the best way to keep the shaman safe was to stay clear of him during the fight. He turned his attention to the attackers and began to swing like a madman. His sword cut and crushed through decayed bodies three and four at a time. He took their energy and released it in tandem, shocking apart skeletal warriors and burning animated flesh. What damage he sustained was instantly healed by the growing aura of dark static about his body.

"So hax!" he yelled and laughed, punched a rider from its horse then cut the decrepit mount in half. "It's like fucking God mode!"

A wyvern crashed into his chest and took him down.

It was twice his size, with claws large enough to clamp down and into both shoulders. Its wing span was wide as a house, with barbs at each tip that used the ground for balance. Huge teeth snapped at his head in an attempt to take it from him, and eyes like silver plates matched his gaze with a feral resolve. From nose to tail, it was covered with thick scales and ridged with sharp spines. Its talons pierced his iron but were quickly repelled, healed as fast as it could harm him. Its tail was again as long as its body, thick as a limb and tipped with a scorpion stinger. He barely moved his head in time to avoid its strike, where rock and earth were skewered a foot deep.

The wyvern roared down at him, its breath frosted in the cold like a stream of snowy cloud. It spit acid across his neck, pitting the iron. Eric screamed against the pain and leveled a punch at its mouth. His fist got caught between the dagger-like teeth. When he couldn't pull free, he instead reached farther in and took hold of its throat. With all his strength, he tore away its bottom jaw. Blood and acid rained over him as the beast fought to get away. He punched again, this time at its exposed chest, and his fist went through scale and muscle. He let loose a charge of dark energy that shook the creature with smoking spasms. Cooked from within, it collapsed on top of him.

The rush of joy at satiating the hunger flushed through him, healed his iron body and brought him near to another transformation. He could feel how close it was, like a building pressure in his middle that would later culminate into an explosion, like taking a massive dump after a week of constipation. He had no other way to explain or compare it, the stress mounting within him, the feeling of being pregnant with possibility, the sudden realization of it happening and the relief of it all passing. Already his mind was swimming with the choices. He knew what he wanted, to strengthen his iron flesh, but the particulars of it eluded him. He could no more specify what material he'd evolve into than he could the color or shape. It didn't matter, though, because he wasn't quite there yet, and the other wyverns didn't give him time to think.

Two more grabbed hold of him, one at each foot, and lifted him into the air with great effort. They carried him over the battle, where the sounds of dying goblins rose up from the slaughter. His head and shoulders crashed through them, banging aside ghouls and two riders. He smashed a dozen goblins before the wyverns lifted him again with jarring beats of their wings. They struggled to keep him aloft let alone carry him up into the storm. Still, higher and higher they flew. It wasn't long before Eric realized they planned to drop him.

He began to frantically shock them out of fear. Forked bolts of black lightning encompassed their bodies, a storm within a storm. Leathery scales smoked in gray plumes, muscles convulsed and split, delicate wing membranes tore and smoldered. One finally let loose its hold and fell away into the fray far below. The other fought to hang on for another moment, shrieked up at the dark skies and fell as well.

Eric plummeted toward the ground, twisting to see where he'd land. He hoped to kill as many undead as he could when he cratered. The fall might have been enough to kill him, but if he could absorb enough magic to heal at the same time...

Another wyvern crashed into him.

It tried to keep them both in air, but the best it could manage was to slow their crash into muddied earth. It bit and clawed at him as they rolled to a long stop. All the while, Eric punched where he could and used the last of his stored magic. No longer able to heal, talons ripped through him. Screaming in agony, afraid to die on this shitty world, he was on the verge of collapse when the combined life force and dark energy of all the fallen on the field struck him from behind like a runaway train.

It arched his body with the pain and pleasure of an orgasmic knife through the heart. His hands clenched from the rush of power, gripped through scale and bone, muscle and tendon. His entire body trembled with the force of transformation. The wyvern in his grasp shook and died, its life force mingling with the rest. Eric threw back his head in exultation. A nimbus of crimson light surrounded him, swirled and coalesced, then settled in his middle like a collapsed sun.

When the strain of it was gone, and the pain finally abated, all it left behind was renewed hunger. A living beast in his gut, it clawed and cried for more. He was on his knees, drenched from icy rain and growing angry at the never-ending cycle. The pleasure was like a drug, an ecstasy and oblivion he could easily succumb to. It was all he wanted anymore, those short moments of pure bliss, the brief eruption of truly living. It was the hunger that pained him, that drove the emptiness to rage. Half again to another change, it still tortured him with wild craving, with the pangs of an unbridled fervor.

Is this what addiction's like? he wondered.

He stood and faced the battle. Fire consumed patches of earth and corpses, defiant of the rain. Slain goblins littered the area, stained the ground with their blood, but the hundred or so that remained stood strong and fought back. Griz was at their center, throwing bolts of magic and barriers of blue light to funnel the undead.

Eric looked down at his hands. He'd lost his sword somewhere during the fighting. A flash from above lit the landscape momentarily. His body was no longer a crude and coarse mass of iron. It was smooth as polished steel, with a black sheen like starless night. It was far stronger, too. He could feel it as he flexed. He walked toward the undead with a renewed vigor for the fight.

"Alright, bitches," he said. "Time to die. Again."

* * *

The rain had let up to a weak drizzle, but the storm continued to rumble overhead. Lightning flashed like a dim heartbeat, brightened clouds enough to highlight their edges in sallow white, while in the distance argent strikes forked down and out in a web of fury. Wind blew from the east, not so strong as to bend a tree but enough to carry the storm's chill and the pained cries of the wounded. Fire and ash licked the air where pyres burned the dead, cleansed the bodies of disease and curse alike. A hundred paces away, the smell of charred rot was still stronger than soaked earth and ozone. More than two hundred goblins had bled the field, drenched the ground where the pyres stood. Magic fueled the flames, spread its touch in a blanket of summer sunset between the mounds and left nothing with which to heal those who had survived.

Eric sat at a campfire with Griz and five others, the

leaders of each clan within the host. There would've been six, but none remained of the grays. Tunnelers, sappers and miners by nature, they were ill-suited for the rigor of direct combat. The goblins ate and spoke for the better part of an hour, of strategy and morale, supplies and the state of gear, but only Eric seemed to notice how exhausted the shaman was, how his hands shook when he drank from the wineskin. There were a dozen more campfires, with goblins huddled together for warmth, the injured on sleeping mats and wrapped in blankets. None of their wounds were life-threatening, but without Griz to heal them, infection would set in.

He had insisted all he needed was a night's rest and would be able to heal everyone in the morning. So here they sat, resting and waiting, despite the lich king, who could easily see their fires from his castle walls.

"If Tragona had more minions," the red general said between bites of what Eric could only hope was jerky, "he'd have sent them by now." His name was Belchburn, though by his own account he preferred to be called Bel. He spit a piece into the fire, where it hissed in protest. "If he's half a wit left, he'll be gone before we get there."

"Aye," Bri—short for Brinecall—agreed. The blue general ran a flat stone across the edge of his sword in long, methodical strokes. "Or he's cooking up a nasty in that dungeon of his."

They were smarter than the other fodder, Eric was forced to admit. They spoke in complete sentences and could hold their own in a fight. He kept listening as the storm shifted overhead but offered no words of his own.

He began to reminisce about home and almost found himself glad to be away. It was quieter here, with no sister and her trail of brainless boyfriends; or his father, the cubicle rat who hated his job almost as much as his life, who only tolerated family because the alternative was too expensive. His mother, who also hated her job, if you could call marketing a job, spent every night in a box of wine and a bottle of sleeping pills.

No, the people in his life he could do without.

Soda, on the other hand... *Or chocolate! Fuck, I could go for some candy.* Playing video games, watching porn, masturbating, and usually in that order, those were the more obvious things he missed. It was the little stuff he didn't expect, the everyday insignificant things everyone took for granted.

Like blinking, he thought, as rain fell across his face in a misted drizzle but had no effect on his vision. The world just wasn't meant to be seen without pause. *It's too damn depressing.*

He touched fingertips to his chest, to the hollow metal with no heartbeat. He felt devoid of thrill, of the constant exhilaration that came from being alive. When he'd killed a newb in pvp, found a legendary he actually wanted or saw a naked woman, his heart would race and blood pump in a surge throughout his body.

Now there was only empty excitement, a feeling less awful than the one before. Taking essence was a rush, but it wasn't *his* rush. It was stolen pleasure, someone else's joy at being alive. There wasn't even escape in sleep anymore. Dreams were a thing of the past. He could lay back and stare out at the storm and stars, try to become lost in contemplation, but it wasn't the same. Nothing in life is like dreaming, no love nor drug, no mirage nor musing. And once the ability is gone, all that's left are frustration and the memory of it to mock you.

The shaman must have seen Eric grow melancholy and tried to lighten the mood with a joke.

"Master," he said, drawing Eric's attention from the rain, "why do dwarven men fear their women more than any warrior on the field or dragon in the sky?" The drawn out silence made it clear Eric had no interest in guessing. "Because their women have larger man parts!" The others laughed uproariously.

"Oh, and beards! I forgot, they have longer beards!"

More ridiculous laughter. Eric didn't even smile inwardly, just gave a light facepalm.

"I thought you were going to say because they bleed for a week every month and don't die."

The laughter dwindled to an uncomfortable lull.

"They bleed for a week?" the brown general asked, looking shocked and a bit frightened. Muckbud was his name, but in Eric's mind he was forever Mudbutt. "What, like from a wound?"

Grimstalk cleared his throat, still trying to wrap his mind around the notion. "Every month?" the green general asked.

Eric laughed. "Don't goblins have women?"

"I'm a woman," Bri said. Eric was dubious; the blue didn't have breasts, though she was wearing armor. Her voice sounded no different from other goblins, either, no femininity to the speech or tone. "What's that got to do with bleeding?"

"Goblins are made, Master," Griz offered, "not born."

"So you don't have sex?" Eric looked down to the smooth space between his legs. "No wonder I look like a fucking Ken doll."

"We can," the shaman replied, "we do. Your lack of man parts was more a matter of modesty and practicality than function."

Man parts? What the fuck, why can't he say dick?

"Yeah," Eric would have frowned if he could, "it'd be a shame to make anyone uncomfortable while I'm destroying their home and killing their loved ones."

The orange general spit his wine with a laugh, then spent the next minute choking and gasping for air while the others laughed at his expense—and at Eric's joke. Bitterbark was what he'd called himself earlier, though Eric liked to think of him as Bitters.

"You know," Eric added, speaking to Griz, "at the rate

we're going, you won't have an army by the end of the week. There's barely a hundred goblins over there, and I doubt half of them could fight a cold, let alone a battle."

"Most of those lost," Mudbutt said, "were untrained or untrainable."

Bri put more wood onto the fire, beneath wide stones stacked in such a way as to protect the flames from rain. "Grays took the brunt," she said. "House Azaren hasn't lost a one since we arrived."

"Nor Bloodfall!" Bel chimed in.

Griz calmed them with a hand, as if to stave off any contest before it could begin.

"You've all done as expected, and the grays, well, they did too. We're not all suited for war," he said to Eric, "the grays less so than others."

This got Eric thinking. "The shamans who helped summon me," he asked, "were they from different clans?"

The old goblin nodded. "There aren't many of us, mind you, and the few we have are coveted by the families they're made for or purchased by. As soon as you were summoned, they all returned home."

There was grumbling among the generals.

"Cowards," Bitters remarked.

"What's up with that?" Eric asked. "Why'd they bail?"

"None of us truly wants to be here," Griz replied. "We do it because it's necessary. There are resources here on Taellus that just can't be found on Xanaranth. Everyone benefits from the goods we send back. Unfortunately, few are willing to help in the endeavor."

"Which is why," Mudbutt added and emptied a wooden pipe against his knee, "we have more grays than swords and little hope of reinforcement."

"Had," Stalk amended. His green skin and dark armor took on brighter hues with the growing fire. "We've plenty swords now that we've no grays."

"That's rough," Eric said. "I almost feel bad so many have

died." *Almost.*

"You honor us with your concern," Griz said and bowed his head. Eric couldn't tell if he was being sincere. "Once the castle is ours, we will send for support to hold it while we conquer the rest of Taellus."

"*Real* soldiers," Bri put in, "no more worm food from the mines."

Griz sighed, looked even wearier. "We take what we can get."

"Xanaranth," Eric said, trying the word out on his nonexistent tongue. "How many goblins are there on your home world?"

"Millions," the shaman replied. "Far more than there are humans in all of Taellus."

Eric scoffed. "That's all? How can a few million take over an entire world?"

"Well," Bitters said, offended, "how many humans are there where you come from?"

"On Earth? Seven and a half billion."

"Million?" the orange repeated, his face perplexed, asking if Eric had made a mistake.

Eric turned to face him. "You got shit in your ears? Billion."

"What's a *billion*?" Mudbutt asked.

Griz replied, "A thousand million."

Bitters gave a snort and looked at his fellow generals, waiting for them to join in on the jest. He seemed to consider the enormity of the numbers and grew quiet.

Eric shook his head and focused his attention back to Griz. "Will they send more shamans, or at least decent warriors? I agree with smurfette here; we don't need any more shit stains clogging up the battlefield. They're a drain on resources, and if the gobs in charge need some convincing, I'd be happy to pay them a visit."

"A generous offer, Master." Griz pulled tighter the blanket about his shoulders. "The truth is few are willing to risk their lives for the amenities they take for granted. There are others far wiser and stronger than we, but they stay at home where they believe they are safe."

Eric was quiet a moment. "You know, you're not what I expected when I woke up here."

The shaman managed a smile. "To say the same of you would be a great understatement."

"No, I mean where I come from, goblins are low level monsters for players to level up on. The idea of them taking over the world, any world," Eric said with something akin to admiration or incredulity, "it just wouldn't happen."

"And now, Master?"

"Well," Eric replied, in a not so modest tone, "you brought *me* here. You just might have a chance." It was good to see genuine laughter from the shaman. It made him seem stronger, healthier, like he might survive long enough to help Eric get his life back. "Speaking of which, tell me more about how I get back into my body, alive and home."

A nod and a squirt of wine. "It is a very complicated spell, one I will need assistance with, aside from the rare and exotic materials—"

"Cut the epic quest crap," Eric cut in. "Just tell me what we need, and *why* we need it. Because I fucking hate quests, and I'm not dragging my ass all over the world on a wild goose chase. If there's a cheap substitute, I want to know about it. I'm not hunting down a unicorn if we can use a plain old horse. You get me?"

Griz nodded. "It will not be easy. First, we need to resurrect your body. There are many ways to do so, but the only way I can do it myself is to sacrifice a human virgin."

"The fuck? Why does it have to be human?"

"Because you are human," he replied with calm, as if used to choosing his words the way one chooses footing while walking upon eggshells. "A life for a life."

"Whatever." Eric was getting tired, or maybe he was just

tired of talking. "Seems wrong to kill someone just because they've never been laid."

"As I said, there are other ways."

Eric asked, "What else?"

"We need to replace your spirit with another's."

"You're going to trap someone else in this thing? Lame." Eric considered. "Why not use the sacrifice? Two birds, one stone."

The shaman shook his head. "Once the spirit has left its body, we will not be able to harness it for the exchange."

"So, you're basically killing two people so far. Can you use one of the retarded goblins?"

"Unfortunately, no." Griz took a deep breath, as if searching for the right words. "It must be someone of strong spirit, or they will die for naught."

Eric nearly growled. "What the fuck, man. Why's shit got to be so complicated? How are we going to know if someone has a strong spirit or not?"

"We could summon them," Griz offered, "as we did you, or wait to see if we come across one in our campaign. Military leaders, royalty, anyone able to wield magic, all would be good candidates. And I can test them to be sure."

"What a fucking hassle. Anything else?"

The shaman hesitated. "Those are just the steps we must take to restore you. I have not mentioned the reagents, any of which could take us weeks to acquire—"

"Fuck it. I don't want to hear anymore," Eric said and got to his feet. "Let's just take dickhead's castle in the morning and wing it from there."

"As you say, Master."

Eric stalked off into the darkness, away from camp, convinced he had a headache despite being hollow.

Eric saw him the moment they passed through the portcullis and entered the courtyard of castle Thrallen. He was taller than expected, nearly seven feet, but any semblance of stature ended there. The lich was beyond decayed, no more than a skeletal memory of a man. What flesh and tendon remained had blackened to a stony shell, unmoving bits of detritus that clung to every rune-marked bone like a disease. The magic etched across his body burned with a violet fire, a trickle of flame woven around and across every surface. Heavy robes clung to his shoulders, tattered remnants of a once nobleman's lavish attire. The deerskin boots were burned and slashed, the soles long gone, revealed bone and inhuman talons. All that was left of his gloves were the leather wristlets, and a large ruby ring seated in gold adorned his right hand.

Aside from the surprise at finding Tragona out in the open, Eric hesitated when none of the goblins reacted. Even Griz approached the castle doors without alarm, as if nothing was untoward. A faint sphere of runes floated about the lich, their light muted by the morning sun. Eric wasn't sure if he was hallucinating—could a robot trip on acid?—or the lich had made himself invisible with a spell.

But if I can see him, why can't Griz? He realized he'd been standing still, studying the courtyard as goblins moved past. He began walking toward the center of the long dead topiary that rounded the yard, not directly for Tragona but close enough to reach him. *Let's see if this dude's as strong as he is ballsy.*

"Hold on," Eric called out, and the assembled goblins halted before the entryway. "Before we go in," he said and took the final step that brought him within grasping distance, "let's make sure everyone—" Eric lunged for Tragona with a half laugh. "Got you, bitch!"

His hands met with an impenetrable shield of magic and a blast of forked energy that scorched his fingers with a noticeable jolt. *Son of a bitch!* The lich turned baleful eyes toward him. Eric saw the invisibility spell fall away in a dusting of light. That's not all he saw, as he shook his hands from the pain. Goblins began to scatter in fear, though Bitters and the other generals stood fast. The cobble circle Tragona stood upon had a ward clawed into it, with runes that flared when Eric had touched the shield.

He actually wrote the spell into the stones, Eric thought for a brief moment. *What a fucking moron!*

Eric brought his foot down with all the strength he could muster and shattered both stones and spell. He grabbed Tragona by the neck with his right hand, spinal column in his left.

"Oh shit, son!" he taunted. "Didn't see that coming, did you?"

Tragona had a hasty spell upon his lips, both bony hands crackling with dark power, as Eric charged for the iron spikes that curved about each window in decoration. He impaled the lich upon two hooks and pulled down with the scream of a frenzied soldier. Tragona's body broke apart in a blast that scorched Eric's chest and sent a dozen goblins flying back toward those cowering. Bones splintered and fell apart, their magic spent. The only piece still intact was the head, which continued to regard Eric with the same menacing stare.

"You are a fool," Tragona said, "if you think you can destroy me—"

Eric crushed the skull in his fist.

"Well done, Master," Griz said, seeming more aghast than impressed by the situation. Perhaps he wondered, as well, why he'd been unable to see the undead mage.

"I know, right?" Eric said and wiped his hands clean in a cloud of lich dust. "Fucker would've probably never shut up. You," he said and pointed to a small group of goblins picking themselves up, "gather all the pieces, and separate them into four piles. The rest of you, start searching this entire place, top to bottom, for any kind of containers. Bring them all here."

Goblins scurried to do as they were bid. The generals stayed to oversee handling of the lich's remains.

"You think he'll have it hidden here, Master?" Griz asked. "Seems brazen, even for this one," he added and kicked a broken femur.

Eric looked up at the castle. "Might be a longshot. Just seems someone who would wait for us like that, even invisible, is stupid enough to hide his phylactery where he lives."

Bel sneezed a puff of bone dust. "A fillo...?"

"Don't strain anything," Eric said and laughed. "A phylactery. It's where liches keep their spirit. Destroying it's the only way to truly kill him, otherwise he'll just heal back together."

"Which is why," Griz added, indicating to the goblins at work, "we want to keep these piles far away from each other. At least, for now."

"You should start looking around," Eric suggested to the shaman, "figure out what it's going to take to fortify and hold this place. Who were you worried about attacking it?"

"Lord Sebran, Master," Griz replied, and Bel spat at the sound of his name.

"Shouldn't you be searching with the others?" Eric asked, his gaze falling upon the idle generals. The way they looked to one another, he began to wonder if they all thought their shared talk by the fire had made them friends. "Don't make me ask twice."

Griz continued, "His lands, Cledford, are small by comparison to other lords in Faradim, but he does command a sizeable army."

Eric watched the five generals disappear into the castle, hoping he'd made his point. "Why would the guy with the smallest lands have a big army?"

"Because of this." Griz toed a pile of lich debris. The pieces looked to be drawing closer and mending together. "King Raynver at Westorval has allotted the lord extra soldiers to keep the lich at bay."

"Why didn't they just kill it?"

Four goblins exited the castle, dragging a human girl in tow. Her dress was dirtied and torn, her hair slick with sweat and skin the pallor of sickness. Eric guessed her to be nine or ten, though malnourishment made it difficult to tell.

She looked like she was dying.

"I suspect," Griz replied, "they would have very much liked to."

More goblins followed after, ooohing and aaahing over the girl, touching her skin and licking their lips as if they hadn't eaten in weeks. Eric quieted them with a glare, almost growled his discontent.

She's a helpless girl, not a fucking hot pocket!

"Put her down and leave," Eric demanded. He knelt so he could study her closer. Something was off about her essence, like it was damaged or intermingled with something else. "It's alright, no one's going to hurt you. I promise. What's your name?"

"I am Ella," she said, her breathing labored, "the daughter and only heir to Lord Sebran." Her eyes were a milky blue, and they pleaded for an end to the pain. "I've been held captive in the broken tower for years, an assurance my father would stay away from these lands."

"What of your illness?" Griz asked and took her frail arm in hand. "Her blood is weak, Master. She won't last the night."

Ella coughed, and her thin lips became flecked in crimson. "I have been ill since weeks after my arrival here. The castle air, it seems, does not agree with me." More coughing and a struggle for air. "It is only recently though that my health has taken a turn for the worse. If I didn't know any better, I'd think Tragona had poisoned me."

"He might have," Eric considered, "if he thought he'd lose his castle. Kill off his insurance policy, so the pissed off father comes after us."

Goblins began trickling out of the castle with a number of items in hand, from jewelry and curio boxes to locked chests, glowing glass phials and beakers on wooden racks to complete dresser drawers, furniture and a broad cabinet that took a dozen of them to lift. They'd literally emptied the castle of every item that even remotely resembled a container.

"You guys don't miss much," Eric said and stood to look each piece over. Some were enchanted, like a handful of clay pots sealed with wax, but none had the look of living essence. "Destroy it all, and burn it." Just in case the goblins were stupid enough to kill them all with fire, he added, "Away from the castle."

He returned to Ella, cradled her frail body in his right hand and waited. The sounds of splintered wood and broken glass echoed back for long minutes before the crackle of flame began to spread. None of them held the lich's spirit, but Eric had already known that. He stared down at her, disgusted at himself and this world he now had no choice but to live in, and wondered if he could bring himself to do it.

"Master?" Griz stood beside him, puzzled. "What do we do now?"

"It's her."

She could barely keep her eyes open but winced at an unrelenting pain. Her condition was worsening before his eyes. If they waited long enough, her death would be upon Tragona's head and not his.

"I see. Well then," the shaman said, as if relieved at the problem being solved, "might I suggest we end this quickly? Two dwarves, one spear. We kill the girl, which destroys Tragona, and then have her for dinner."

Ella's eyes opened at that, wide with fright and a growing delirium. Eric had no words at that moment but fought against a sudden rage and every impulse to crush Griz where he stood.

You're lucky I need you, he growled inwardly. *The fuck am I going to do?*

"Please," Ella pleaded, her voice losing its strength

"See, Master, she wants to die. It would be a mercy."

"No." Eric shook his head. "I gave her my word. Isn't there any way to get it out of her?"

Griz looked back at the piles of Tragona. "It must have taken him a very long time to weave a spell into her spirit, to transform her into a living phylactery. We would have to convince him to craft another, and even then, the spell may kill her. To undo the binding without Tragona's aid would take twice as long, if it were at all possible. I'm afraid the only way to set her free is..."

She squeezed Eric's hand. It was the barest of a touch, but he felt it deep within. Tears carved dirty rivulets down her cheeks, and she looked up at him with a firm set to her chin.

"I understand," she said. "It's alright."

"No," Eric insisted, his voice breaking. "I can't do that."

She smiled despite the pain, met his gaze with a strength he'd never seen in another.

"The good of others," she said, "has always come first in my family. We sacrifice for those we love. We give to keep them safe. I only ask one thing."

Eric took a deep breath, lungs or no, and tried to find his way to being as resigned as she.

"What is it?"

"I want to be buried beside my mother." Ella looked off to the east, toward what must have been family and home, though the court was blocked by stone walls. "Don't let them eat me."

"Technically, that's two things," Eric said, eliciting a pained laugh that led to coughing. "Sorry, bad habit."

The way she looked at him, her touch, as if he wasn't truly a monster, made him feel something he hadn't experienced in a very long time. He cared. More than anything he wanted to help this girl, who had gotten dealt a shit hand and was willing to die to prevent others being hurt as she had. He wouldn't say the words, but he nodded assent.

A calm came over her then, as if the pain had slipped away and an almost smile settled in her features at the thought of being at peace with her mother. She closed her eyes and lay back into Eric's hand, a final gesture meant to let him know she was ready.

"Griz, how do I..." Eric began and nearly choked on the words, "you know, so it doesn't hurt."

"Her neck, Master."

Eric gave a curt nod, growing numb to the ordeal. As much as he wanted it to just be over, he'd hate himself for the rest of his life if he caused her undue pain. He put thumb and forefinger gently to either side of her head.

"I'm sorry, Ella."

A quick twist and her chest no longer labored to draw breath. Her whole body became instantly still.

The influx of essence was immense, a flood of power that overwhelmed his senses in a sea of argent black. The first transformation came upon him with such speed and intensity, a spherical blast that sent goblins flying outward against the walls, that he had no time to choose before the second was fast on its heels. He knew what he wanted, had no idea if it was possible but wanted it all the same. Eric wanted to be human again; not to be put back in his old body but to somehow make this new one flesh and blood. He hadn't made a clear choice when he felt the magic subside. He didn't feel any different, certainly couldn't see any change. All he saw was the girl whose life he'd just ended.

He set her head back in place, so it looked like she was resting and stood, cradling her limp body.

To Griz, he said, "I hate this fucking world of yours."

The shaman wisely chose not to speak, only bowed his head in respect.

"Secure the castle," Eric told the goblins, who were still struggling to pull themselves up from the floor. He began to leave, with Ella in hand, knowing Griz would be beside him. "Show me where her mother's buried."

Together they left the courtyard and headed east.

Midday sun did little to brighten the foggy hillocks between Thrallen and Cledford. Dark clouds still roiled overhead to the distant rumbles of thunder. They cast a pall over the land, where everything seemed a dismal shade of gray. More mud than grass, the ground looked as if it had been trampled by countless boots at one time. Scattered and broken palisades were spread across what remained of earthen ramparts lost to weather. Whatever battle had taken place between men and the undead, it left marks upon the land like the notes of a chilling story.

The field continued far to the east into heavy mist and a tall, crenelated stone wall. Knights patrolled on horse along the outskirts, blue livery over their armor, lances held high. Pikemen in leather stood watch at either side of an iron portcullis, while archers leaned on their longbows behind the parapet above. Even at this distance, Eric could see and feel the glow of each of their essences, more orange than red and shot through with charges of silver-blue.

Hunger clawed him from within.

"Their cemetery," Griz said and pointed southeast to a copse of leafless trees, "is over there, Master. Perhaps it would be best if we remained unseen for the time being." He relied heavily upon his staff as they walked along the road. "At least until we've buried the girl and are rejoined by the others."

Eric could've walked up to the gate, delivered the girl to her father's men, but he felt obligated to bury her himself. Besides, he doubted they'd listen to what he had to say. He didn't want to fight them, had no intention of killing humans. Given his appearance, though, he had little doubt they'd attack. He left the road and headed toward the cemetery, careful not to be seen—well, as careful as a fifteen foot metal monster could be. While he was still somewhat distraught over Ella's death, another pestering thought kept needling its way to the front.

"I had two transformations," he told Griz, "after I...after Tragona died."

"Excellent, Master," the shaman said. He gauged the golem body with his good eye. "What did you choose?"

Eric was quiet for a moment, his feet making sucking noises in the mud. Rain began to fall as the iron fence around the cemetery came into view off in the distance. It was south of the walled keep, away from patrols.

"I wanted to be human."

"Ahh," Griz said. "I see. And what happened?"

"That's just it. Nothing happened!" Eric replied in anger. He wanted to make a fist but held Ella in both hands. "I spent two transformations on nothing."

The shaman considered. "Perhaps not, Master. When your glyph evolves, it grows larger to compensate. You grow larger. You say you underwent two transformations, but I see no change in size."

"So I got screwed. I wished for the impossible, and now I'm shit outta luck. For fuck's sake!" Eric fumed. "I could've *used* those changes, to be faster, metal claws, rocket boots… Literally anything would've been better than nothing."

"The golem is bound to your spirit," Griz explained. "Nothing is impossible, Master. Highly improbable, yes, but not beyond the realm of possibility. I think what you desired couldn't be done in so short a time. I can no longer see your runes, but if I were to hazard a guess, I'd say they were reduced in size to make room for future changes."

"Hmmph."

Eric wasn't convinced. He certainly still wasn't happy about it. It did make him slightly less pissed off to think the transformations hadn't been wasted.

They entered the cemetery through a stone archway with carved statues of robed figures on either side. Eric was forced to duck as he passed through or smash the stonework with his head. There were dozens of graves, with each headstone done in marble or granite and inscribed with delicate artistry. One among them was larger with a fresh white flower across its top. It belonged to Marjory Sebran and had unclaimed plots on either side.

Eric knelt beside the blank headstone on its right and began clawing a deep enough space for Ella with one hand. He refused to put her down in the mud. Griz did what he could to help, digging with one end of his staff. His time might've been better spent keeping watch.

A guard came upon them from the north. He was carrying a handkerchief full of cornbread and little slices of cheese and apple. Head down, stuffing his face with stolen food from the pantry, he didn't see either until he was nearly upon them. He yelped and dropped his food, fumbled for the sword at his belt. Eric looked back over a shoulder but continued to dig.

"Seriously?"

Dude comes face to face with a giant robot, and his first thought is to stick his dick in its face?

Griz moved behind the headstone, used it as a shield and

held his staff out toward the guard.

"Be gone," the man shouted, crumbs falling from his mouth, "evil spirit!" He did finally manage to pull free the sword, though.

Eric sighed and stood, faced the guard still holding Ella. The man's eyes were wild with fear beneath the hood of a wet cloak. He wore a leather vest over a white shirt and knee-high black boots with frayed soles. There were so many laces, up the vest, along each bracer, even the shirt, that it looked like he'd spent half an hour getting dressed.

"Look, Ren Faire," Eric warned, "I don't have time for your shit. Unclench, turn around and walk the fuck away." The guard stared back, his blade shaking. Eric added, "Or I'll make you eat that sword."

The man wiped rain from his eyes and looked closer at Ella. "Is that the lady—"

Griz fired a bolt of lightning at his chest.

The guard let out a short shriek, frozen in place, and fell over onto his back like a board.

"Aww, wut!" Eric looked back at the deadly muppet. "Did you kill him?"

Griz shrugged. "I thought he might alert the others to our presence."

The guard groaned. Smoke rose from off his chest into the rain.

"Oh. Good," Eric said. "Leave him for now. Let's just finish this and go."

"Yes, Master."

They finished digging a decent enough hole, just a few feet deep, and placed Ella inside. He didn't cover her with dirt, because he figured her father would just dig her right back up. Whether to verify it was her or to see his daughter one last time, the result would be the same. Eric didn't want her to be disrespected like that.

"Let's go," he said and started back toward Thrallen. "You should get everyone ready to deal with Sebran. He's going to show up sooner or later looking for answers. My guess is sooner."

The shaman was quiet with his own thoughts for a short while as they walked.

"Master," he asked hesitantly, "is there a reason you didn't want to kill the guard?"

"Yeah. The fantasy's been fun, but I don't want to kill people. I'm not a murderer. I don't need shit like that in my head, playing over and over like a not safe for life video."

"I see." From his tone it was clear he didn't. "What about dwarves? Or elves? Gnomes? Avoiding the humans won't be easy, but there are many other races—"

"Those are people, too."

"Are we people, Master? Goblins, I mean." He added, "I don't mean to sound sensitive. I'm just looking for clarity."

"Where I come from, you're monsters," Eric replied, gave it some thought, "but after talking to you and some of the others, I'm not so sure. Don't get me wrong, I'm still pissed at what you did to me, and most of you are beyond the short bus. Looks aside, though" he said and made a noise as if weighing the idea in imaginary hands, "I guess you're people, too."

"It will be difficult, Master, to conquer the world," the shaman said, "without killing those you consider people. Defeating monsters will help you grow strong, but in the end, it helps neither of us reach our goals."

"Probably should've thought of that before you stuck me in your killer robot. You would've been better off with a sociopath. Ya know, someone who doesn't give a shit about anyone but themselves."

"We did, Master," Griz said, "and we chose carefully. There may have been a mistake in the casting, but the soul we settled on derived great pleasure in tormenting others. He stalked the weak, attacked from stealth, took countless lives without a thought."

Eric laughed. *Sounds like me playing my rogue*—He

stopped and faced the shaman.

"Dude! I am *not* my Warbones character. That's just a game! It isn't *real*." Eric fumed. "Un-fucking-believable! You ruined my life because I like pvp? That's just great. I guess I should be thankful I wasn't on a roleplay server. Who knows what fucked up rules you would've put on this thing," Eric said and banged his hollow chest. He began to mimic people LARPing like lords and ladies with excessive bowing and a terrible British accent. "Oh no, after you, Milord. Right this way, milady." He kicked and punched at nothing like a child mid-tantrum. "Fuck!"

"I can see you're upset, Master." Griz did his best to stay clear while also trying to calm him. "It may not have been real, as you say, but the lives you affected, the misery you inflicted, the sense of purpose and joy you garnered from it all...that was very real. We could sense it across realms. I can understand your hesitance to take the life of another human, or anyone you see as people, but Master, they will not look upon you the same way or give you the same consideration. They will see you as they see us, as monsters to be destroyed."

Eric was slowly settling down, his growls more like heavy breathing than the outburst of murderous anger. *It's just a game.* The thought repeated itself in his mind, as he recalled how many times he'd ganked new players for the fun of it. *It doesn't make me a bad person.*

One thing was clear. He looked like a monster. If he didn't plan on finding all the ingredients and doing all it took to be human again, what was the point of going on? What was he supposed to do now? He could kill more monsters in the hope that the golem could *become* human—or some magical approximation of it. Would that be good enough for him? Could he live in this shitty world? How long would that take? Could they send him back home if he had a magical body?

"Fuck," Eric said, defeated before he even started.

* * *

They returned by nightfall to the orange glow and fading crackle of dying flames outside the castle. The goblins had made a bonfire and gathered around it for warmth. To Eric's surprise, there were reds standing guard and greens out scouting for intruders or any sign of remaining undead. They'd secured the castle, searched every inch of it and were ready to close the gates once the meat was all cooked. Apparently greens were made to be hunters, skilled at tracking and trapping. A handful had set out and brought back wyvern for all to eat. They dressed the corpses in the field, carried back all the meat and hide they could. They'd go back for the bones later. Rooms had been assigned, for sleeping, crafting, cooking and spoils.

"The upper levels are yours, Master," Bel said. It was difficult walking up the stone stairs but not impossible. Eric was getting more and more used to his new size. "We only assigned what space was needed. It won't be long before the humans realize Tragona and his forces are gone."

Bitters snorted. "Master, send me and my gobs. We can sneak into Sebran's castle, tonight. By morning, any one resembling a leader will be dead, and all their food and water poisoned."

It seemed oranges were assassins.

"Yes," Bel said and sniggered. "Picking off the rest will be easy. A few carefully placed fires, funnel them toward Master..."

The other generals joined in the laugh.

Now they even sound like gremlins. Eric rubbed at his head. He didn't care about the mechanics of having a headache, only knew that he felt throbbing behind the glow of his eyes. *What would I do if this was a game? Assess resources, strengths and weaknesses, figure out what's coming next and plan to deal with it best I can. Hope for the best, plan for the worst; hope was a sucker's bet.*

"Once that meat's done cooking," Eric told them, "I want the fire out. Close and lock the gates. Post guards in the courtyard, along the walls and inside the castle, just in case. Keep scouts on the lookout, especially from the east. Sebran *will* be coming. Rotate people as best you can, so no one falls asleep when they shouldn't." He considered barking at them to go, when none of them moved to immediately follow his orders. Instead, he said, "You guys did a good job while I was gone. Keep it up. Dismissed."

They looked to one another, gave nods or bows and left downstairs. Griz remained behind. Nothing was left in the long hallway but torn paintings and falling purple drapes over the windows at the far end. The bedroom doors were all open, the furniture dragged outside to be burned.

"There's probably books, tools, instruments, potions and who knows what else a lich might hoard. Find them," Eric told him. "Use what you can to help us, throw away the rest. We have two goals from now on: make me human again, one way or another, and get the resources needed to satisfy your mission here. Send your people a message. We took a castle, suffered losses, and now we need reinforcements. Tell them whatever you think will convince them to help. You can stay up here with me. I think it's best you stay by my side as much as possible." He didn't say it out loud, but the intimation was that everyone else was more or less expendable. The shaman nodded and turned to leave when Eric said, "Hold on. Tell me about goblins and their colors. It's not random, right? Each type is made for a specific purpose."

"That is true, Master," Griz said, "and very perceptive of you to notice. The most common, grays, are not very intelligent. They're easier to make in large numbers and are used for menial labor. Some do specialize, though, in mining and sapping. It takes a long time to train them, but no one else is willing to work with explosives. Reds are our soldiers and guards, disciplined by nature and trained to work in units. Blues tend toward a solitary life. Their particular disposition makes them ideal as duelists and gladiators, combatants for sport and glory. Oranges are assassins and spies, tricksters of a sort that thrive in times of pressure. Given enough time to prepare, they can render an enemy indisposed without lifting a sword. Greens are our hunters and scouts, with keen eyes and a head for the outdoors. They make excellent trackers, and some specialize as animal handlers. Unfortunately, we have none of those with us.

"Browns, like myself, are nearly as abundant as grays, though with quite a bit more brain than brawn. That being said, browns who favor violence end up as brawlers or mercenaries. Most, however, are made to be craftsmen. Any caste can become a skilled worker, any sort of smith, armorer, woodworker, and the like, even a shaman, though the chances of that are very low. Only one in a thousand ends up with the temperament and acuity to work magic. It is extremely difficult to form a goblin with the intent of fashioning a shaman.

"There are other castes on Xanaranth, some not even limited to one color, but none of those are with us. I assume you're asking to take a measure of our remaining forces."

"Yeah. Interesting," Eric said. Wheels were already turning in his mind. "What does it take to make a goblin? If we need to cut ties, could we make our own?"

"Possibly, Master." Griz looked off in the distance, as if considering how it might be done. "Normally, it would take the concerted effort of many shamans to work the magic. That might not be an issue with access to a proper nexus. The truly limiting factors are the rare stones and metals." He hesitated to add, "Plus we would need to sacrifice... people."

Eric groaned.

"The more people," Griz said, "the better outcome. You can fashion a dozen grays from a single human, but..."

"You get what you pay for."

"Yes!" the shaman said, "Exactly that, Master."

This place is determined to make me a murderer. Even if I don't do it myself, anyone they kill is on me. They're following my orders—for now, anyway. I don't doubt for a second they'd turn on me if they could. None of them can be trusted. Not even Griz. The only thing I can trust is that they'll work out of self-interest. As soon as I start wanting things they don't, I may have to take a more drastic approach to leadership.

"Alright," Eric said. "Go send a message back to your people. Take a closer look around the place for anything useful. Then rest. You look like shit." The shaman bowed his head and turned for the stairs. "Griz. I kind of like you. I definitely need you. But I'm not above saying 'fuck it' and killing everyone. I know things didn't turn out the way you planned...just, don't fuck me."

Griz looked up into the red glow of Eric's eyes. He spent a long moment in quiet thought, and when he finally spoke, there was none of that pandering bullshit in his tone.

"You have my word."

Eric waited outside the walls near the road facing east. He didn't need sleep or the comfort of a building to feel safe. Sebran and his men were coming. Despite the dark and persistent rain, it was one of the few things he felt sure of.

It was just a matter of time.

Storm filled the skies in a quiet blanket of gray. The stars were completely hidden, but occasionally the moon would light the edge of a cloud in muffled silver. Eric could see fine, though. Whatever magic enhanced his senses made it seem as if the world was lit by the bright of a full moon in a clear sky. Sounds carried to him as well, the dull hiss of light rainfall, the muted strike of drops against mud or their splash into growing puddles. He heard the heartbeats of six reds standing guard behind him in the castle and four greens skulking the low hills in front. They reeked of unwashed bodies despite the rain, of mud and blood beneath the oiled leather of their armor. He could still smell the cooked wyvern, the char of ashes from the bonfire, the rain and storm.

All this, but he felt nothing. It was cold and wet across the surface of his body, as he stood still within wind blowing in from the north. Water pooled at his feet, where his weight had forced him down several inches into mud. He felt the world upon him but had no feeling inside. It was all just a growing numbness that ate away at his caring. It was more troublesome than fear of death or any pain from coming battles. If Eric wasn't careful, apathy would transform him into a monster far worse than the one he already looked like.

The problem was what to do going forward. This world wasn't about to give him anything he wasn't willing to literally fight for. This wasn't some after school special euphemism for facing hardship. If he ever wanted to be human again, to go back home, he'd have no choice but to take—money, resources, lives. Was there a better way without killing? He could try to explain, to people like Lord Sebran, ask them for help, open himself up for the inevitable disappointment and abuse. People could be good, generous and kind, but if the internet and politics had taught him anything, it was that shit rises to the top.

No one with power is going to want to help me, he thought and clenched his right hand into a fist. *I'll have to make them...somehow.* He looked down at both hands. *And no more wasting transformations. I need a weapon, a shield, magic. Power. If I can't convince, I'll have to threaten. If people are scared enough, they'll do what they're told. No one has to die.*

The lie sounded hollow, even to him.

He felt them before he heard the rushing beat of their hearts approach. Their presence prickled his skin like a static charge, five men trying to sneak across the field.

"Can you hear me, Master?" a green whispered. Eric held up a hand, signaling that he could. "Men from the east, at least three, could be more. Engage?"

"No," Eric said, his booming voice carried throughout the field. "Don't kill them." The men had stopped, hearts racing with fear. "I want all five of you to go back and tell Sebran to come talk to me. I don't want to kill anyone, but if he brings an army here...I won't have a choice." They hesitated, possibly waiting to see if he'd say more. "Go!"

They fled back to Cledford, and nearly an hour had passed before three horses approached. All three riders wore full plate, but only the outer two carried lances. The one in the middle must have been Lord Sebran. When they came into view, Eric noticed their liveries were green with white griffons. The knights in blue patrolling the keep must have been sent by King Raynver.

They stopped a hundred feet or so away. Even at that distance, Eric was making the horses skittish. Sebran didn't wear a helm with full visor like the others. His had a long green plume on top. He took it off to reveal a weathered face with a thick mustache. His hair was dark, down to his shoulders, and a scar ran along his right cheek.

"I am Lord Jessop Sebran of Cledford," he said by way of introduction, "loyal protector of the crown and rightful heir to these lands. To whom do I have the pleasure?"

"I'm Eric."

"What are you?" he asked. It was still raining, but the wind had died. "A creature in armor, or some sort of golem?"

The fuck?

"Yeah, actually. Golem." Eric wanted to move closer, though he could hear them just fine. Something about talking so far apart felt adversarial. "I'm sorry about Ella. She was...nice."

The knights with him shifted, struggled to keep their horses in line. Sebran's mustache bristled at the mention of his daughter, but his anger didn't seem to be directed at Eric.

"The lich. Is he dead?"

"Yep," Eric replied, "along with all his minions."

"Horseshit," one of the knights murmured beneath his visor.

"You see an army of undead, fuckstick?" Eric yelled at the knight. "Notice any change in the weather? Yeah. You're welcome."

"Apologies," Sebran said with a narrowed gaze. "My man spoke out of turn." In a tone that promised reprisal for his underlings, he added, "It won't happen again."

Eric shrugged. "No big."

No big? Eric berated himself. *Ugh. You're so fucking stupid! Get your shit together.*

"Yes, well, perhaps you could tell me how you came to be this way?" Sebran cleared his throat, as if he was trying not to be insulting. "You don't seem like any golem I've heard tale of."

"I dunno. We don't have golems or even magic where I come from. I was brought here by an army of goblins." The knights shifted, started to whisper, but Sebran cut them short with a gesture. "They took my spirit and put it inside this," Eric said and thumped his hollow chest. "Lucky me, right?"

"That's dreadful!" Sebran said. "We've dealt with goblins before but never anything like this. Golems are typically magical constructs. To force a soul into one…it's unconscionable. If I may ask, what were you before?"

"Human. Still am, I think. I'm from another world, though." Eric looked around at the storm and mud, the castle behind. "I don't know this place at all."

So far, so good. He doesn't seem like too much of an asshat. If he was an NPC, I probably wouldn't kill him.

"I'm sorry, that sounds terrible." He tightened his grip on the reins and said, "We have sages and scholars, practitioners of the arts. If it is within my power to return you to your body, I will do so. You have my word."

It reminded Eric of Griz's promise.

Was he betraying the goblins? He'd made it all too clear

56

that all he cared for was being human again and getting back home. Why did he suddenly feel dirty?

"Thanks," Eric said to fill the silence. "That would be awesome. No offense to your world, but I'd rather be in mine."

"Completely understandable. Tell me, what happened to my Ella?" Sebran leaned forward, as if bracing himself for something he really didn't want to know. "How did she die?"

"The lich," Eric replied, "Tragona, he...used her as a phylactery. He kept his spirit inside her and locked her in the castle. As long as he kept her alive, he couldn't be killed. When we attacked, he must've poisoned her. She was dying when we found her, in a lot of pain. There was nothing we could do." Eric thought back on that moment with a cold sense of dread knotting his middle. "Before she died, she made me promise to bury her beside her mother. It was the least I could do."

"It was poison then." His voice seemed tormented by the loss. "Healers weren't able to determine what had damaged her organs so severely." Sebran looked directly at Eric. "And her neck? What caused that?"

"Oh," Eric said. *Ah fuck, he knows.* "That was me." The lord's jaw tightened. *Did I just fuck this up? Was that a deal-breaker?* "It was the only way to kill the lich. And the pain. She was...hurting a lot. She wanted me to do it."

"I see. So it was a mercy." Sebran had to quiet his men again, though he seemed less angry about their outbursts. "Well, I'll have men come secure the castle on the morrow. We can discuss—"

"That's not gonna fly."

"Pardon?" Sebran asked.

Eric said, "The castle. It's mine now. Until I'm back in my body, back home, I have no choice but to live in this world. The goblins listen to me, do what I tell them to. I gotta keep them somewhere." Eric waved his arms around at what used to be a magical wasteland, filled with the undead. "I cleared this place myself, so I'm gonna keep it."

"That is...disappointing," Sebran said. "This land once belonged to my father. It is by all rights mine, but as you say, you cleared the land, rid it of a terrible evil. We are in your debt," he said with a slight bow of his head. "I gave my word. I will determine if anything is to be done about returning you to your body. Perhaps then you will see fit to return my castle."

"Sounds like a deal."

Lord Sebran bowed his head once more and led his men back toward the east.

Huh. That went better than I expected.

* * *

Eric was starving.

He'd spent the night outside, making sure there were no shenanigans on the lord's part. *It wouldn't be the first time some NPC promised one thing while plotting a dick move behind the player's back.* No one else from Cledford came, no scouts or spies, no immediate plans of betrayal.

It was almost disappointing.

He wanted Sebran's help getting back into his body, but it would've made everything so much easier if the guy had been an ass. He was so understanding, so polite that Eric almost didn't know how to react. If Sebran went back on his word and attacked in the cover of night, it would've been all that much easier to fight back—to kill them. To ease his hunger.

It would've been self-defense, Eric reasoned. *This is my home now,* he thought and looked at the gothic nightmare of a castle, *shitty as it is. I have to protect it...and my goblins. I need them.*

Guards and scouts were changing shift as the sun began

to rise. Eric returned to the courtyard where many had woken and gathered, awaiting morning meal. Others were still asleep on scraps of cloth in one of the rooms. With all the clanging of metal armor and pots in the kitchen, the low voices and stupid laughter, the cursing and shoving, it was a wonder they got any sleep at all.

Children, Eric thought. *They're all basically children, with the exception of a few. Scary, cartoonish, fucking murderous children.*

Eric called Griz and the generals to a meeting by the portcullis. He'd doubled the guards around and within the castle, plus scouts outside the wall, until further notice. As much as he wanted to trust Sebran, he had a sinking feeling the lord would just as soon attack to have his lands back than do anything to help the monster that had broken his daughter's neck. Compared to Tragona and his undead army, the goblins must have looked like a safe bet.

Griz arrived first.

Eric asked, "You find anything useful in the castle?"

"Quite a bit, Master," the shaman replied. "There is a laboratory in the lower level with its own cache of stores, an abundance of rope, candles, dried herbs and various spell reagents. Tragona experimented on humans to a torturous degree, though I cannot say what it is he was trying to accomplish. Their remains were so disturbing, so tainted by magic that they're meat has become rotted and poisonous."

"Gross," Eric said, more about their wanting to eat dead people than the experiments. "Probably something to do with using people as phylacteries. Anything else?"

"Yes, Master, there is also a small reliquary." Griz fished the lich's ring from a pocket. "It has a collection of potions and other enchanted jewelry, such as this. I'm fairly certain he intended to use this ring to contain his spirit once the girl died."

"Crafty fucker."

"Indeed, Master." Griz put the ring away as the other generals were approaching. "The reliquary includes a collection of semi- to precious stones, with quite a bit of diamonds. They're common but useful if we ever intend to make grays."

"Grays are made from diamond?" Eric asked. "That doesn't sound like cheap labor."

"Diamonds and iron, Master. The stones are terribly rare on our world but in abundance here on Taellus."

That's something, I guess. Dunno what I'd do with an army of grays, though.

He addressed the gathered generals.

"I want a full accounting," Eric said, "of our current situation. How many goblins of each color do we have? What are they using for gear? How much food and water do we have stored? What do we know about the lands on our borders, on all sides?" He looked to Griz. "And most importantly, where can I find something to kill that isn't murdering innocent people?"

"Well, Master," the shaman hedged and shifted his weight, "we had hoped to be working our way east by now, but—"

"Yeah, no. No eating potential allies. They might turn out to be useful—" *What is that?* A smell struck Eric as he honed in on the sound of streaming. He turned to see a brown relieving himself against a courtyard wall. "Hey! No! Don't do that here!" The brown was wide-eyed with fright but couldn't stop. He ran toward the backside of the castle leaving a trail as he went. "The last thing we need is for this place to start stinking of shit and piss."

Bel cleared his throat. "I'll have my reds dig a proper latrine outside the wall. There's twenty-eight of us in all, Master. We all have steel swords, some chainmail but mostly leathers. We have ten shields we rotate for guard duty."

"Thirty-one," Mudbutt said proudly. "Err, browns, that is, Master. Also steel swords but no armor."

"Relax," Eric told him. "It ain't a competition. Does that include Griz?" Mud confirmed that it did, so Eric asked Stalk, "Greens?"

"Just twelve, Master," the green general replied. "Scouts and hunters weren't a high priority when this host was formed. We have hunting knives, short bows and a limited supply of arrows."

Eric looked beyond the gate. What few trees survived the magical storm that had plagued the land were black and twisted. He doubted their wood was of any use for fletching arrows.

"Right," he said, "so we need to keep an eye out for healthy trees, keep a stockpile of wood for fletching and fires."

"Riverwood is best, Master," Stalk said, "along clear streams and rivers, some ponds and lakes. They don't grow very tall, and the wood is more pliable."

Eric frowned—inwardly.

"Good to know," he said with growing irritation. He really was trying not to lose his patience. There was just so much noise going on around him, and every cackle or scuffle made his hunger seem all the more pronounced. To Bitters, he asked, "How 'bout the oranges?'

A shadow fell across the goblin's face, either anger or embarrassment. "Nine," he said sullenly then quickly added, "Master. We lost quite a few during your arrival."

Oh. Well, shit. He gave a mental shrug. *I didn't think any of them were important back then.*

"My bad." It was about as much an apology as he'd ever give. "Gear?"

"Steel short swords, daggers, throwing knives, and we each maintain our own herb kit for mixing poisons. Four of us wear silk padded leathers for infiltration. The rest have a mix of leather and cloth."

"Nice." Eric sounded impressed. He wondered when they might be useful for more than swords on the field. He looked to the blue general, who still didn't look all that feminine to him. As much as he wanted to keep calling her smurfette, she just didn't fit the description. "How many blues?"

"We're sixteen, Master," she answered. "We all have steel swords and long daggers, some hardened leather armor like mine. Most are used to going without it. They think it hampers movement. We can use more than just swords if the need arises. Blues are trained to use any weapon at hand."

Alright, so... Eric did some calculations in his head. *We have ninety-six total.* He looked over those gathered in the courtyard. The goblin host was much bigger when he first arrived, but what remained was leaner, the actual army. *We're better off. They would've just been a waste of food. Still, we gotta find a way to keep these guys fed. The way they're eating that wyvern meat...*

"What's the land like around us?" he asked. "Aside from the obvious," he added and indicated the range of mountains stretching west to north off in the distance. "Have you done any scouting?"

"We did, Master," Griz replied. "I believe the castle to the south was rebuilt here once it was destroyed. Most likely because beneath us is a convergence of two ley lines. Its magic helps strengthens the stones."

Eric could feel the ley lines as a steady thrum, like the bass of a song he couldn't quite make out. That electric thrumming was always there but subdued enough that it didn't take hold of his attention. The way they flowed far below, always in one direction, was like rivers of pure magic reaching up toward the surface with their splashing. He wondered what it would be like to tap directly into such power. If he could use it to fuel his transformations, he'd be human again in no time.

"To the east," the shaman continued, "is Cledford. There are small towns and farming villages spread throughout the land surrounding it farther east and to the south. North of it is a river that runs along the range directly north of us. It rounds a forest that continues east for many days. West of us is a fully enclosed valley. We haven't been able to scout very far in, as it's been completely barred by the undead until recent."

An entire area blocked off by mountains, with this castle guarding the only way in. Is that why Tragona was satisfied with staying put? What the hell is he hiding in there?

"Stalk, can you send someone to check it out? No more than three days. If they encounter any danger, tell them to turn around and report back." The green general left to see it done. "Bitters, is it possible to get someone inside Sebran's keep without being seen? Just watch and listen, see what they're up to. I mean, I know you guys don't exactly blend."

"Absolutely, Master," the orange general replied, as if his own skill had been called into question. "I'll send Marbit. She's an excellent spy. If she needs to, she can pose as a human child."

Marbit. Isn't that what they call those stale ass marshmallows in cereal?

"If you say so." Eric watched him go as well. They seemed happier to have a task. He might just have to do the same with some others to keep them busy and their minds off eating humans. "What's south of that ruined castle?"

"Dense forest," Bel answered gruffly, as if recalling a bad memory, "Master. We almost lost a patrol there our first day. Luckily, my gobs recognized the smells and got out in time. It's infested with trolls," he explained and scrunched up his nose, as if he could still smell one. "They won't risk leaving the forest—not without a shaman venturing out to secure a new totem."

"Great!" Eric said, his stomach roiling with quiet pains. "Stinky troll forest is the one to beat. What's in the forest north—"

The crystal on Griz's staff began to slowly pulse.

"Hmm," the shaman muttered, concerned.

Eric asked, "What is it?"

"It's the foundry, Master. I set an alert spell for the others to use in case I'm ever needed."

"That place is still around, huh?" Eric gave it some thought. If it wasn't already destroyed by demons, they should probably move it. "What all do we have there? How many smiths and weapons? Come to think of it, what are they doing for food and water?"

"We have seventeen Master craftsmen, Master," Griz said with some pride, "and another twenty-five with many years of experience. They make all of our weapons, armor and tools. In exchange for allowing us use of their land, we provide the demon army with all the weapons and armor they need. Karron additionally provides us with resources, from processed ores and hides to all that is necessary for our craftsmen to survive."

Sounds like a sweet deal, so long as the demons aren't treating them as slaves. I wonder how much of what they make they get to keep.

"Alright then," Eric said. "Let's go see what's up."

Griz nodded and began summoning a portal.

When they arrived at the foundry, Eric was surprised to see a demon already there and inside the protection of the magic barrier. It was crouched over the spot where Eric had killed the other demon. Gouge marks in the stone floor and a drop of blood in particular had caught its attention.

While the first one Eric had encountered was a foot soldier, with thick limbs and a wide chest, covered in heavy dark plates, this one seemed more of a scout. It was lean and cunning, with a feral intelligence behind the eyes. Bright red with vertical slits for pupils, they seemed to gauge and take in all with practiced care. It must have stood twelve feet tall, with slender but muscled arms and long legs bent backwards at the knee. Its scales were dull crimson edged in black, more oval than diamond shaped and tightly spaced for protection. Rather than plates across its back, there were finned spines a foot long, from obsidian black to orange and black again at the tip. Its chest was striated with corded muscle beneath a harness of steel spikes worn crosswise like a vest. Its hands and feet resembled claws, with long talons and barbs along the backsides. Its maw was draconic, a short snout with pointed teeth and a series of nostrils across the top. It had no ears or hair, just a head covered in tiny black spikes.

Within seconds its essence was overwhelming. The bright of its crimson aura washed over Eric like tingles across his front, tantalizing parts he no longer had. It was summer warmth on the face, the breathy intake of fresh baked goods and the numbing rush of realization one was about to have sex. However strong the soldier had been, this demon's essence put it to shame.

It was increasingly difficult to think of anything else.

"Greetings," Griz said and bowed to the demon with the deference of a diplomat or politician. "To what do we owe the honor?"

The other goblins kept working, heads down to avoid eye contact. The incessant sound of hammering rang out in time to glowing sparks and the bright glow of freshly poured molten metal.

There was a feel of magic coming off the demon, not as strong as its essence but there all the same. It was like stepping into a strong electrical field, one that could jolt outward and strike at any moment.

It warned of danger.

How the hell did it get in here? The thought was hazy in his mind, beneath the shouts and sudden screams that wanted the demon's power, like a barrage of his own voice demanding, *Do it! Just do it!*

"A servitor has gone missing," it said in a voice more rasp than whine, the slow paced speech of one who gave thought to every word. The demon eyed Griz and stood to its full height. It completely ignored Eric. "I tracked his scent—" the demon pointed toward the gouges— "to here. Explain."

"There must be a mistake," Griz said. "I've not seen a demon here since collection. Perhaps he was one of those who helped carry arms back to the citadel."

Damn, Griz. You go, boy! Eric had to admit, it was a pretty smart explanation. He had trouble keeping his own thoughts in check, though, was clenching a fist to fight back the urge to attack. The demon noticed but said nothing. *Just fucking kill him, already!* Eric growled inwardly at himself. *Shut up, goddammit. Shut the fuck up!*

"Seekers do not make mistakes." The demon stepped forward and faced Eric, looked up into the glow of his eyes as if trying to gauge intent. "Considerable strength would be needed to best a servitor."

Son of a bitch. Eric knew they were playing a ruse to save the foundry, but the sudden proximity... *You better back the fuck off!*

"Indeed," Griz agreed, "so much so that I can't think of many creatures even capable of it. Isn't it more likely that this soldier is out on the hunt or has taken the fight to the fey on his own terms, rather than a highly unlikely loss to a mysterious predator?"

"What purpose does this serve?" the seeker asked and tapped Eric's chest with a talon. "It looks awkward, clumsy and lacks the finesse of your usual work. Surely, it is not meant to fight."

If Eric didn't know better, he'd swear the demon was trying to goad him. It *wanted* him to attack. All he had to do was reach out and grab its spindly throat. Its face was so close he could feel its breath across his face.

"That's just a worker," Griz assured him. "We goblins are not known for our strength. We need such things to help with heavy lifting."

The demon dragged its talon over Eric's chest, filling the air with a low pitched screeching and several sparks. It only slightly marred the surface but enough to enrage Eric. It was all he could do to keep from striking out in a frenzy.

"It is a tool then," the seeker said, "a stupid thing to be used. Give it to me." It kept its gaze upon Eric and grinned.

"As a show of a good faith."

Griz seemed at a loss but managed to finally say, "I cannot. It is just a tool but an invaluable one. I can offer you anything else you see here, for your personal use." He headed toward a collection of fine steel swords pegged to a wall separating the foundry. They hung over bundles of numerous, more common weapons ready for the next collection. "These are our finest," he said and pointed to a row of masterfully crafted long and great swords. "I could even add an enchantment for you, given enough time."

The seeker seemed to consider but never looked away from Eric. Its talon continued to etch a path across his dark metal.

"No need. I will let you keep your toy."

The seeker shoved Eric back a step, hard enough that a less coordinated creature would have stumbled and fallen. The demon was much stronger than it looked. Eric's eyes flared bloody red.

"Oh, dear," the shaman said.

Eric smashed his head into the seeker's, sent it reeling back but kept it close by grabbing hold of its neck with both hands. He growled in anger, a fury spurred by the demon's taunting and a desire to take its essence. Eric squeezed with all his strength and forced the seeker downward.

Eyes narrowed, one foot braced behind, the demon looked as if it had expected the assault. It immediately raised both hands to grab hold of Eric's wrists. There was no denying its strength, but the gurgled struggling meant it was fighting just to breathe.

Talons raked Eric's wrists. They marred the metal but couldn't reach the runes inside. The seeker raised both arms and smashed down into the crooks of Eric's arms. Magic formed in one hand as a ball of swirling violet. It plunged the sphere into Eric's face, and it broke apart as a burning flash of wild flames.

Eric didn't need the false approximation of eyes to see. He

68

used his entire body to sense his surroundings. The magic jarred that ability, though, like overcharging all his sensory input. Momentarily blinded, ears ringing, hands extended just for balance, vertigo threatened to send him down onto his back.

The demon grabbed Eric by one leg and pulled, drove an elbow into his chest to propel him even farther. Eric felt himself go down and crash hard against the floor. Stone cracked outward beneath his weight. The demon was suddenly on top, clawing wildly at Eric's eyes and throat. It reached back with both hands and called magic to them.

Eric caught both wrists as they came down. Two more spheres crackled with black lightning just inches from his face. Whatever magic this was, its intent was to kill. Eric squeezed, forced both wrists back, but the bones wouldn't break.

All the goblins but Griz had fled to the lower level. The shaman was moving his staff through the air in a small circle while quietly chanting.

Is this his chance? Eric thought, also wondering if he'd taken on more than he could handle. *Is he gonna help, or is he gonna fuck me?*

"You have broken our pact," the seeker said to Griz, his voice strained from the struggle. "When I do not return, Karron will know of your betrayal. He will seek to destroy all of goblinkind. Not only on Taellus but on your home world as well."

Eric changed tack and brought the demon's hands together. The magic clashed and exploded into bright shards of ebon flame. A flash of blue rose up between them. The demon screamed in anguish, its hands all but destroyed. Some of the bones and bits of muscle still remained but the dark magic was spent. Eric rolled, forced the seeker beneath his weight. He held the demon down by one hand at its throat.

"You talk too fuckin' much," he growled and grabbed its

face with his other hand. Eric pushed for all he was worth with both hands. "And those goblins are mine!"

The seeker's neck snapped in two places.

Eric was barely able to breathe a sigh of relief, to let loose his hold, before the change came upon him. Like a spike of adrenaline, it seized his every thought in a mix of sated hunger and dying pleasure.

It's the fucking hunger that kills me. I can't take it anymore. I'm no good if I can't think straight.

And with that his choice was made.

The exultation faded, and so did the hunger. Eric still wanted to feed on essence, but it no longer drove him. As much as he wanted other changes, he would never again be a victim to that unrelenting desire.

Eric sat up and looked at Griz.

"Shit," he said. "I fucked up. I just couldn't take it."

"No, Master. You did the right thing." Griz moved to stand before him, as other goblins were starting to come out from hiding. "He forced our hands."

Eric snorted. "*We* didn't do shit. I'm the one who killed it." He looked the shaman over, though he wasn't really all that surprised. It's not like they were friends. "For a second, I thought you were gonna help."

"I did, Master," Griz said. "I knew you would turn the seeker's magic against him. I shielded you from the blast. The spell he was casting...it would have torn you apart. It was the best I could do, given the circumstance."

Huh. Eric recalled the flash of blue light as the demon's magic exploded. *Guess he did help.*

"I didn't realize," Eric said. "Thanks." He got up to his feet and looked around at the foundry. "Well, this place is burned. Start packing it all up. We'll make a new one at the castle."

* * *

70

Eric helped carry anvils and weapon bundles back through a portal, but the massive forges would have to be remade. The crafters began setting up a temporary workspace for smelting and forging. The castle was built on two ley lines, which was serviceable for most tasks. Crafting masterwork weapons would require scouting a new location, a proper nexus of ley lines to draw magic from. They'd also need to find new sources of raw ore. A search for deposits could take time and require most of their forces. While it was true the goblins were no longer forced to forge weapons and armor for the demon army, their own was still underequipped.

Plus we'll need those ores and minerals to make new goblins at some point, Eric realized when he approved the order to begin surveying. Luckily some of the craftsmen had experience and knew what to look for. *That'll be nearly half the browns out looking, with a good chunk of reds and blues to keep them alive. Even more once they start digging.* His little army was dwindling, not that he relied on any of them near as much as Griz. *Can I even trust them to come back?*

"Something amiss, Master?" Griz was coordinating browns and where to put the last bits from the foundry. There were still quite a few tools, die casts, mounds of uncured hides and numerous other things the goblins could carry on their own. Griz had taken charge and was directing them all. "You seem quiet."

They stood by the open gates, where Eric's focus was on the east. He didn't know when or if Sebran was going to return or even if the lord was coming to help him or attack. He felt like an idiot for hoping.

"Just thinking," Eric said. Midday had already come and gone. Winter sun was setting between the clouds, just over the mountains behind him. "Can we trust that Lord Sebran guy?"

"Of course not, Master," Griz said without hesitation. "He's human. Always in a hurry to die, as if they don't already live short enough lives, and they care little for anyone or anything but themselves."

Fair enough.

"You know I'm human, right?" He was more amused than annoyed.

The shaman wiped his brow with a sleeve of his dirty robe. "I thought you would prefer honesty, Master."

"I do," Eric said, "as long as it isn't *too* insulting. I just never took you for a racist."

"My opinions are based on experience, Master," Griz said, "not the other way around. I don't think any less of humans for their behavior, or we would never use them in our golems. I'm simply aware of their behavior and act accordingly."

There are other golems?

A reverse whirring filled the air and ended abruptly with what looked like the face of a mirror folding in on itself. From the split in space, a goblin in white and gold silk clothing appeared as if he'd been standing there all along. He wore breeches, a tunic, a vest, short leather boots and a piece of cloth over his shoulder like a mini-cape. He wore gold-rimmed glasses over his wide, thick nose and carried a white walking stick topped with a large gold encrusted crystal. He wore a number of gold rings in a row on his long, tapered ears. More unusual than his ensemble was his caste.

The goblin was white.

From his skin to long hair tied back into a knot, his eyebrows to pointed teeth, he was a varied palette of snowy white. Even his eyes seemed to have a pale glow in the fading light of day.

"Grizzletongue!" he called out and began assessing the gathered goblins in the courtyard with a raised brow.

"Auditor Blanchbottom," Griz said to the new goblin with a bow of his head in respect. He walked over to stand before him. "I am glad to see you well. How are things at the conservatory?"

Blanchbottom? The guy's name is literally white ass? Eric fought back the urge to laugh. He wasn't sure if this was like the situation with the seeker, where it would be better if he pretended to be an actual golem. *Figures it'd be a white guy in charge,* he joked to himself. *I wonder what they're made for and why we don't have any.*

"As well as can be expected." Blanch seemed like one of those office types, polite but impatient. "If we could skip the pleasantries, I have seven more of these yet to do today."

"Of course. You received my report—"

"What are they doing?" Blanch asked, tilting his head down to look over his glasses at the browns carrying material past. With a flick of his wrist, his walking stick became a scroll, which he opened and perused. "These items, that portal...what happened to the foundry?"

Griz faltered for a moment before explaining, "It is no longer safe there for us. I'm afraid our agreement with the demons is no longer tenable."

The auditor gave Griz his full attention.

"Why not?"

"They tried to take our golem," Griz said truthfully. "With all we've given them and continue to give, I saw this as going beyond the bounds of our agreement."

Blanch checked whatever was written on his ledger and eyeballed Eric.

"Take it back," the white said. "Make the deal."

Griz shook his head. "It is too late for more dealing. I'm afraid we've...collapsed that particular passage."

"Unacceptable." He pointed a long nail at a list for Griz to see. "This expedition is now operating at a deficit. The benefits of our accord with Karron's army cannot be offset by the cost of this golem. Even if your conquest is unsuccessful, the resources gained by that pact are enough to recoup our initial investment and make staying here profitable."

Ahh. So the whites are some sort of bankers or accountants or something. Useless.

Eric stepped forward and looked down at the goblin in his pristine outfit. "We're not goin' back," he said with finality. "And you might as well be talkin' to me. I'm in charge."

The scroll snapped back into a walking stick, and Blanch backed away.

"What is this?" His tone had decidedly changed. With genuine fear, he asked Griz, "What have you done?"

How did he get here? Eric wondered. *Was it a spell or that walking stick?* He hadn't created a portal, like the way Griz travelled to Inexium and back. *If I take the stick from him, can I use to go to Xana-whatevers?*

Griz tried to explain. "There must have been some sort of mishap with the summoning. The spirit we bound remained conscious, in control."

"Control!" Blanch's eyes were wide, and he continued to back away. "You've lost control of this expedition!"

The shaman's voice remained calm. "The expedition is still on track. It's just...under new leadership. I asked for reinforcements, because I believe we can still conquer this realm and beyond. Eric needs its resources as much as we do."

Blanch frowned and stopped moving, as if he'd found his backbone.

"You gave it a name?" One of his eyes twitched, like he was about to pop his cork. "You're taking orders from a human!"

Eric laughed.

"Please, Master," Griz said. "You're not making this any easier."

Blanch took firm hold of his walking stick and tapped it against the ground, like a judge banging a gavel.

"Your charter is hereby revoked! You are to cease all activity and return to Xanaranth at once. I will give my final report to the council immediately." He leveled a grave look toward the shaman. "If you still honor your house, I will see you at the next Gathering."

With that, he disappeared into a folding of space.

Has to be the stick.

"That went well," Eric said. "What's the Gathering?"

Griz took in a deep breath and let it out. The whole encounter obviously hadn't gone the way he hoped.

"It is a time, Master, when all heads of house come together before the council to discuss laws, agreements and any grievances. This occurs every second full moon, which for Taellus is twice a month—or roughly every other week."

There was something to his voice as he spoke, a hint of sadness or regret. From what the white had said, if Griz didn't show at this next Gathering, there would be repercussions. It sounded as if he, too, would never see his family again.

"You gonna go?"

Griz had been lost in thought, looked up from his reverie in confusion.

"You would allow me?"

He didn't say 'Master.' Does that mean something?

"Sounds important," Eric said.

Griz looked around at the other goblins. They kept working, even though there was no doubt they'd just heard they were all fired. He looked proud, not of himself but of those he led, those who chose to follow him.

"House is very important to a goblin, Master," Griz said wistfully, "as much as blood relations to a human. I believe in this expedition, in you, Master. I know we can conquer Faradim and all the realms beyond. We can get you what you need and fulfill our charter in the process. But if I go to the next Gathering," he said and let the thought hang.

"They won't let you come back." Eric gave it some thought, his army of level ones and his epic quest to regain humanity. "I'll tell you what. Give everyone the opportunity to go home. Send them back if they really want to. I'm gonna keep going. I don't have any other choice. At least this way you guys do."

Eric watched from a hilltop outside the castle walls, as browns passed through a portal. Its wavering glow cast shades of beryl over the courtyard walls, like an emerald reflection of water. The first rays of morning sun were stretching across his back, lit the drops of frozen moisture on his metal in orange bursts. He'd ordered the goblins out surveying to return, so they could decide if they wanted to go home or continue.

Honor and house were important to goblins, as Griz had said but less so to those who were made for manual labor. Browns were just a step above grays. Their esteem and familial ties, by nature, were not as strong. They took pride in their work, not in those they worked for. All of the others had chosen to stay. To return home meant admitting failure. Continuing the expedition, charter or no, at least offered the hope of redemption and regaining favor with their respective houses.

All but twelve browns had decided to leave. Two were

Master craftsmen, and five were many years on their way toward the same goal. Mudbutt stood proud among the five remaining fighters.

It was a terrible blow to their morale, losing so many skilled workers. They could still function, survey and find new mines, produce arms and armor, but their odds of success had been greatly diminished.

Griz ordered a new team back out and headed over to join Eric. Barely a dozen remained in the castle, a few reds, oranges and greens. They could keep watch, guard the gates, but it was up to Eric to maintain their hold of it.

If Sebran attacks, I'm on my own.

Eric would have rather some of the others had left, instead of the browns. He needed workers more than fighters. Without them to find mines, extract minerals and ores, they had no hope of making new goblins. As much as he wanted a weapon and shield from his next changes, Eric thought the ability to wield magic, to help Griz expand their army, would be much more useful.

I dunno if it's even possible.

"Explain magic to me," Eric said, as the shaman sat down beside him. "Like, what is it? How does it work? How come some people can use it but others can't? Is it an intelligence thing or like some innate ability thing?"

"That's quite a large topic, Master," Griz said, as if surprised by the sudden interest, "one that usually takes many years to fully grasp."

"ELI-five it for me. Gimme the wiki version."

"Alright, Master, I shall do my best." He took a brief minute to compose his thoughts and explained, "Magic is a force of nature most like gravity or magnetism. It is inherent to a place, in its ley lines, though I cannot say what determines its strength. The magic here on Taellus is strong, when compared to say Inexium, but pales in comparison to Xanaranth. Some have theorized this has to do with the number of ley lines present, their direction of flow and density—"

Eric cleared his throat.

"Apologies, Master. To wield magic is to channel, by way of a focus. The basest of users employ cumbersome foci, like exhaustive rituals and complex casting, while the most skilled seem to use no focus at all. They're able to use their minds and body to channel and direct."

"Magic can also be stored," Griz went on, "within an item or enchantment. Do you know what a rune is, Master?"

"Err, yeah, like a letter."

"Precisely, Master, although in this case the letter of a magical language." Griz used his staff to draw in air, and where he wrote, golden runes appeared and hung in place. "Runes are individual letters. Sigils represent concepts. Both can be used to create a ward, a simple spell." He kept scrawling golden runes with his staff, as if writing out a sentence in a foreign language. "Wards can be joined to create a glyph, a complex spell. The more wards a glyph contains, the more complicated the spell. Glyphs can be worked together to create a construct, an interlocking system, but it is incredibly difficult, requires countless hours of planning and preparation and a great number of skilled users working in tandem."

When Griz finished the last rune, they all flared to life as one and faded into golden mist. Below the spell, where its magic rained down, a stem sprouted from the mud about an inch tall. Two small leaves grew out from its middle, like the promise of spring.

"You can create life," Eric mused. The little sprout wouldn't survive winter, but the notion stuck with him. "Can anyone do it?"

"I wish I could say yes, Master," Griz replied sadly, "but it has been my experience that is not so. It has little to do with desire or practice, as far as I've observed. Some are simply born to it. Discipline, desire, practice all determine how well one does it, not whether one is able."

If his golem body could one day be human then why would using magic be any different?

"If I spend a transformation," Eric asked, "or however many it takes, do you think I could use magic?"

Griz considered his answer as if he saw beyond it, to what Eric truly wanted.

"Anything is possible, Master, but it would take a great deal of practice and study to help me with the ritual." He appraised Eric with his good eye. "That is why you asked, because you wish to create more goblins?"

Eric nodded.

He'd been thinking of those that left. Their loyalty wasn't to him or even their expedition. But if he could make his own goblins...

"Why were you and the others so quick to follow me?" Eric asked. "Aside from the fear of dyin' and all. Why stay? Or why not just take off on your own? Why continue to serve me?"

"Survival is a factor, Master," Griz admitted with a chuckle, "but we all serve, one way or another. It is the single most important tenet goblin society is based on."

"What about your leaders? There's always someone at the top, even if it's a council or whatever. At some point, there's a dude who doesn't answer to anyone."

Griz said, "Even those at the highest level, Master, who make the most important decisions, ideally serve the people. As I said earlier, the expedition is still underway. It's simply under new leadership. Either way, we're still serving society."

Eric got to his feet. Even though it hadn't been long since Sebran agreed to help, he was getting restless. He didn't want to sit around waiting. His hunger had been reduced to little more than an imagined grumbling, but acquiring essence to fuel more changes was his highest priority.

I feel the need for xp.

His vision wandered south toward the ruined castle he

was summoned in. If there was a forest full of trolls beyond it, he could potentially get to work. He neither needed nor wanted to risk what remained of his army. It was better they gathered resources and watched over their new castle, rather than follow him toward their possible deaths.

Nah, I got this.

Eric headed toward the ruined castle.

"I'm gonna take a walk," he told Griz. "Don't wait up."

* * *

The forest was visible from beyond the ruined castle, though it stood a few miles off. Eric trudged through fields along the way with a sense of foreboding, as if the darkness between its trees was somehow watching. It was impressive, the dense woodland, with leafless tops that came close to reaching into the storm clouds. Mist clung to the ground made muddy by rains but couldn't hide the thick trunks just ahead. Even the smallest of them was many feet around at the base, with thin bark and a wide bough of empty branches. A few of their roots broke the surface, bent the earth in small crevices that pooled water and debris.

It was the larger trees, however, that caught and held his eye. They were few and far between but stood out in stark contrast. Massively thick trunks, easily fifty feet in diameter, these bigger trees dwarfed the others in size and scope. It was these that stretched off into the gray of winter skies, with craggy black limbs that bent at sharp angles. Their skin was rugged with age, cracked and broken, blackened between the splits. Wide knots stretched across their surface in a pattern like watching eyes or the howling spirits of creatures long dead within the trees.

Stepping into the forest brought with it a cold dread, like slipping from a dream into the depths of a growing nightmare. The air became cold in a way that slowed his steps, not for the chill but out of caution. Old discarded limbs crackled underfoot, mixed with sodden earth in a ploy to grasp. The echoed snaps and breaks were all the more unsettling for a lack of any other noise. There were no birdcalls, no insects, none of the sounds that signaled wildlife. That emptiness was like a vacuum, sucking up every noise he made and amplifying it like a beacon.

Might as well be blowing a fucking air horn.

If there were trolls, he couldn't smell any over the heady scent of rain. There was a bitterness in the air, that came and went with the wind, but that seemed to be coming from the larger trees. Eric was working his way toward one. The smaller ones had grown too dense for his size. It wouldn't have taken too much time to go around, but his first instinct was to push one over. He didn't really expect it to move when he tested one with a push.

A single crack, like a lightning strike, rang out with enough force that Eric jumped and pulled his hand back. The tree didn't fall over but was bent enough to reveal mottled striations in its pulp. The splintered wood looked sick, was greatly weakened by disease or whatever had tainted its insides. Dust from the break seemed to linger in air, gray to black tiny flakes that cascaded in a slow descent. It was similar to the bitterness, sharper and sickly sweet. Even its sap had an odd coloring, more gray than golden with black flecks floating within. Eric left the tree and went searching for another way forward.

When he finally came face to face with one of the big trees, it was so wide he couldn't see around it, was more wall than tree. Its top branches stretched another three hundred feet or higher above the others. The acrid scent he'd been following was from a tarry substance between the cracks in its bark. There was too much to be sap, though that's exactly what it looked like. It was as if the tree was bleeding, a dark jelly-like blood that filled every crack and crevice. Sticky to the touch, it left streaks with shades of crimson across his fingertips when smeared. Oddly enough, his fingers tingled where it had touched.

Eric washed it off in a puddle at the base of the tree. In a world filled with magic, there was no telling what he was dealing with. It felt like everywhere he looked, magic gone awry had somehow tainted the land.

Is that what this was? Where were the trolls Bel had spoken of? Or any other living creatures for that matter? This place wasn't a forest; it was a cemetery.

Another crack sparked off farther east. With a cover of fog taller than he was, densely packed trees and the slope of small hills, it was difficult to see all that far in any direction. Where'd he come from was gone behind a wall of misted white and overlapping trunks. He had a general idea of where he was, felt confident enough to get back out, but navigating the forest wasn't as easy as he'd first thought.

More breaking of branches sounded out.

Eric began carefully working his way toward what sounded like frantic scrabbling through fallen branches. It had started off a careless mistake and now seemed an all-out pursuit. His own noise became less a concern the louder the others grew. There was a hoarse breath like ragged growling rising in strength the closer he drew. The cold sense of dread intensified, as if his hollow had filled with ice. Steam rose off his body as he ran. It was then he could hear it, the muffled cries and jolts of a voice fleeing in terror.

It's a chick, he could tell and ran even faster. Trees cracked and fell aside, shouldered away in haste. More cries, and he cursed. It sounded like his sister that night at the park... *God dammit.*

He came bounding through the trees, slid down a low gully into a clearing and nearly struck her. She was on all fours, crawling his direction in desperation. Furred hides shredded and muddied left her nearly naked to the cold. Long black hair down to her waist had been braided into folds, were now disheveled and come loose. Her skin was a pale green, smooth with youth, smeared with dirt and blood. She was painted in white across both arms, shoulders, down neck and back. Her exposed muscles were fit, tensed with fear and determination. When she looked up to see Eric, her wide eyes were a bright violet beneath a delicate brow. She had two blunted tusks in her lower teeth, but there nothing coarse about her. In a word, she was beautiful—troll or no. She nearly backed away before what chased after her came into the clearing.

It stood a foot taller than Eric, six more than her, and carried itself with a strength born of madness. It was impossibly thin, each rib and knotted joint clearly visible through a long and tattered gossamer wrap. Chalky skin, black eyes, a mouthful of fangs, it looked a nightmare spirit become flesh.

Each croaking breath shook its body, expanded its fragile chest with a shuddering of clicks. It gave pause when it saw Eric, flexing jittery hands with black talons as long as each finger. Its hair was a mass of curls that fell all about its body, floating in air with a swoosh and swoop as if submerged in murky water. Its ears were two feet long, twice that of the troll girl's, and tapered back to a sharp point. When it moved to attack, its whole body disappeared into a shattering of smoke—a dark cloud that creeped its way forward.

"Get behind me," Eric told the girl.

Instead she fell back and scrambled away from them both. Thorny roots sprouted up from the muddied earth, grasped at her legs and arms. They snapped, whipped out, caught a wrist and held fest.

Eric stepped up, swung into the cloud. It was like a flutter of roiling ash, swirling as it moved. He'd done no damage he could see and felt nothing as it encompassed him. Roots grew at his feet, tried to grasp and take hold. He broke free with little effort. He wanted to help the girl with her bonds but had to keep the creature focused on him.

"Is this the best you can do?" he asked. "Some vines and smoke rings?"

It materialized behind him, raked a hand across his back. It left gouges three feet long and deep enough to hurt. Eric spun and swung a backhand, but it was gone again into a burst of smoke. The girl fought to break out, bled from wrists and ankles where the thorns had bitten deep. Again it appeared, raked his back in a crisscross of excruciating sparks and was gone from his wild swings. Any deeper, and it might break through to his runes.

He faced the girl, left himself open, waited for the rush of cold. When he felt it begin to take shape, he put all his strength into an elbow jab. A sharp twist of his torso, and he grazed the creature's shoulder. Brittle bone crunched, elicited a hollow scream that clawed his ears from within. He quickly jabbed at its throat, poked his fingertips just under the chin. The creature choked, flickered into smoke and back, as if it couldn't hold the form any longer.

"You need air to shift?" Eric reached down and filled both hands with dirty water. He threw toward its mouth and got some in just as it flickered. "Not so tough now, huh?"

He jumped for its throat, but a vine slapped his hand away. More and more rose up, cumbersome roots lined in heavy thorns and leafy vines like agile limbs. Both sought to trap or trip him, encase his legs and arms, anything for a few moments where the creature could catch its breath.

The troll girl cried out. A root had wrapped around her throat, and its thorns were cutting in. Blood ran from the row of wounds, a darker green than her skin. Eric growled, pulled free one limb after another and rushed to save her. If the root around her neck tightened any further, she'd bleed out in front of him with nothing to be done for it. He pulled the root apart, used both hands to keep it from puncturing her throat any further. He broke the others the same way, pulling outward with care.

The cold came again all too quick.

Eric's world exploded into pain and bright lights. His runes had been exposed. Talons raked his back in a dual frenzy of echoed shrieks. Sounds had become muted. The pain was like a burning that crippled his legs, hot embers in his middle flaring outward. He swung wildly behind, each time at bursts of smoke. It was chilling, the sudden calm at odds with his anger. Another part of his conscience came to fore, a detached piece of being that watched on without actually taking part.

So this is how I go? it seemed to say. *At the hands of a crazy bitch I can't even attack?*

Fuck you! Eric screamed inwardly. The pain was too much. It was too difficult to think. Flailing his arms in a weak attempt to hit back only wore him out faster. *Do something useful instead of whine! Like, come up with a fucking plan!*

Pfft. Whatever. Fine. Crawl to those trees. There were smaller ones all around. *Break 'em. Fill the air with that dust. You don't need to breathe. It does.*

His legs wouldn't work. Even troll girl had lost her fear of him, was looking at him with concern, wanting to help, knowing she couldn't. Eric ignored it all, the look of pity, the relentless talons tearing him open from behind. He put one hand in front of the other, pulled himself through the mud toward the trees.

He reached the first and smashed it over. It cracked, split down the middle and toppled against another. Dust spat out into a puff of lingering ash. He punched another and another. The creature halted of a sudden. He turned into the cold as it sputtered. He grabbed hold of its gauzy wrap. Eric pulled the creature toward him as it struggled for air. He forced a hand over its nose and mouth, squeezed to keep them closed. Talons clawed at his arms and back, his neck, his face. His other hand was at its throat, thumb pushing into the hollow. He'd never seen the wide-eyed fear, the frantic spasms of one dying in the throes of suffocation. Its attacks grew weak until they eventually stopped. Arms sagged, legs ceased kicking, and its essence rushed to fill him.

Eric was in ruin. Without the foundry, without dark magic, he had no way of healing. His runes were exposed in half a dozen places, torn open and raw against the pain of his damaged glyph. There was no other choice. He either healed or he died right there in the mud.

His choice had been made, the change had taken place, but his body was healing at a much slower rate than he'd hoped. Minutes went by before he could even understand what she was saying, knelt over him at the chest, looking so worried.

"– what to do! I don't know how to help you."

"You can speak?" Eric asked. He could still feel his metal mending, but the largest wounds had closed. The runes within him were whole again, his glyph fully healed. "I always thought trolls just sort of grunted and stuff."

She snorted a short laugh. She'd been helping him to sit up but let him fall back to the mud.

"Did you just call me an animal?"

"What? No! No," he said and sat up on his own. Sitting this close to her made him a little uncomfortable, but he was able to see her face much more clearly. She truly was beautiful. "I've never actually met a troll before. I've just... heard stories." Her brow eased, but she still looked insulted. "I didn't mean to hurt your feelings."

"Taliana," she said and stood, offered him her hand. He took it and was surprised at how strong she was. "My tribe is to the east, just beyond the river. I...don't know what you are, but you saved my life. I owe you a debt. I would introduce you to the others and offer my thanks with food and fire. Will you return with me? My pledge of gratitude must be made before a totem."

Great, Eric thought. *Trolls are people too.*

"No, I—that's not really necessary. I don't exactly make a good first impression. I mean, I'm kind of...I'm a monster."

"Don't be ridiculous." Taliana took hold of his hand and pulled him east. "You'll see. I will explain everything. No one will say an unkind word." She looked back up at him when he wouldn't budge. She looked puzzled. "Trust me. I won't let anyone hurt you."

"I can't," he said as an excuse. "I need to get back. I was just exploring when I heard your cries. What was that thing, anyway?"

"A fey," Taliana said and reluctantly let go his hand. "They infect our forest. I thought I was still close enough to the totem, to its protection, but I must've gone too far. Or the fey are growing stronger. We've tried to drive them from our homeland, but the best we can do is keep them at bay." She seemed to search his face but there was no sign of emotion there. "We could use your help, uh..."

"Eric."

"Eric!" she said and laughed. "That sounds like a human name. If you come with me, maybe you could help?"

Part of him really wanted to, though to be honest, just to spend more time with her. She was hurt, in need of first aid, and all she wanted was to thank him. Eric wished he could actually feel what her hand was like. His metal could feel pressure, temperature and pain. It just wasn't the same as living flesh.

"I have other concerns to deal with, too many to be honest. I would like to come back and see you, though. I'm just not sure when."

Taliana gave a nod. "I understand. I would stay and talk more with you, but it will be dark soon. I must get back and tend these cuts."

"Okay. It was nice meeting you, Tali."

She narrowed her eyes at him. "You may not call me that. Such familiarity is for mates. If another heard, you would be forced to seek my hand."

Eric laughed nervously but her expression didn't change. "Holy shit, are you serious?"

Taliana crossed her arms. "Yes. And it's impolite to assume someone is telling an untruth."

"I—No, that's not what—"

She laughed at his expense.

"So serious. If I didn't know better, I would think you *are* human. Thank you again," Taliana said, took hold of his hand in both of hers for a final squeeze goodbye and let go. "I must get back. I do hope to see you soon."

She's pretty funny, too.

"So do I," Eric said and waved, as he watched her walk away. "So do I."

Eric sat with both arms on his raised knees before a magical bonfire in the courtyard. There was nothing left to burn, so Griz had conjured the large flame. Aside from the tingle of magic, it looked like any other fire, with more green than orange at its center. It didn't crackle like burning wood, but its warmth didn't waver. The feel of it on his front, across his face and arms, reminded him of summer and the constant heat of noonday sun.

"I almost died today," he told Griz, in the same way he might have mentioned finding a cool rock.

The few goblins in the castle were either resting, on guard or out on patrol. The shaman sat beside him with a carving knife and a small piece of wood. He'd been whittling the individual links of a chain. Griz paused and gave Eric a look of concern.

"How did that happen, Master?"

Eric chuckled and asked, "Have you ever seen a fey?"

"Oh, dear," the shaman said. He looked as if he might put

down his whittling then continued to work at the first link. "You know, Master, just as *demon* is a general term for the many races upon Inexium, *fey* is also a general term for those who come from Twilight. What you faced could vary greatly from what I've seen or even read of."

"Twilight," Eric repeated in distaste, "like the crappy teen romance novels? I never read the books, but the movies were fuckin' terrible. Chick was dumb as a rock, and the sparkly vampires were ridiculous."

Griz kept working at the first link until it finally came free. He blew the shavings from the middle and looked pretty pleased with himself.

I swear he just ignores half of everything I say.

"Twilight is a dreamscape, Master," he said and started working the next link, "a world between worlds, a realm where thoughts and desires can manifest into reality." He gave Eric a meaningful look. "It can be a truly horrific place. If you encountered a fey, it could mean their war with the demons is bleeding onto Taellus." He set back to work and asked, "What did it look like?"

"Like a crackhead, grandma zombie." When Eric saw his description wasn't helpful, he added, "It was almost as tall as me, super thin, all white skin, black eyes, with crazy fuckin' hair and nails that tore me open like a goddamn burrito."

The shaman actually stopped to consider. He looked worried and confused, as if he was trying to piece together a motive for crazy.

"What you're describing, Master," Griz said and put down his whittling, "is a collector. They gather souls for the Hunt, a host of fey that prey on those with weak or damaged spirits."

Why go after Taliana then?

"What do you mean by damaged spirit?" Eric asked. "Like some kind of trauma or mental disability or actual damage to their soul?"

"Yes." Griz had a far off look as he answered. "All of those, Master. Fey can cross realms in a number of ways, but collectors...they dwell inside and move between marked trees."

Those big trees with the diseased sap?

"Marked how?"

"By stalkers, Master," Griz replied. "Like scouts, they are vanguard to the Hunt, seeking out the greatest number of prey."

Eric said, "You say stalker, I hear crazy ex. What the fuck is a stalker?"

"Stalkers are spirit hunters, Master. They can sense suitable prey. They leave their mark and move on, let others pick up the scent." Griz scratched at his forehead. "All of this is highly unusual. Something drastic must have changed."

Should I go back? Eric wondered. *Is Taliana marked by one of those guys or just the trees?*

Eric rubbed at his back. Even though he was healed, it still ached.

"How is it my runes can be damaged," he asked, "but I don't die? I mean, it was so bad...I lost the use of my legs, but I was able to keep going."

"Well, a simple enchantment, Master," Griz said and drew a gold ring in air, "can be like a circle. If the circle is broken—" he smudged a piece away, and the ring fell apart— "the enchantment is broken. However, a complex enchantment," he said and drew multiple rings, each one connected to the last, "like a glyph, is a collection of circles. If one is broken—" he broke the first circle, and none of it fell away— "the glyph, as a whole, is damaged but not broken."

Eric considered how many rings of runes were across his body before he turned them inside. There could be even more, what with how many transformations he'd undergone.

"So to die," Eric guessed, "I'd have to have all of my circles broken. Either that or some are too important and can't afford to be broken."

"The latter, I'm afraid, Master." Griz wiped clear the air of golden scrawl. "Your body is a masterwork of art, an incredibly complex enchantment, but it is not without flaw. Break one, and you'll lose the ability to speak; one more and your ability to walk. Who is to say which of them all contains the spark that is *you*."

Eric sighed at the thought of his own mortality.

"That's just fan-fuckin'-tastic."

An orange goblin ran through the gates, panting and out of breath. She was wearing breeches and a tunic, with a leather hooded cloak. Eric recognized her as the one Bitters had sent to spy on Sebran.

"Marshmallow!"

"Marbit, Master," Griz corrected. The orange stopped before them, trying to catch her breath. "Easy now. What is it?"

"Body...the body. *Your* body, Master," she said to Eric and gasped. "They have it."

* * *

Eric fumed.

I knew *he was gonna fuck me!* He also felt stupid for not keeping track of his own body. *Now what the fuck do I do?*

"What can he do with it?" he asked Griz.

The shaman looked frightened, both at Eric's obvious anger and what Sebran might do. Wheels were spinning behind that one good eye.

"With the appropriate spell and materials? Master, he could potentially force your spirit back into its original body. It would be difficult, much more so without you there, but not impossible."

"But it's dead," Eric complained. "What in the fuck happens to me then? Do I just die, like all of this was for nothing? Do I become a goddamn zombie or something?"

Marbit backed away. Eric had been clenching his fists without realizing it. He wanted to scream, to reach out and crush something...anything.

He wanted to kill Sebran.

"I—I don't know, Master." Griz straightened with resolve. "We need to get it back. Whether he plans to use your body to blackmail you into doing his bidding or force your spirit back into it, so he can claim the golem for himself, we need to take it back. If we recall everyone, we can march on Cledford as soon as they return."

It was stupid to think they could ever resurrect his body, epic quest or no, and put his spirit back inside it like changing a pair of clothes. His meat suit was dead. Keeping it around was a liability, something to be used against him. So long as he had hope, of bringing it back to life, he was weak, exposed.

Too bad I can't use the hollow part of me as storage. It'd be easy to keep it safe if it was inside me all the time. No, his best bet was in the changes. *Level up enough times, and I can make this thing human.*

"How many?" Eric asked Marbit. "Guards, knights, archers, anyone with a weapon. What are we up against once we break through the wall?"

"Fifty-seven archers, Master." The orange squinted, looking up as she recalled and ticking off numbers on one hand. "Thirty-four knights, fifty-one pikemen, a hundred and sixty-three foot soldiers—" she ran out of fingers, since goblins only had four, and cycled back to her thumb— "fifty-two guards, eighteen squires, three casters and over three hundred peasants. Most of the soldiers are from Raynver, but they follow Sebran's orders—for the most part, without complaint."

Eric cursed and Griz whistled in appraisal.

"That's a lot of dudes," Eric said. "You weren't even there all that long. How are your numbers so precise?"

Marbit lifted her chin with pride. "It's what we do, Master. I disguised myself as a child, worked in the kitchen, served food and drink in the hall, cleaned the stables—

"It doesn't sound like those last two would go well together," Eric said, "handling food and cleaning shit."

"All humans smell of piss and shit, Master." Marbit said it like a fact. "It's an impossible odor to escape. Only the lord bathes with water. The rest rub themselves with dirt."

Great. Hygiene lessons from a gremlin. How the hell does anyone mistake that *for a child?*

"Either way," Eric said, "it's too many. I don't wanna risk our guys like that. They shouldn't be able to hurt me. It'll be easier if I bust in, grab the block and leave."

Griz warned, "This could be what he wants, Master, to lure you close enough to complete the ritual. Rather than a frontal assault, we could send in oranges to do what they do best. With the right poison, we don't have to kill anyone. They'll all be too sick to fight back."

"We don't have that kinda time," Eric said. "If they can put me back in my old body, then what's to stop them from putting someone else into this one? Then I'd be royally screwed, assuming I don't die in the process. No, I've gotta go by myself, smash the place up good enough he doesn't think about fuckin' with me again. Just be ready," he told Griz. "If any of them follow me back here...you can kill 'em."

"Very well, Master."

Griz gave a single nod, like a salute, and was off. Marbit followed after, albeit slower, still exhausted from her run.

It would be morning in a couple of hours. Assuming most people would be sleeping and he could run there in time, it was possible he could get his body back without too much of a fight. He still didn't want to kill anyone—except Sebran.

That douche wrote his own obituary.

Eric began to run.

Being a hollow metal golem, he moved with relative ease and speed. Running was only slightly faster, but he never grew tired. He could maintain that pace for as long as needed. It was sort of a terrifying thought, being chased by a metal monster that could run forever, crash through stone walls and kill with a punch.

Even transformers needed to recharge. Hmm, can I go forever without running out of fuel? Does consuming essence recharge me? Eric considered as he ran. *I'll have to ask Griz next time I see him.*

The ground wasn't as muddy this time, had been hardened some by the morning cold, though the clouds always seemed to be threatening rain. Rumbles in the distance, the occasional bright flash between clouds; it seemed a storm was ever present, just waiting to open up.

Eric's senses had been heightened but did nothing for his sense of time. Without a watch, he had no real way of knowing how long he ran. The stars were hidden behind clouds, like a perpetual gray blanket to match his mood. When the keep walls came into sight, he wasn't sure how long it was before first light.

There were twice as many archers as last time but no guards outside the closed gate. He didn't sense sentries along the way, nor were there knights out on patrol. The keep was closed up tight.

They were expecting him.

A call went out. The twang of loosed arrows ensued with the pitched whizzing of their arc. Eric paid them no attention. He kept on for the wall. The iron portcullis was too difficult an ask and would only slow him down. He chose the stones directly next to it, turned his head and shouldered through.

Stones and mortar exploded outward in time to the cries of falling men. The wall collapsed where he'd passed and continued to fall apart at either side. Some of those who came down with it were bloodied but alive. Others were not so lucky. Eric had no time to give it thought before their essence rushed toward him.

"Finally!" Lord Sebran said from in front of the keep steps. He and two others in long robes stood before a fire pit with Eric's body. The amber was still intact. "Finish the ritual," he ordered the two beside him. They looked like stereotypical wizards, pointed hats with wide brims, hair and beards down to their middle. The glow of runes hung in air between them, an incomplete spell. "The rest of you, keep that thing back!"

The courtyard was full of men. At least a hundred in various armors, chainmail and leather, with long swords or pikes, they lined the bottom of the walls and stood ready to attack. Every knight at Sebran's disposal moved to bar Eric's path. Some carried sword and shield, both heater and tower, while others chose two-handed great swords. Each wore livery of blue or green, though most were in blue. Atop the walls stood every archer, ready to loose a volley before men got too close.

While not as large as the courtyard at Thrallen, this one was much busier. There was a stable to Eric's left, with a handful of horses, and an empty smithy to his right. There were workers and servants, both female and male, but they did their best to stay out of the way. Only one caught and held Eric's attention, a filthy beggar just outside the stable. Clothes torn, he was sitting in a pile of horseshit with no real understanding of where he was. More than his apparent history of head injury, old scars and stitches covered him head to toe, as if he'd been taken apart and put back together. Even more unsettling than his Frankenstein's monster impersonation, there was magic coming off him, but something about it was off. If magic was a chorus, his was a barrage of horrified shrieks. Like most other magic he'd encountered out in the world, this one's seemed tainted.

A call went out, and arrows were loosed. They'd done little

to no damage to him earlier. Their scratches had already healed. The beggar, on the other hand, would be skewered. Eric jumped in front, did his best to shield the poor guy with his body. No one deserved whatever had happened to make him look like that, let alone be killed by arrows from his own lord's archers.

"Fuckin' assholes!" Eric yelled. Arrows bounced off him and struck the floor. One took the beggar in his right leg. He didn't flinch, but tears fell from his vacant eyes. "You could've killed him!"

"He's already dead," a knight said and approached. "Soon you will be, too."

"That a fact?"

Eric was ready to barrel them all aside to reach Sebran and the casters. He didn't want to kill anyone he didn't have to, but those wizards had to go.

"Back to that lard ass you call a body," another said.

"And that nub you call a pecker!"

"Hope it kills you, too."

So they don't know if it'll kill me for sure? Eric was trying to ignore all the insults. *Well, that's something, I guess.*

He was about to charge through, when he saw a fey climb over the wall.

"Fuck me…"

It was similar to the collector, tall and spindly, pale skin and very thin. It moved like a spider, though, over the wall and across the ground on all fours with crazy speed. No one around it seemed to notice, and it moved between them with precision, careful not to touch. Its eyes were completely covered, the top half of its head hidden beneath a white carapace with spikes. The shell-like skin continued down its back in overlapping square ridges.

It's invisible and *blind?* Eric wondered. *It doesn't move like it's blind.*

"That's right, asshole," the lead knight said and swung his sword. "Fuck you!"

Eric moved back out of reflex but the sword edge still clanged against his chest. It left a hair-length gouge that immediately started to heal.

His attention was on the fey. It wore that same gauzy material, like a tattered snowy gossamer. Its pelvis was covered in a dark material beneath the wrap. He thought it might be another collector, until it stopped before a woman with a wicker basket looking on. The fey touched her on the forehead and slipped back between the crowd, searching out others to mark.

It's a fucking stalker.

A golden glow emanated from her brow where it had touched and slowly spread all through her veins. The glow was gone from her forehead but lit up her veins in the early morning dark. It stayed there, like a beacon, calling out for other fey.

Taliana didn't have that. Eric had been avoiding and ignoring attacks, keeping track of the stalker. He was relieved she wasn't marked, but that meant other trolls were. It's the only reason a collector would be out in their forest. *Should I go back later and warn her?*

Eric was surrounded, taking scratches from all sides. He pushed through the knights like they were children to keep from losing sight of the fey. It had touched three more in the crowd of those watching on. Their veins, however, were not glowing gold. They were blackened, like poison, their marks somehow marred.

The two casters were chanting loudly, as if their spell had reached a crescendo. The fire in the pit was glowing blue and violet. Eric needed to stop them, but the fey was to the right, on the other side of the yard. For every one marked in glowing gold, another ten were webbed in black across their faces and exposed skin.

"Knock it off, already!" Eric yelled and backhanded a knight into the wall. The man struck with a loud thud, armor bent, stones cracked, and slid to the ground with a groan. He wasn't dead, but he didn't move. Eric yelled again, to the people in the crowd oblivious to the stalker. "Watch out! He's right there!"

It didn't matter. They couldn't see it. People began to comment that the ritual was making Eric insane. He pushed others aside with enough force to take them out of the fight without killing them.

Sight of his old body trapped in amber caught his eye. It was naked, with short hair, and the skin looked gray, even dark at the lips and eyes. He saw the flabby stomach in rolls and couldn't recall being so fat. It was like looking at a stranger and judging who he'd been. He felt anger and disgust, as if he'd taken his old life for granted, just as the goblins had taken it from him.

All he wanted now was to take it back.

Eric headed for the casters. Their spell in air was a collection of spinning runes and sigils, rings of golden shimmer within rings. Magic filled the space between each mage and the solid block of amber. Men struggled in vain to keep him from the fire, from interrupting the spell, but their strength and weapons were no match. Even mighty blows from a great sword left but a scratch and were healed in less time than it took to swing again. Despite Eric's resolve, he couldn't help but watch the fey slip through the crowd of soldiers and servants, marking one after another.

Why the fuck is he marking so many?

There was a scuffle, as a woman marked with gold was shoved aside on accident and scratched along her arm. She cursed the fool who'd done it, one marked in black. And then it happened. Her mark began to change. As if it, too, had been tainted, her golden glow darkened to black.

Is he killing them? Fuck! I don't understand what's going on here. Why should I even care? He looked to Lord Sebran, and his anger flared. *I should tear that fuckin' mustache off his face!*

Eric seethed, but beyond the three at the fire pit, he could see the stalker marking prey. If they were all weak or had damaged spirits, then something else was terribly wrong. With the number of people it'd marked, it would only be a matter of time before collectors or the Hunt came to kill them all.

"Goddamn it!" Eric pushed passed Sebran and the two casters, knocking them over. He headed straight for the stalker. "Get out of the way! How do you people not fucking see it?" He pointed at prints in the mud, saw it jostle shoulders as it skittered like an insect. Ordinary people, and some soldiers, were in a hurry to move from his path, while men in heavy armor continued to attack him from behind. "For fuck's sake, you're all useless!"

Eric grabbed hold of the fey by a leg, tried to pull it in closer. It fought back, pulling for all it was worth to break free. Violet fire grew in one of its palms, and it threw the flames at Eric's face. It struck him full on, sent magic back and out as it burned across his metal. There were outcries of panic at seeing magic erupt but not until it had already struck his face. Eric used both hands to swing the fey in a half circle and threw him against the wall. Stones went inward from the force, and cracks spread from the impact. Wooden support beams split apart. It looked like that section of wall was going to crumble.

"He's gone mad!" a man shouted from the right.

"Get him under control," Sebran ordered, "before he brings the entire wall down!"

Shoving knights aside, Eric was back at the stalker. He tried and failed three times to grab it. At every turn, someone was in his way, inadvertently or not. People were shoved and knocked aside by the fey but were all too quick to blame each other. Two more knights got bashed aside for blocking his path. Eric didn't know what was more frustrating, that the stalker refused to fight him or the stupid people getting in his way.

"I'm trying to save you, damn it!" he yelled at them and

smashed another knight, crumpling the armor.

The stalker had scampered itself into a corner as Eric shoved a group of guards to either side with both arms. Its only option was to climb. Eric leapt and caught it by both legs, brought it down hard into the mud and wouldn't let go. With deliberate care, he grabbed farther up its body one hand at a time. If he could get a hold of its neck, the fight was over. Arms and legs kicked out, their talons leaving deep gouges and flying sparks. Magic went up and out, again and again, scorching his metal blue, blinding him with purple flames.

He could take the pain from both, knowing he'd soon win. The fey had no hope of escape. It was frantic, wild in its attacks. Even the knights had finally realized that something was amiss, as mud and sparks flew as if of their own accord. They'd kept a safe distance, suddenly more afraid of what it was they couldn't see. Eric was reaching for its neck when the ritual took hold.

The edges of his vision blurred. It was like the wave of sudden haziness that comes from taking oxy, all fog and no warmth, the distant pull toward sleep without the drowsy. It felt like the world had become a tunnel, and he was being pulled back toward the entrance. The light slimmed and dimmed until at last it became nothing.

When next he could see, his world was filtered in waves of dirty gold. His vision was still blurry, behind the bubbles and swirls, within the block of amber. There was no breath, no beat of heart, no flow of blood...just regret. The golem stood empty, beyond the gathered faces, out of reach. One face took center stage, with a cocky voice and bristling mustache.

"I kept my word," Lord Sebran told him. "I put you back into your body." His satisfied grin was both cruel and mocking. To his men, he ordered, "Toss him in the lake."

At least I didn't die, Eric thought, as men gathered rope to tie around his block. He felt hollow, even more than when he was made of metal. *And I got my body back.*

He saw the golem standing still. Soldiers were poking it with swords, while others brought chains to bind it as well. Fear and sadness rose within him, the sort that came from the realization he'd made a horrible mistake.

My body...

– 10 –

Eric sank into the water by late of early morning and watched the boatmen row away. He wasn't able to turn his head and look around as light faded, only saw the occasional fish as darkness grew from below. By the time he struck ground, light of day had become little more than a muted glow at the top of his vision. Disturbed earth clouded the water in great swirls all around him. Once they had settled, he was alone in the somber dark.

He no longer had enhanced senses, could only rely on what he saw through the encasement of solid amber. He felt nothing in its embrace, no chilling cold, no aching pain or driving pressure. His everything was numb in the deafening silence.

Why are my fuckin' eyes open, anyway? Did I die this way? Somehow he doubted that. *Or did those two mages open them for me during their ritual? Seems like the sort of thing a dick like Sebran would do, a final* fuck you *before burying me alive.*

His body was dead, so he didn't need to breathe. He supposed that was better than an eternity of suffocation, like living in the endless throes of drowning. His biggest complaint was that he couldn't move. No matter how hard he tried to break free, to wriggle a finger, the amber held fast. Its spell wouldn't budge.

What if I get an itch? Thought of getting one made him wonder if that might *cause* an itch. *Damn it! Happy thoughts, happy thoughts...*

He was alone with those thoughts for some time.

Is this my life now? Eric tried to see anything in the water that could distract him but was unable to squint or even focus his eyes. *Is this forever? If I really am a zombie, will I ever die? Zombies have to eat to survive, don't they? If I starve, will I die?*

Eric wasn't afraid of dying. He was looking for a way out. He began to consider what he might do if he got free. Was there some way back into the golem, a ritual Griz could perform? Would Eric want to if there was? Could he still be resurrected if he was already *in* the dead body? He didn't know the particulars of the spell, but that seemed problematic. Maybe he could make life as a zombie work—assuming he didn't have to eat anyone to survive. People were gross enough on the outside. Either way, should he stay on Taellus or go home? What was there for him, anyway? Years and years of more schooling, dead end jobs, being overworked for shit pay, crushing debt and misery? The only things worth having or doing in life tended to kill you with the cost or cause death in the long run. What was the fucking point of it all?

At least here they have magic.

Considering magic, why did it behave so differently in some places or instances? The land around Thrallen, Taliana's forest to the south, those people at Sebran's keep, all seemed...unnatural, corrupted. Either magic worked differently for different people, or something was affecting how it worked. If the golden glow caused by the stalker was a person's spirit or soul, it looked like that one woman's had been infected by a scratch. Why else would it have turned black like the others?

And what was with that jigsaw dude at Cledford? Griz had said Tragona was experimenting on people in his laboratory. *Could he have been one of them?* Those experiments might explain why the land and magic all around the castle were tainted. *If he was fucking with people, sure, but what about the land? Was he messing with ley lines, too?*

Light of day had faded to total darkness. Eric had nothing to do but think...about his past, what he'd done, the choices he'd made and why. He could picture imagined futures, ease his mind within the fantasies, but all of them were all a lie.

Hope was a lie.

It all circled back to where he was, what he could do at that very moment—which was nothing.

Eric began to miss being in the golem, its enhanced senses and strength, the surge of essence from a kill, the thrill of transformation and the well of choices that came with it. He realized he'd taken it all for granted, even if he never asked for it.

The faint glow of a new day came and went. None of it mattered. He was still alone with his thoughts, trapped in his own choices, unable to move. He didn't even have the comfort of his own heartbeat to pass the time. It was all just numbing silence.

He'd been talking to himself, reliving old memories, seeking solace in the past, but on the third day an odd thing happened, an unsettling thing.

His voice answered back.

It was disconcerting to hear a voice, even if it was his own, talking inside his head of its own accord. It was like one of those studies he'd seen in a video, where people had their left and right brains physically separated. Both sides had an internal voice, but only one could speak. The other was trapped, a silent passenger, a prisoner in its own body. It was able to think, make choices, but unable to take action.

Relax, the voice said, *I'm not here to shit on your parade. I just wanted to cheer you up. The golem is too valuable for the goblins to just eat the loss. They're gonna come for you.*

Eric disagreed.

Ehhh, I don't think they need me anymore. I mean, it took a whole bunch of shamans to put me in there in the first place. Griz probably won't be able to do it on his own. They'd be better off forgetting about me, maybe get some help from Xanadu—

Xanaranth.

Whatever, Eric thought sardonically. *They should just put someone else in the golem, if they can get it back. Or make a new one altogether.*

Their charter was revoked, the rational voice pointed out. *Xanaranth won't help them. They're only option now is to get you back into the golem. No one else can use it. It's been marked. You pissed all down the leg, on the inside. It's claimed, man. It's yours.*

The other voice wouldn't go away. When Eric refused to respond, it went on for hours about how cool it would be to use magic—as if Eric didn't already know that. His numbing silence had been invaded but in the worst kind of way. He never realized what a self-absorbed asshole he could be.

Eric never thought he'd miss the quiet.

On the fourth day, just hours past the faint rising of morning glow overhead, the voice had finally stopped. A shadow broke through the light, and a strange tingling filled the water. Bubbles began to rise all around him. He could feel the block pull free of the lake's bottom and gently start floating up toward the surface. Rays of daylight grew broader and brighter as he rose, the water more clear, and there were *voices* from above. Muffled by the lake, their sounds still carried through the amber. Eric never thought he'd be so happy to hear other people.

When the block broke the surface, it bobbed up and down until it came to rest upright. Only its top half stuck out of the water, where a boat sidled up and revealed five goblins. Griz was there, eye closed, casting a spell. Two in back were blues with oars, and the others were reds. They reached out and tied rope around the amber block. Once it was secured to the boat, they helped the blues row Eric back to shore.

The entire expedition had come to save him. Griz continued casting until the boat struck against mud, where at least a dozen pairs of hands were waiting. It wasn't until they'd pulled the block out and lay Eric on his back that Griz ended the spell. An immediate sense of weight came over the amber, enough that Eric could feel it press upon his front. The shaman casted another spell, and the amber fell away.

Eric was finally free of it.

He slapped his arms and legs up and down in the mud, laughing and hooting. Sunlight touched his face, and he could *feel* its warmth. He still wasn't alive, but this was the very next best thing. The goblins gathered around him laughed along, though some in back were still afraid. He was, after all, undead. Eric sat up, got to his feet, beaming like it was the last day of school.

"I am so fucking glad to see you guys," he said and laughed again. It felt weird, though, forcing himself to breathe after so many days without air. "Like, seriously." To Griz, he added, "I'm also kinda surprised. I...didn't think you'd come for me."

"That was not even a consideration, Master," Griz assured him. "You're a part of this expedition. We would never leave someone behind." The generals and other goblins gave headshakes and grunts in agreement. "I do apologize it took so long. It took time to find you, and we've...had a few setbacks along the way."

"It's Sebran, Master," Bel said with a furrowed brow. The red general was clearly upset. "He's taken the castle and moved his men inside."

Bri was right beside him. The blue general added, "And he's brought your body with him, Master."

Bitters spat out of anger, along with many others.

"His casters, too, Master," Stalk said in an ominous tone.

"We think, Master," Griz clarified, "they're going to try bonding it to a new spirit, to control it."

"Master," Mudbutt pleaded, "we need to attack right away, regain the castle and get your body back."

That's twice now, Eric thought.

They kept calling the golem his body, as if he wasn't already in one—the one he'd been born to. That's when Eric realized the goblins had never seen him as a human trapped inside their golem. They saw him as their leader, stuck in a dead human.

Eric nodded and they took it as assent. The generals gave orders, and their respective gobs took off to perform the assigned tasks. While a temporary camp was being built, Eric started planning.

"Can you do the ritual," he asked Griz, "by yourself? Can you get me back into the—my body?"

"It will be difficult, Master. I'm not sure, honestly, but I'm willing to try if you are."

Eric chuckled. "What's the worst that could happen? I'm already fuckin' dead. Besides, being a zombie might be useful."

"You're not exactly a zombie, Master," Griz pointed out with some hesitation. "Your spirit is trapped inside a dead body, and that body is no longer preserved. It *will* start to deteriorate. Any damage you sustain now cannot be healed, unless you were somehow resurrected."

"Can I be?"

"No, Master," Griz replied, "not while you inhabit it."

Eric shrugged. "Meh. It's starting to stink, anyway."

"Your best chance for survival at this point, Master, is to go back into the golem."

Bel agreed. "It's where you belong, Master. You were born to wear that body."

It was so strange seeing them with human eyes. The golem's senses were so enhanced, that vision sometimes took a backseat. He'd seen the goblins before as a sort of amalgam of sensory input. Shape and color, smells and sound, all sort of rolled up into a single image. Here he was simply seeing them for who they were.

They were little people, in their own way, as varied in size and shape as humans. They stood two to three feet tall, with tapered ears both short and long. Some were bald, some had hair, some thin or stocky, slight of frame or muscled, with bulbous noses or long and pointed. Even the colors that defined caste were disparate in hue, with reds that ran pale and oranges dark. They were individuals, smart and fierce, and they deserved a good leader.

"Let's get to it, then," Eric said with enthusiasm. As Griz left to prepare for the ritual and the other generals started to disperse, Eric asked Bel to stay behind. "What's our situation?"

Bel hooked both thumbs in his belt. "We're far south of Sebran's keep, Master, but it is still his lands. There might be a patrol at any time, so we've set up guards, scouts and patrols of our own. We lost the castle, true, but it's not all bad news. Our survey team did find a few promising spots for iron and copper deposits. Once we retake Thrallen, we can begin mining. Scout report of the west details a village overrun by some kind of monsters. We could ransack the place for resources, while you fed."

"Nice," Eric said, impressed. "That is good news. Hmm, how many of his men did squirrel-lip bring to the castle?"

"As far as we can tell, Master? All but a few guards."

Eric snorted. "Well that was fuckin' stupid, leaving his

ass exposed like that. We should raid the keep before we go after the castle, cut off their food and supplies. We take everything worth having, all their weapons and armor, any metal and jewelry, anything we can use. Try not to kill anyone if you can, disable anyone who gets in your way. Don't burn or break his house, but make him wish he'd never left."

Bel grinned. "Yes, Master."

"I'll probably wake up in the castle courtyard," Eric said, "hopefully before they try to stick someone else in. I'll force them out of the castle. Take a roundabout way back, so you don't run into them on the road."

"Are you going to kill them, Master?"

"Not yet." It rankled Eric, but there was no denying he might need them. "As pissed as I am and as much as I hate Lord Semen, bigger trouble might be on the way. While I was at the keep, I saw a stalker."

The red narrowed his eyes. "A fey? They shouldn't be here on Taellus, not while Twilight is at war."

"Shit's about to get ugly," Eric agreed. "Let the others know to keep an eye out. Do what you gotta do. Be ready to march the second Griz finishes his spell. I'm gonna have some fun before I send those assholes packin'."

"Consider it done, Master."

Bel set about making plans, while Eric went looking for Griz. The shaman was seated by a fire at the center of camp. Eric didn't want to disturb him, so he quietly took a seat and waited. It seemed his time underwater had at least taught him some patience. He was so glad to be free, he didn't mind all the chatter or clatter of metal, the hushed cackles and joking, the goblins being themselves.

Hours passed in that bustle, as Griz meditated in total silence—or did whatever he was doing to mentally prepare. Winter days were short, and night was already falling when he opened his eye. He gave Eric a confident nod and used his staff to climb to his feet.

111

"I'm ready when you are, Master."

Eric stood as well. Even naked, he wasn't cold.

"I've got mud in my crotch," he said, "and up my ass. I am *so* ready to be done with—" he indicated his flabby body— "all this."

Everyone gathered in a circle around them as Griz began to cast. He scrawled the first rune, an unfamiliar symbol in gold shimmer. It climbed into the air above the fire and spun in place. More and more joined it, until they formed a complete circle.

That's the first ward, Eric thought.

Another circle went up in air, just below the first and at a tilt, so that its runes spun through. They weren't joined by any rune or sigil but were interconnected. Two more circles went up in the same pattern, each more tilted than the last. The joined wards seemed to form half a sphere, which Eric assumed would be the final glyph.

Crazy, he thought and watched Griz scrawl them one by one. *How the fuck does he keep track of it all?*

Once the sphere was complete, Griz pushed it aside to make room. He began a new circle, one connected to the sphere but outside. Eric realized the shaman wasn't merely scrawling a single glyph.

Griz was casting a construct.

Sweat beaded across his tiny brow, and Griz's arm began to shake. His other hand was tightly gripping the staff, using it to hold himself up. Eric couldn't fathom the toll it was taking. Working magic wasn't just writing words in the air. It was fueling a spell with magic, with power from inside the caster.

Shit. Eric knew it would be difficult, but he didn't know how much. It wasn't until that moment that he began to worry. *Can he even do this?* Griz was struggling just to stand. The new runes he scrawled came out dull, as if they weren't as powerful as the first—or he was running out of steam. *There's gotta be a way to help.* Eric offered a hand to steady him.

Griz completed a circle, but it didn't flash like the others had. One of its runes began to crumble and fall away into mist. Griz quickly went back to correct the mistake, before the entire circle fell apart. Eric could tell it was too much. With the strain of casting so many wards, Griz was losing focus, making more and more mistakes. The construct was too complex for him to manage on his own.

Soon he wasn't able to keep up with correcting the failing wards. Two glyphs were complete, but the third was an utter mess. Eric knew it was only a matter of time before the whole construct collapsed.

Eric's heart sank.

He'd truly hoped Griz would be able to finish the ritual on his own. He wasn't mad at the shaman, was actually grateful that he'd tried. The toll it was taking, the sheer amount of effort he was exerting, Griz was doing all he could to make it work. It only took a moment for Eric to come to grips with the fact that it wasn't going to happen. With the golem out of the equation, he started thinking of what was next. He didn't want to spend whatever time he had left as a rotting, undead corpse waiting to fall apart. He'd always wondered if there was an afterlife. Or did everyone die and become nothing?

Despair had taken hold.

Eric might as well have been back in the amber block. He was trapped again, unable to move forward, a prisoner to his choices. His mind went back to the same conclusion he'd reached at the bottom of the lake. Hope was an indulgence, a fantasy for the weak. The strong worked with what they had, saw the world with clear eyes and recognized when they were out of options. He didn't see the point in going on.

Eric put a hand out to the flames, watched it catch fire across his palm and curl around in bright orange. It didn't even hurt, as the pale dead skin blackened and burned.

Nearby goblins rushed to stop him, but even as a dead human he was too strong.

Griz collapsed from exhaustion. The spell collapsed with him. Golden light rained over the fire as Eric took a step forward. Goblins let go, backed away with arms raised, as Eric went up in flames. Bel tried to reach him, burned his hands in the attempt, but the fire was too strong. It took only a few moments to engulf him head to toe. The flames were so loud as they consumed him, it was like the silence of the lake, drowning out all other noise and complaint. In a way, it was peaceful, a blinding light so bright that it began to fade at the edges. It took the strength from his legs, the light from his vision.

Eric fell to his knees and into darkness.

Eric stood in a dark room.

The floor below his naked feet was pure black, glossy like polished marble, cold to the touch. Faint silver light shone from above, like a broad ray of moonlight. The ceiling and walls, if there were any, couldn't be seen.

Frantic mumbling caught his attention. Eric turned to see a tall column of glass. Seated at its center, rocking back and forth, hugged knees to chest, was a naked man with his face hidden behind his legs. His hair was dark, cut short, with curls gone wild from lack of care. Eric couldn't tell what the man was saying, but he appeared to be clearly upset. Eric saw in that anxious rocking the physical signs of madness that would have overcome him in the lake had he been able to move.

Water began to rise within the column.

"What?" The man rushed to his feet, looking down at the water. "No, no, no, no. This can't be happening!" He was backed against the glass, used both arms to hold himself up. His fingernails had been noticeably chewed bloody. When he saw Eric, his eyes went wide with fright. "No! You can't be here. You have to leave!"

Eric raised a brow. *Someone can't handle their shit.* He took a closer look at his surroundings. *Where the fuck am I?* The last thing he remembered was catching fire—when he'd killed himself. He was dead. He'd always thought people who committed suicide were selfish and weak. Yet, here he was. Eric frowned at the distinct lack of electronics. *If this is the afterlife, it fucking blows. Even hell has to have an xbox. Or an ipad. Something...*

"Please!" the man pleaded in a strained voice. The water had reached his ankles. "You have to go. Now! Before it's too late."

"Bad news, chuckles," Eric said. "It's already too late. You're gonna fuckin' drown if you don't climb out of that thing."

"I've tried!" He came over and banged at the glass with a fist. "There's no way out. Nothing I do works."

"Huh. Maybe this isn't *my* hell," Eric said. "It's yours! Who are you, anyway? And why the fuck am I in your hell?"

The man banged the glass again. "I don't know what that is!" He got down on all fours and tried to find where the water was coming from. "My name is Jaken," he said in a voice both panicked and pleading. "I know I'm being punished, but I—I don't deserve this! It was just a loaf of bread. I hadn't eaten in days! Please, sir, help me. I beg of you. If you won't go, please, at least set me free."

No one had ever called him sir. He kind of liked it. Not that it made a difference.

"Seriously, dude. I *literally* just got here." Eric looked up at the top of the column but couldn't tell if it was enclosed. "I don't know what the fuck is going on any more than you do. If I could leave, I would. I don't even know how I got here in the first place."

Jaken got to his feet and tried kicking at the glass with a

heel. It sent up all his jangly bits in an unpleasant display.

"Ugh!" Eric held up a hand to block his vision and turned his head away. "C'mon, man!" Jaken hugged his arms to chest and began to sob. The water had reached below his knees. "Alright. Hey, c'mon. I'll see what I can do."

Eric searched the glass for seams, anything that that might open. When he found none, he banged his fist against the glass. It rang back in response but didn't budge. He couldn't tell how thick it was, just that it was solid. Without tools, there was no breaking through. The way Jaken's voice carried made Eric think there was no top. He might be able to climb up and help him over. Eric jumped for the lip, but it was easily two feet out of his reach. It was almost as if the column had risen to avoid his touch.

"Look," Eric said, "it's not that big a deal. The water's gonna keep rising. You just gotta swim 'til it reaches the top. Then you hop over the edge." Jaken looked up with a sense of hope. "You can totally do it, dude. Just let the water carry you up. No biggie."

"I—I can't swim, though."

Eric sighed. "Of course you can't. Cuz why the fuck would anything start being easy now? Do this," he said and waved his arms in front of him like treading water. "When the water starts to lift you, kick your feet a little. Or better yet, just lean back with your arms out. Try to float."

The water had reached his waist.

Jaken worriedly asked, "Are you sure you can't just leave? I—I won't tell anyone you were here. I promise!"

"Sorry man." Eric shrugged. "None of this is me. I'm just here for the ride, like you."

When the water level went above his neck, Jaken tried to lean back as Eric had instructed. He floated on the surface, breathing in and out like each one might his last.

"Relax," Eric told him. "You're doing fine, man."

Kicking his feet a bit, breathing more steadily, Jaken seemed to be getting the hang of treading water. He rose higher than Eric and even let out a nervous laugh at his success.

"I'm doing it!" Jaken shouted.

Then he smacked against a glass ceiling.

"Oh, shit!" Eric started banging against the column again. "Hold your fucking breath!" He turned sideways and tried smashing his elbow through. Nothing seemed to work. "I don't get it. How the fuck did you not run out of air if it's enclosed?"

Jaken was drowning, and there wasn't a damn thing Eric could do to stop it. He wanted to save the poor guy, but he was helpless against the glass. Jaken struggled for air, let out bubbles as he clawed the top.

"Fuck, man. I'm sorry."

It didn't take long for Jaken's struggles to cease. He simply went still and slowly started sinking. His eyes were open as he settled to the bottom, an endless stare into the beyond. Eric put a hand to the glass, a farewell and final apology.

The cylinder disappeared.

Silver runes came alight in a charging buzz one by one across the distant walls. They joined together to form a circle, one after another. Eric saw he stood on a wide platform, looked over its edge and saw wards reaching as far down as they went high.

"Ohh," he realized, and the world snapped into place.

Eric was back in his body—his golem body.

He was in the courtyard at castle Thrallen before the gate. Apparently Jaken, inside an incredibly powerful magical construct meant to conquer kingdoms, had been made to stand guard.

Did I kill him? Eric wondered. Jaken had looked trapped, like he was in the golem against his will, a prisoner. *Is that what was supposed to happen to me?*

He wondered what was different, why he had free will and could control the golem like it was his own body. He looked down at his arms and chest, where runes were once inscribed across their outer surface.

Did those two mages fuck with my glyph?

He had no way of actually seeing the runes, nor could he tell if they'd been altered. How were they able to control Jaken then? Why wasn't he off rampaging the countryside, like the goblins had intended? Was the golem just a stupid animated hunk of metal that followed simple orders? Or did it have a set of instructions written directly in the glyph?

Regardless, he had to admit he was happy to be back inside. He'd never thought he could be driven to take his own life, to fall into such a pit of darkness that the only way out was to end it all. It gave new perspective to all the others he'd thought of as weak...his cousin Sarah, who'd been a cutter and finally went all the way. There was a kid at school, a freshman, just a year behind Eric, who'd already had mental issues before the bullying.

He put them from his mind. It did nothing for him to dwell. It just felt so damn good to be back! He flexed his fingers, felt the strength, all the power running through him. He wanted to never be that weak again, to feel that helpless and alone. He reveled in the enhanced senses, let the world come rushing in.

Eric looked around to see men standing guard and immediately saw they'd been marked. Not all of them, but enough, and every one of them in black. Their veins stood out in an ashen glow, like a corruption in their bloodstream. Half a dozen pikemen lined the gate on either side. They looked as bored as the task sounded, leaning heavily on their pikes or simply struggling to stay awake. It looked like every archer from the keep was manning the wall. Knights patrolled on horse outside, and sentries had been posted farther out along the hilltops. Sebran must have been expecting the goblins to attack.

He felt a tingle of magic pull his attention toward the gate. Beyond the metal bars, purple fire seemed to burn in the shape of a large claw mark. He wasn't able to see its glyph, but he was sure the enchantment was meant to mark the location. It had the same feel as magic the seeker had used against him. Could one have found its way to the castle? Did that mean more were coming?

Awesome, Eric thought sarcastically. *Not only do we have to deal with the Hunt, once I evict this jackass, we've got fucking demons with a vendetta on the way.*

He turned and headed for the castle entrance. The pikemen didn't seem startled or even ask where he was going. Either they were used to Jaken following orders without verbal command, or none of them cared. There were workers moving about the courtyard, carrying wood and rolling barrels, tending horses or fetching water from the well. Soldiers stood at either side of the steps. No one seemed to pay Eric any mind as he strode past them all and into the castle.

Most everyone was outside, with the exception of servants in the kitchen and soldiers asleep in the other room on his left. Eric could sense their essence through the walls. There were two more upstairs, one using magic, and a third far below. If the mages were in the castle, he'd have to deal with them first.

He did his best to walk lightly, but each step across the stones rang out much more loudly than he'd wanted. It was one of those disadvantages to being metal—he'd never be a true rogue. Any chance of stealth was simply out of the question.

Eric went upstairs toward the room he sensed the two people and magic. He stopped at the end of the hall, so they wouldn't hear. It sounded like they were arguing or at least having a heated discussion. One of the mages was no longer able to work magic. They were trying to discover why, but frustration was getting the better of whichever of them had been affected.

He could be infected, Eric thought and slowly moved toward the door. He tried to recall everything Griz had

120

told him about working magic. It had to be focused from somewhere, a ley line or from within themselves. What if inner magic was channeled from the spirit? If the black glow meant corruption of the soul, it made sense his magic would be affected too. *Good. Means I only have to kill one of 'em.*

Eric was suddenly worried *he* could be infected. His runes, his glyph, were protected on the inside, but where was his spirit? If someone infected scratched his metal, would it spread to him? Or did they have to touch his runes directly? It didn't seem likely, but if his soul was corrupted, if he lost access to its magic, would he die? Or was the golem completely separate from his spirit, fueled by the essence he took from others? His head swam with too many unanswered questions.

He more broke through than opened the wooden door. The handle was too small to work, so he simply pushed the door open. There were more splinters and twisted hinges than he expected. While the doorway was spacious, it wasn't made to accommodate golems. He had to duck to step into the room. The ceiling was unusually high, just like everywhere else in the castle, but none of the rooms were perfect squares. There was only one section, by the door, where he could stand without lowering his head. The rest of the room sloped toward the window. Both mages sat on either side of a table. One was working a spell, while the other wrote in the air to no avail. They both seemed annoyed and surprised to see him and were rightly outraged by the broken door.

"You were not summoned!" the one with magic said, only half paying attention to the splintered mess in the doorway.

"Why are you here?" the other demanded. He kept shaking his hand out, as if his fingers were to blame for the lack of magic and not the ashen glow running through his veins.

Eric hunched as he walked over and still managed to scrape his head along the slope. He grabbed each around their neck and shoulders. His hands were so large they completely covered the mages' fronts. The spell the first had been working fell apart in a golden shimmer. Their heads poked out of Eric's grip, as if a squeeze could pop them off. He used just enough pressure to prevent them from yelling for help. Both started to turn red, which meant they couldn't breathe either. It was difficult to gauge his strength sometimes, especially with brittle old men.

"Oh, ya know," Eric replied casually. "I was just out for a walk and thought I'd stop by to shoot the shit. Feels like it's been *forever* since you guys buried me in that lake." Eric laughed. "Good times, good times. So, how ya been?" He eased up enough to let them breathe. They gulped in ragged gasps through their ridiculous wizard beards. "Catch me up! What have you fuckers been up to?" To the one who could still cast, he happily warned, "If you try to cast a spell, I'ma pop your head back like a pez dispenser."

The corrupted one sputtered, "Lord Sebran has only reclaimed what was rightfully—"

Eric choked off his next words.

"How did you reconnect with the golem?" the one in his left hand asked, afraid but genuinely interested. "What happened to the woodcutter?"

"Oh, don't you worry, Gandalf."

"I—I am Balzak."

"Right, right. That's what I meant," Eric said. "Don't you worry, Ball Sack. Jaken is just fine. He says 'Hi,' by the way. Ya know, before he drowned. So, what do you guys know about the Hunt?"

The second mage was turning a shade of purplish red. Eric decided to relax his grip before the old man passed out. The mage gasped and choked, fought to take in air, while the first stammered out a reply.

"Stories of fey stealing souls...it is for children, bed time tales to make them behave." Ball Sack sounded like he believed he was telling the truth. "It is a fiction, a fantasy.

They are not meant to be taken literally."

"That true, Saruman?" Eric asked the second with exaggerated interest.

The mage hedged, as if unwilling to correct him. He must have known whatever name he gave, Eric would find a way to twist it into a mockery.

"Yes," Saruman agreed, "as far I am aware. Fey have not been seen in generations, and rarely more than one. They were never as bad as stories made them out to be."

"If the Hunt was real," Ball Sack said with a little too much incredulity for someone in a position to be choked by a giant hand, "word of it would have spread. There would be bodies everywhere."

"If they were real," Saruman pointed out, "it would not matter. The barrier construct at Westorval shields the entire world, not just Faradim. No magic transport can get through to Taellus in large enough numbers to be of consequence. Not even fey."

Eric stressed, "But something *can* get through."

"In theory," Ball Sack replied grudgingly, "anything is possible, but in the real world?" He scoffed and shook his balding head.

It made Eric wonder where their hats were. Somehow the whole situation would be more satisfying if they were wearing them. It turned out Saruman was smart enough to finally ask the right questions.

"Why are you doing this?" He narrowed his aged eyes. "Why have you not killed us and been done with it? What are you really after?"

Eric asked the broken mage, "Aren't you just a little bit curious why your magic isn't working?"

"How did you..." Ball Sack began to ask.

Saruman gave a hmph! "What has happened? You must already know. Tell me."

"First," Eric said to Saruman and drew their heads close together, "I want you to bite Ball Sack on the cheek, and you better draw blood. Your lives depend on it. Now, kith," he said in his best Mike Tyson voice and brought Saruman close enough to chomp his friend. When he did, Ball Sack cried out and cursed in a very unwizardly-like fashion. Eric pulled them apart and saw the bloody bite mark. "Excellent!"

He let them both go. They fell back onto the pieces of broken wooden chairs Eric had dashed when he grabbed them. They both worked to their feet, which took a while without their standard issue knotted wizard staves, and brushed off disheveled robes. Ball Sack wiped at his cheek with a sleeve of his robe. He wasn't marked, so his veins hadn't been glowing. He was, however, infected now. The magic coming off him began to turn, became just as sour as Saruman's.

"Try to cast a spell," Eric told him.

Ball Sack raised a brow but went back to working whatever magic he'd been at before Eric came bursting in. His eyes narrowed when nothing happened and then widened with realization.

"Good," Eric said. "Now I don't have to kill you. I was trying to tell you at the keep, but you fuckers wouldn't listen. There was a stalker there, marking all kinds of people."

"A fey?" Ball Sack asked, more confused and fearful than surprised. He shook his head against the notion. "That is not—"

"You've been marked," Eric told Saruman. "That's not all, though. Something else is going on. Your spirit is corrupted."

Saruman flinched, touched his face and chest, as if he could diagnose his own soul.

"My spirit," he asked. "What do you mean?"

"I mean the first person I saw marked had her veins all glowing in this golden light. Most everyone else was in black. I saw her get scratched," Eric said with emphasis, and feigned scratching Ball Sack's cheek, "and hers turned black too. Just like you."

"Am I marked as well?" Ball Sack asked. His hands were trembling. Eric shook his head no. "But you made him infect me. That is why I cannot work magic. Why would you do that to me?" He seemed oblivious to the whole part where he helped stuff Eric's spirit back into his corpse and dropped him to the bottom of a lake. "A contagious infection of the soul...How is that possible?"

Eric would have rolled his eyes if he had any. "Don't you remember? Anything's possible," he said in imitation of the mage's voice. "I don't know why or how, but I think it's got somethin' to do with the lich. Tragona was experimenting on people here in the castle. I saw a dude at the keep who looked like he'd been torn to little pieces and sewn back together. He wasn't marked when I saw him, but his magic was definitely off. I could feel it, even smell it. It's like... magic is a stream, and someone farther up took a shit in it then pissed just in case."

Ball Sack's shoulders slumped, like he'd been told he had cancer and only months left to live.

"Your analogy," he said, "though crude, may not be far off. If spirits are being infected in such a way their magic is hampered, their impurity could carry back to the ley lines. One person would have little effect, but thousands?"

Saruman leaned on the table from the weight of his realization. "The Academy...if this infection has reached Westorval—"

"The barrier," Ball Sack finished. "It could fail."

Eric said, "Sounds like it already has. Aside from the stalker at Cledford, I ran into a collector in the forest just south of here."

Ball Sack was visibly shaken, his voice weary with concern. "We must warn the Assembly. If you have seen two in so short a distance, there must be many more elsewhere. If the barrier has already been compromised enough to allow so many through—"

"It is only a matter of time," Saruman said, "before it utterly fails."

"Yeah, that's rough," Eric said. "Well, good luck with that! I've got a lord to go murder."

He waved and headed back out of the room.

– 12 –

Eric had a difficult time getting down the spiral stairs to the laboratory, but once he reached the bottom, the ceiling was fairly high. There was at least another three feet above his head, less so where arched stones ran the length between support columns. There were a number of sturdy wooden tables across the center of the room, with a series of iron chains and shackles. The varnished surfaces were worn to a paler shade, as if many had been restrained against their will. Etched lines were carved within the centers and led toward one end, where dried bloodstains speckled the table legs and floor. Brackets on that end held clay bowls in place, where body fluids were somewhat contained and collected.

More tables lines the walls. Those to his right held various tools and instruments for cutting, sawing, slicing and breaking—all manner of grisly surgery that could be imagined. They weren't the gleaming silver of surgical steel one might have found in a modern hospital. Their edges were visibly sharp, but all the rest was coarse. The handles were bound in leather and worn smooth over time. The best way to describe them was *well-used*. If the lich had had a favorite, one wasn't apparent from looks alone.

The next two tables beside that held rotting limbs in neat rows and organs preserved in clay basins. There were hands and feet as well but oddly no heads. The grim collection of body parts had been carefully removed and placed, as if categorized and set aside for later use. Eric noticed tiny bite marks in one decaying leg, where it looked like a goblin had tried but didn't care for the taste.

The table beside that held a number of books. One was already open, its pages yellowed and wrinkled. It held a fairly detailed map of Faradim with converging concentric lines drawn all throughout. From the sheer number of them on the page, with arrow ticks noting directional flow, Eric guessed they represented ley lines. He found Thrallen on the map, saw the two lines passing through and wondered how accurate it truly was. Far off to the east, right beneath Westorval, dozens of lines converged to a single point. A notation scrawled in ink called it a nexus.

Tables on the other side held a meticulous collection of stones and minerals, many of them unfamiliar. There were metals too, shaped into rods an inch thick and a foot long. They didn't have seams, like they'd been cast, but were perfectly smooth. Eric could still sense a hint of magic about them. They didn't hold magic within but had been used for spellwork at some time. The books on this side of the room were anatomical in nature. They held detailed drawings of the human body, of muscle structure and bones, tendons and joints, organs and veins. From the way the last had been drawn, with the directional arrow ticks, it looked as if the artist was drawing similarities between the bloodstream and a ley line.

Eric sensed men enter the castle. The mages might have finally packed up and gone for help. He followed the essence he felt still below but saw no other way down. He went to one end of the lab where there was a separate chamber with a well. Otherwise, there was nowhere left he could see to go.

A breeze touched upon his front, while facing the dead end. Eric stepped across and began feeling for any latch or catch in the stone wall. When he found it, a rock where the mortar would have allowed for two fingers to fit inside and pull, Eric used brute strength to make up for his lack of grip. The rock came out a few inches to reveal an iron hinge. A mechanism clicked, but the wall remained still. Eric used the rock as a handle and gave a pull. The wall slid outward with little effort and touched against the well. There was plenty of room for a normal-sized person to fit through. For a metal golem almost three times as large? Not so much.

Eric sighed and forced his way through, careful not to make too much noise. He might never again enjoy the advantages of stealth, but a part of him wanted to catch Sebran by surprise.

Mortar gave and crumbled, rocks slid and tumbled. They dropped one by one at first, light thuds against bare earth, and became a small albeit quiet collapse. They only made noise when rocks struck one another, which Eric tried to mitigate with his hands.

The rough passage on the other side was much larger. Eric was able to stand without trouble, and the walls on both sides gave room enough to stretch his arms. It went on in a straight path a few hundred feet before turning back and continuing farther down.

When Eric reached the next level, it looked bare but for the statues and tombs along each wall. Eight on each side, the likeness of the men and women buried within the stone encasement before them were finely carved in a white marble with bluish streaks. From wrinkles in noble clothing to the creases upon skin, each looked like they'd been captured in time. None appeared very old, so Eric guessed they'd been portrayed as they had when in their prime.

At the end of the grand chamber were open double wooden doors, reinforced with thick iron bands and the remnants of enchantment. Flickering light bled out into the room where Eric stood. He approached the massive doorway and pushed one of the doors. It slid quietly open on oiled hinges.

Sebran was inside, at the far end of what looked like a treasury of sorts. Shelves lined both sides of the room, thick slabs of wood held by chains and iron support bars beneath the outer edges. The wood was longest at the top and grew subsequently shorter with each lower shelf, so that the supports formed a pattern drawing in toward the center. It reminded Eric of the giant organ being played at church, back when they still went, many Christmases ago.

The lower shelf on his left held three coffers filled with coins. First gold then silver and what he assumed was platinum, they were each stamped with a crown on one side and crossed swords on the other. Above that were smaller chests filled with jewelry and cut gems, a wide array of gold and silver necklaces, bracelets and rings— many of which looked all too similar to what Tragona had been wearing. The gems he could recognize looked like rubies, emeralds and diamonds. Those he couldn't were black, purple or yellow. The shelves above those continued on with other valuables, gold plates, silverware, bejeweled cups and urns, decorative jewelry boxes and all manner of masterfully crafted trinkets in marble or metalwork.

Shelves on the other side amassed a wholly different sort of treasure. Eric saw and felt them with awe and a longing to claim them all. Glass jars six inches tall lined every shelf three deep. They were as wide as they were tall, with glass stoppers sealed in wax and imprinted with a family crest. Each one was spelled shut with an enchantment he could feel but couldn't see until he tried to touch one with a finger. Its glyph lit up in a golden sphere around the glass, both protection and a warning to be cautious.

Within each jar was swirling light with charges of static silver. Most all of them were vibrant orange, with faded crimson in the mix, while some were red as blood or deep blue with whorls of green. Only one among them was all black, in a section at one end by itself, placed apart as if out of fear of being too close to the others. It bore a striking resemblance to the infectious corruption. Their collective force was palpable, a power urging to be taken.

Every one of them contained essence.

Sebran was at the far end of the room, knelt before a jar on the lowest shelf. A leather necklace with a single diamond had been placed around the jar, accompanied by a white flower on its top. He had a hand to the glass but made no move to lift the jar. It was almost as if he was mourning at a shrine.

He saw the golem and knew but didn't say a word. His jaw stood out with tension, as he swallowed hard his emotions and got to his feet. He smoothed the front of a silken shirt and leather vest done up in gold buttons. He wore a brown fur cloak across his shoulders for warmth, and his breath frosted the air.

"It's you," the lord said with frustrated contempt. He still hated Eric for ending Ella's life. "I can tell in your manner. Even trapped within metal, you have the bluster of a drunken braggart."

Eric stepped closer, towered over him with menace. Sebran didn't flinch as he looked up into the crimson fire of those eyes.

"Yep. It's me again, asshole."

Sebran may have seemed consigned to his fate, but his casual demeanor belied a mind hard at work. What or whoever was in that jar meant something to him. If a confrontation was inevitable, he was all too keen to have it elsewhere.

"How is that possible?" Sebran asked and clasped his gloved hands in front. He wore a sword sheathed at his belt, for what little good it might do him. "Even if you managed to escape the amber, how did you get back inside the golem? Only one spirit can occupy an object at a time."

How the fuck do you know that?

"Jaken's dead," Eric replied, "thanks to you." He gave a nod toward the jars. "What are these?" He pointed at one with a finger, caused its glyph to flare to life. Sebran didn't seem to care about the others. "Looks fragile."

The lord stiffened, raised his chin. His mouth even twitched a bit beneath that ridiculous mass of bristles he called a mustache.

"No?" Eric grabbed hold of him around the neck with his left hand, knelt down and brought Sebran along. He slowly dragged his index finger toward the jar enshrined with a necklace and touched the metal tip against its glass. "How 'bout now?"

Sebran's nostrils flared, but he wouldn't budge.

He may be an asshole, Eric thought, *but he's got a pair, that's for sure.*

Eric poked the jar again, a series of metal *tinks* that grew louder each time.

"I will break it," he promised. When the lord still refused to talk, he grabbed hold of it in his right hand. "Fine, then."

"No!" Sebran pleaded. "Wait! Wait...don't. Please put it back. I'll tell you."

Eric put the jar back within the necklace, let go of Sebran and stood. He was still blocking the only way out. There was no getting past him, and he wasn't leaving without answers.

"My family has a strong bloodline of casters," Sebran explained and straightened his clothes again. "We keep it secret because nobility are not permitted to use magic. Those who govern have power enough, in the eyes of the

Assembly."

Eric recalled the name from his talk with the two try-hard wizards. That meant magic was governed by a separate body, possibly a council of magicians at some school in Westorval. So did the King answer to them, or was it the other way around? Exactly how did they enforce these rules?

"That doesn't explain the jars," Eric said, "or why they look like they contain essence."

"My family," Sebran reluctantly admitted, as if he was ashamed or afraid of being judged, even by someone he despised, "aren't just skilled practitioners. They're spiritists. It's a forbidden form of magic. They harness souls to work magic. It's far more potent than channeling ley lines," he added and looked down at the jar he cared for, "but it's also cruel and despicable."

*Wait...*Eric began to piece together an uncomfortable thought. *Is essence a soul? I thought it was just like life force or something.* He wondered if what he'd been taking to fuel his changes were actual, supposedly eternal, souls. *Is that what makes the golem so powerful? So, does that mean if I take someone's essence, their soul no longer exists? Am I stealing their afterlife?*

He was never a true believer in life after death. The entire notion of heaven and hell seemed as ridiculous as an immaculate conception. But if souls were real, what did that mean for what comes after living? He had proof they existed, had seen and felt it with his own senses. If souls were real, there must be something more...to life, to living, to death and beyond.

"You sound like you don't approve," Eric said, "like you can't or won't use the magic yourself."

"I can," Sebran said, "but you're right. I refuse. I've seen it destroy lives, twist the good intentioned into true evil, turn love into ash." He shook his head with heartfelt sadness. "I could never do that."

"And the jars? Why do you have them?"

Eric could understand the sentiment, was feeling it himself, but that didn't explain why Sebran had enough souls to fuel a dozen transformations.

"We take—" Sebran began and corrected himself. "My family used to take the spirits of criminals and debtors, tax evaders and the like, and stored them for later use."

Like batteries?

Eric pointed toward the lone jar. "Why's that one black?"

"An experiment gone awry," Sebran answered. "No one has ever been able to duplicate the results."

Except Tragona, Eric thought wryly.

Sebran continued, "There's something wrong with the spirit, like it's been fouled by torture and torment, dark emotion to such a degree that it's become unusable. Its magic is warped, too volatile to employ or risk release into the ley lines."

"Experiments," Eric said, "like the ones Tragona was doing in the lab above us."

He looked back at the golden rings on a shelf to his left. Something clicked. The lich might not have known about this hidden collection of souls, but what he was doing bore a striking resemblance to what Sebran had been describing.

"It's not a coincidence," Eric accused, "that he chose this castle. Who is he to you?"

Sebran had the look of someone caught helping a murderer. He knew what he'd done was wrong, had known all along, but said nothing to protect his family name. He put reputation above others, risked the lives of those loyal to him, even those who loved him...like his daughter.

"He was my uncle," the lord admitted and bowed his head. Sebran took in a deep breath, set it loose in a long exhalation. "He was cast out of the family, exiled from Faradim on pain of death. My father put him on a boat headed east for the Red Isles. When he returned years later, after my father had died, he seemed a changed man. I was

134

a fool to have ever trusted him, but I learned that lesson far too late."

Eric was more interested in the experiments than the family drama. All that game of thrones shit was about as useful to him as an enema.

"What exactly did he do?"

"There are countless books in our library," Sebran said, "of experiments my forebears have performed in the past. They were always done in the interest of better harnessing a spirit, of getting the most from a body or purifying the essence to a more potent form." He looked to the jars, as if he saw them as imprisoned people and not contained magic. "My uncle was too extreme. He was trying to alter the soul, remake it into something else that could be bent to his will. He went through subjects so quickly that it was noticeable people were missing—innocent people. He became indiscriminate in who he took. He had to be dealt with."

Oh, sure, Eric thought with sarcasm, *it's fine to forever kill criminals and the poor, but once you start fucking with rich people, shit's gotta stop!*

"What about that one?" Eric asked and pointed to the shrine. "What's so special about it?"

Sebran smiled at the jar, a faint turning of the lips that faded with accompanying memory.

"Her name was Marina," he said, as if he could still see her in his mind. "She was a farmhand, a beautiful young girl, full of life and joy."

It was clear he'd loved her and still did.

"But you're a lord or whatever," Eric finished for him, a noble drama for the CW in the making. He rolled his eyes inwardly. "Cuz poor people are just the worst."

Sebran's brow furrowed. "It was my father who had disapproved. I didn't care for station or lineage. I only knew she made me happy. We were married in secret." He started to speak again but choked back the words. Eric started

135

to feel shitty for making fun of him. After a moment, he added, "Father took her spirit as a reminder not to break with tradition or ever go against the family's wishes.

"That's why you wanted the castle back so badly," Eric guessed. He didn't have to, but he wanted to set the record straight. "Look, I tried to save your daughter. She was in pain, already dying and there was nothing we could do to save her. She *asked* me to end it. I didn't have to go out of my way to bury her next to her mother. It's what she wanted, and if I couldn't save her, it was the goddamned least I could do."

Sebran gave a curt nod in recognition. "I was just so angry at the loss, even though I knew it would one day come. You do have my thanks for that, no matter what you choose to do next."

"I'm guessing Tragona didn't know about this," Eric said and indicated the stockpile of souls.

"No, he was never trusted with that knowledge before he was sent away. Otherwise," Sebran said with a heavy heart, "he would have destroyed Marina's spirit out of spite."

"Trust me," Eric said and eyed the blackened soul, "I think he woulda done a lot worse."

He was tempted to smash the jars himself, take their essence and channel the transformations into becoming human again. Then he could finally return home and be done with this world. But he couldn't bring himself to do it. Even though they were dead, it felt wrong to take their souls. They were people just like him, and they deserved whatever peace they could find in death. He may have lost his human body, but he hadn't lost his humanity.

"Is there any way to free—" Eric started to ask but was interrupted by distant screams.

– 13 –

Eric was still blocking the entryway. Sebran looked at him in askance, clearly wanting to go see what was the matter but uncertain of his own fate. At some point during their discussion, Eric had decided not to kill him. It was easy to see this world as not real, with it having no consequences he should care about, but that wasn't the case. It wasn't some video game he could be an ass in and hide behind the anonymity of a character. It was a face-to-face, tangible existence with people just as real as everyone back home. There was no need to go burning bridges while there was a chance he might still need help from unlikely places.

Eric stepped aside and let Sebran go, followed after as the lord ran. More screams rang out, echoed back from within the castle.

He may have been a dick, Eric reasoned, *but I did kill his daughter.*

Eric tried to imagine what he'd do if someone hurt his sister Emily. What he'd done. Memories of the park came rushing back, of her and her friends drinking with *them* when she was supposed to be watching him, the crowd of guys later pulling her far away from the group and into a van, his ten-year-old self yanking open the back doors with a stick in his hand, like a goddamned hero trying to rescue his older sister and being beaten by kids five years older than him badly enough to be put in a hospital for a week.

He growled and forced the memories from his mind, which drew an odd look from Sebran. His childhood, his family life, all of it had been shit. It wasn't something he wanted to think about—not ever. There was a damned good reason he played Warbones as much as did.

They reached the laboratory and were heading up. Eric slowed to traverse the steps without stumbling but was right behind Sebran as he entered the main hall.

There was blood spattered across the stones as if more than one had died, but no bodies could be seen. Men who'd been sleeping in the next chamber ran for the courtyard with swords in hand. A servant came rushing in from outside, panicked and out breath, saw Sebran and headed over.

Eric had expected to see demons beyond the doors because of the mark outside the gates. What he saw was wholly different.

"How many?" Sebran demanded of the servant in an authoritative tone. He didn't slow and continued past for the doors.

"Just one, Milord," the man answered and followed after, still trying to catch his breath. He stopped just before the exit, clearly planning to stay inside. "But everyone it attacks...they become just like it."

Sebran had stopped listening, threw the doors wide to survey the attack for himself. The lord paused for a moment, unsure of what he was seeing. He straightened his back and started barking orders.

Eric noticed their essence right away, dark with the

faintest hint of crimson, shot through with violet charges and much stronger than a human's. Their aura was so powerful it caused the air around them to waver, like the shimmer of intense heat rising off a stone.

Whatever monsters they were now, it was clear they were once human. It looked as if the corruption had been taken to an extreme. Their skin was blackened in forked paths along each vein, lightning strikes that branched out across pale flesh. The dark patches had become scales, reflective like metal and sparked when struck by steel.

They ran on all fours, snarled and leapt on prey like starving animals. With nails grown long and black, sharp enough to slice through steel, one tore through a knight's armor like it was paper. Their bare feet had become more animalistic as well, longer and wide, more suited to leap and with curved talons at the end.

Teeth like sharpened bits of coal, eyes a glassy black, a dark fluid seemed to leak from both. Whether it was blood or the corruption, Eric couldn't be certain, but neither did it matter. Even a wound by claw caused the victim to change.

They had filthy hair where the metal scales hadn't spread across their heads. It had the look of pseudo-armor, like the unfinished costume of a horrific cosplay. Crazed and feral, the handful Eric could see were trying to feed on the nearest exposed flesh. They were mindless attackers, caring only for their own hunger.

One had multiple wounds across its back from pikes striking at a distance. The flesh had parted but stopped when the blade touched against scales. Even the wound, its blood and muscles, were dark as onyx. What oozed down its back was thick like foul syrup.

A horse whinnied and bucked through, kicked a man against the wall and tried to bite another. It too had been changed. It barreled a soldier over, bent down over him and tried to feed.

To Eric they looked like nightmare fiends.

"We can't allow any to escape!" Sebran shouted. To himself, he added, "If they can turn others to their side with a wound, they'll take everyone in Cledford. They'll be unstoppable."

Eric said, "This is some zombie apocalypse shit right here. But worse."

The fiends were alive, they were fast, and the change was almost instant. All of them were trying to feed, to satisfy a ravenous hunger, but once they took a bite, the victim began to change. It took only moments for the corruption to spread. Once the victim became a fiend, its attacker lost all interest. Both would then look for others to feast on.

There was a critical mass, however. When three or four attacked the same person, there were too many wounds, too much blood lost. The victim died before they could change. The same was true of a fatal strike, either a bite or claw to the neck. When someone died, nearby fiends broke off their attack to join the frenzy, if they weren't already feeding. It was a momentary distraction at best that allowed Sebran's men to attack freely from behind.

For every fiend killed, three new ones took its place. Sebran's army of three hundred was being consumed before his eyes. No matter how much the fiends fed, they were greedy for more. Their hunger reminded Eric of his own, when his need to take essence had been the only driving force that mattered.

They were insatiable.

"You don't owe us anything," Sebran told him with a begrudged pleading in his voice, "but if you don't help us here, all of Faradim may be lost."

Eric watched over the carnage, men pulled down to their backs and savaged with teeth and claw. He'd drawn the line at killing people, knew in his heart he wasn't a murderer— even if he'd joked about it. He knew anger might one day drive him over the edge, but until then his humanity was intact. His dilemma now was in deciding whether it was the same to let them die as it was to kill them himself.

"If anything, you owe me," Eric told him. "This isn't my world."

"You still have to live in it."

Sebran left to join the fight, to hold back the tide of teeth and death overwhelming his men.

Eric called after, "This isn't over between us."

He headed down the steps and was hit by lingering essence from the dead. The sunny rush of a few humans paled beneath a violet surge, where the combined spirits of three fiends brought him close to a transformation. It was an incredible flood of power washing over his runes, intermingled with conflicted emotion.

Now that Eric knew what he was taking to fuel his transformations, he felt guilty for doing so—even those he hadn't killed. Especially those. Had he stolen their chance at an afterlife, in heaven or whatever happened to someone when they died? He'd thought of himself as an atheist, though he was raised catholic. Now, he was no longer so sure. If souls existed, didn't that mean there *had* to be something after? What happened to the souls he used? Were they gone forever, or had they become a part of him?

Where exactly is mine? he wondered and punched a fiend across the shoulder from behind. It was trying to bite a soldier who'd fallen to his back. The man was frantically struggling to keep it away from him. *Is it inside the golem or somewhere else?*

His punch had broken bones but did little to slow the fiend. It turned to sniff at Eric, to scent if he was worth eating, and quickly went back to snapping at the man trapped beneath.

Good thing they can't eat metal.

Eric pulled the fiend off him by the neck. The guard scrabbled away still on his back and was jumped by another. The fiend was heavier than it looked, with arms and legs flailing, as it tried to reach back and claw Eric. Its nails were three inches long, jagged at the tip but metallic like its scales. The gouges it left in his hands and arms were not near as deep as those caused by the fey but enough for alarm. If he couldn't keep away from its attacks, give himself time to heal, it would eventually expose his runes.

Chaos reigned around him. The iron gates had been bent and torn open. Arrows sped past him, some hitting their mark but many striking earth. More and more men fell to fiends, became fiends themselves. Heavy armor was a hindrance, as evidenced by the knights outside the wall fighting off their own horses. Prolonged battle in plate was wearing them down.

Eric squeezed the fiend's neck with both hands but found it harder to kill than expected. It was stronger than it ever was as a human, sturdier and difficult to break. With the way it wriggled in his grasp, Eric worried it would get free before he could manage to snap its neck. There was magic at work but not the sort it could directly use or throw his way. He forced it down to its stomach, so all it could reach were his hands. With a knee to its back, he grabbed around to its chin and pulled. A resounding *snap* sounded out, and the fiend became still.

The feel of it rushing in overcame his other senses. Its essence was easily three times more potent than it'd been as a human. Whatever magic changed its body had drastically altered its spirit as well.

A change of his own was upon him, dulled the cries and shouts around him. His existence became burning, a power within aching to be spent. It was an odd sensation in his middle that tingled up his back, a surging pleasure that threatened pain if he let it linger for too long.

Eric wanted the ability to work magic, to channel it into spells and enchantments, to craft wards and glyphs. If anything could make this whole experience worthwhile, worth losing his body and being trapped in the golem...

Nothing happened.

Fuck!

It was like wishing to be human all over again. He didn't know how many changes it would take to make it happen. He just hoped it wasn't all a waste of time and transformations that could've been put to better use. The changes he'd spent toward becoming human hadn't been *totally* wasted, he admitted. They did bind him to the golem. So what did this one do for him just then? He didn't seem any taller or feel any stronger. As far as he could tell, nothing had changed.

He turned his attention back to the fight.

The fiends ignored him, made it easier to walk up on them from behind. He went for those nearest, brought them down with an arm around the neck or a makeshift weapon to the throat. Smashing their heads with a fist only worked if most of the skin hadn't been corrupted. Their scales were too hard to cave in with one blow. It took five powerful strikes when he tried, and the creature still twitched. Eric decided the neck was his safest bet. Better to finish them off than risk leaving one alive. He had one down on its back, a knee holding it in place, and drove a heater shield through its throat. A twist to either side was all it took.

Pikemen and guards were doing their best to hold their own. Many fought back to back for protection, while others worked with shields to drive fiends toward the wall. Orders were given and men followed, despite visible fear. It was going well until fiends topped the walls. The archers were unprepared and ill-suited to defend at close range. Within minutes, dozens more fiends were leaping down from all around.

Eric picked up a steel great sword, which in his hand was more a dagger, and drove a fiend to its front with his foot. His grip was so large that his fingers didn't fit the pommel. Two rested against the blade with the guard between the next three. He plunged the sword down for a swift kill, pulled it free and caught another with in a backswing through the shoulder. Held in place, it was an easy target for the three swordsmen it'd been fighting. He didn't wait for thanks, nor did he hear any called after.

Hands slick with their blood, Eric went for another. He didn't tire, didn't weaken and couldn't be infected. At least he hoped so. Two more fell to his blade before it shattered at the middle and became useless. A second change came upon him. He endured its burning and again chose to wield magic.

And again nothing happened.

It was taking more essence each time, like filling an experience bar. Each level he gained made the next one all the more difficult to obtain.

While he didn't understand how the corruption was altering their spirits, making them so much more potent, he felt a twinge of guilt for a momentary thought. If he let them all become fiends, who knew how many changes he could fuel with their essence. Of course, he'd probably be overrun and torn apart. The way the fight was looking, he might not have to make that choice.

Too bad, Eric thought. *It'd be a hell of an exploit.* Given enough people, in a controlled environment—*Not that I'd ever do that...*

He continued left, took one down in his right hand by the neck and drove it down into the mud. He reached out and pulled another toward him by its leg. The guard it was atop saw his opportunity, flipped around onto all fours and stabbed it in the eye. A blade to the brain, it turned out, was quite effective. Eric pushed and broke the other's neck.

He'd been clearing the courtyard by moving back and forth it as he crossed west to east. More had sprung up behind him, but they were far less in number than when he'd started. It gave the men struggling for their lives a bit of room, both to breathe and to keep fighting. The fiends ahead of him were winning but had reached an upper limit. Too many of them were on single targets.   They   were killing instead of infecting.

Three packs were clustered over victims in front of him, noisily tearing into flesh, flinging blood and bits in a grisly halo around the bodies. He considered climbing the wall and jumping down on top of one. With his size and weight, though, he'd likely bring the wall down.

From the corner of his vision, he saw the two mages exit the castle. They had no magic to lend, would only get in the way and become two more fiends he'd have to deal with. Eric was about to wave them back inside when Ball Sack pulled a crystal orb from the velvet of a metal box. He let the box fall and threw the clear orb at a pack of fiends.

It shattered upon impact and engulfed the immediate area in green flame. The blast of fire condensed across the pack in a blaze of brilliant emerald. It spread up and over them, all around, consuming flesh between their scales. They'd barely had time to cry out in pain before collapsing into char.

"Whoah! Fuck, yeah!" Eric shouted at the two. "Do more of that!"

The combined essence struck him, nearly knocked him over but hadn't been enough for a change. He went after the closest pack, pummeling from behind, brought two heads together, drove his foot down upon a neck. So long as the fiends ignored him, so long as they fed, they were much easier to dispatch.

While Eric fought his pack, a handful of polished white rocks landed among the cluster to his left. The earth was already muddy, soaked through with blood. When the rocks struck, the ground became momentarily akin to marsh. The corpse and fiends sunk inches within then became trapped when it all turned to stone. They would have kept feeding, had the body not been buried. With frightening speed, a rough white spire for every rock thrown jutted out three feet long. It looked like a stony bramble had erupted and impaled every fiend.

It was enough to send Eric into a change. He was still on one knee, finishing the last of his pack. The bliss rose up from his middle, swept across every rune inside him. It was a fire of promise, a burning pregnant with choice. The power swelled to a painful crest and was spent with a single thought.

Eric felt it this time.

Like the sudden waking from a bad dream, he opened his eyes to a new level of clarity. Colors became brighter, sounds crisper, as his spirit did more than merely bind with the golem. It connected. It was as if he'd become complete, his hollow brimming with a warm glow. He felt alive at last, more so than he'd been in a very long time. The ever present emptiness that had defined him was now filled with something new. He had hope. Transforming into a human no longer seemed so farfetched.

Eric held out a hand, knew it was within him. He just didn't know how to call it forth, how to put it to use. He scrawled in the air, as he'd seen others do. Rather than runes, he used letters, but they fell apart into gold sparkle.

He growled in frustration, walked toward more fiends feeding on the dead. There were close to two dozen packs with barely a handful of men left in front. Those behind him still struggled but were at least winning out. If Eric didn't deal with those clustered before they finished their meals, the resulting onslaught would spell the end.

Fire, Eric thought, imagining it in his mind. *Fire*. He recalled the green flames, wanted to bring them forth. *Fire!* He saw their every detail as he continued to walk. The liquid lick of its light, the emerald glare of its blaze, consuming all it touched...

"Fire!" Eric shouted, and his world became flame.

It exploded outward in a plume of beryl madness, so intense it baked the mud to cracked earth in an instant. Flames swept from off his body, tore away metal into flecks that flared to viridian embers. The air itself was on fire, swirled and whooshed with a deafening voracity as it turned. A whirlwind of destruction, it claimed all within its grasp.

Fiends reared and cried out, blood spattered maws turned to ash. The burning spread farther down, a new corruption of growing black. In the span of a few breaths, their flesh was gone. It took longer for scales to bubble and drip, for their remains to become slag within the dying of fire.

Eric dropped to all fours in utter agony. He'd felt pain before but nothing like this. He been stripped, metal flayed and consumed by the wildfire. It left his coloring in shades of green along lines across his body. The fire was gone, but the ache of it lingered long after. He took in deep, ragged breaths, despite not needing air. It helped him endure while his body healed. The pain had been so intense he didn't realize its core burning was a change waiting to be spent.

He looked up and saw four more packs descend on what was left of the men trapped on that side of the yard. He had magic now but no idea how to use it properly. Another attempt like before might be his last.

No, he needed a weapon—a sword. One he could call at will and send away. It would have to be strong, like his star metal. Steel would only break. And it had to be large enough for him to wield.

Power fled his middle.

Better able to breathe again, Eric stood and saw the carnage his magic had wrought. Six clusters had been decimated. The char of their passing clouded the air with foul odor and ash. Melted metal had pooled with bits of blackened bone. All else had succumbed to the emerald fire.

Eric held out a hand and willed his sword to it. A layer of metal came away from him, as it had when the flames came. Tiny flecks and flakes swarmed together in his hand. From pommel to tip, they formed a star metal greatsword. It took only a brief moment to fully form. It felt good in his hand. The blade was even taller than him, which was considerable since he'd grown another three feet. Its metal was dense, far heavier than steel, and even though the sword was huge, he was able to wield it with one hand.

It's a tradeoff, he realized, *for now anyway.* Forming the sword weakened his armor, made his runes more vulnerable. *Probably wanted too much. I can take care of it later.*

He went after the remaining packs, swinging the sword just as easily as a man might a steel blade. From behind, he did his best to cut away heads. Where the sword struck scales, it wasn't able to slice through. Still it was enough to end most he attacked. He finished those out of reach of his swing with stabs, through the chest or an eye, whichever was easiest. Unfortunately, the last two clusters finished feasting, and Eric stood between them and another meal.

All thirteen rose at once and swarmed him like rabid animals. Four leapt at his shoulders, three more right behind, and toppled him by sheer force. The others were at his legs, clawing madly at his metal. Blood and spittle fell from their mouths, as all of them grunted with the effort of trying to tear him to pieces.

Eric rolled onto his front, trapping one beneath him and raised his sword for a fatal strike to its head. He threw fiends off him one after another, forcing them from his arms. He grabbed one off a shoulder, brought it down and killed it as well. As much as it felt like he was making headway, his time was running short. The pain behind his legs, across his back and shoulders, grew with every claw swipe. Their gouges were cutting deeper. His runes were in danger of being exposed.

The few guards and pikemen left, the pair of knights who still remained, were fighting off a last handful of fiends on their end. Even if they managed to succeed, they wouldn't reach Eric in time.

He threw off as many as he could at once and stood, drove

his shoulders toward the wall to crush those he wasn't able to shake loose. Stone crumbled beneath his charge, and debris rained down. The wall had collapsed inward, was on the verge of tumbling. Eric struck again, killing the fiend between and brought a section of wall down. Rocks smashed with disregard. He was up to his knees in stones, but a few fiends had been momentarily trapped. He finished those off with quick stabs to the head.

Of the seven that remained, five snuffled the air and caught scent of the men still fighting. They ran off before Eric could do anything to stop them. Two still clawed at his middle, flailing both arms in frenzied swipes that would only abate with their deaths—or his. Metal parted beneath the furor, revealing silver light and a trickle of golden shimmer. What fell from the open wound looked like the glowing cascade of a failing rune.

Everything went dark.

He felt the pain all too keenly, could still hear, smell the blood and ash, but his vision was gone. Eric grabbed at one with his left hand, caught hold of it by a shoulder and punched it to death with the guard and blade of his sword. The other kept at the wound, not to further a weakness but because it was a mindless killer. Eric doubled over to protect the opening with one arm, swung out with the sword. He knocked the fiend aside, heard it come right back at him. He dropped the blade, reached out and caught the fiend around the waist. Eric brought it to his front, wrapped both arms about its back and crushed it against him. He didn't stop until he heard its spine crackle beneath his grip.

It took long minutes of healing before the wound finally closed and his runes were fully mended. His vision returned in the same moment, like opening eyes.

Three fiends were held back by shield and pike, while four more had pushed men to the opposite corner. One among them was Sebran. Eric was surprised to see the lord fight beside his men, had taken him for the sort who let others do the dying.

Eric picked up his sword, pulled free of the fallen rocks and headed across the courtyard. An angry swing ended the one on his left, cut through from shoulder to waist. Another swing took out the one on his right, an upward slash from underarm to opposite shoulder. Three pikes simultaneously caught the middle in the chest, as Eric swung and lopped off its head.

Less than two dozen men remained. They all turned as one and rushed to help their lord. They made quick work of the four, attacking from behind. When all the fighting was done, there were only somber nods, claps on the back and men falling to the mud in exhaustion. They were relieved, visibly glad to be alive, but grieved by the loss of so many.

Though he'd expected to hear cheering, he had to admit it would have seemed out of place. Maybe if the enemy hadn't been fellow soldiers...

They gave Eric sidelong looks, but not one of them was grateful. Only Sebran approached.

"You have my thanks," the lord told him. His clothes were in ruins, torn and covered in splatters of dark ichor. "We saved more than a collection of mortar and stones this day. We saved a kingdom."

You're still not off the hook.

Sebran had spoken as if they were on the same side. Eric quickly cured him of that notion.

"That's two you owe me," he said. Eric considered the jar. "Actually, make that three. You can take Marina, but get the fuck outta my castle."

The lord's mood swiftly soured.

"My men and I," he said, "are but the tip of a very long and very dangerous spear. There is no more army of undead to hold this land. If King Raynver decided to take it back, thousands would be at your doorstep. You would be wise to let this be and find refuge elsewhere."

Eric laughed. "So instead of fighting an *army of undead*,"

he said in imitation of the lord's speech, "you think your king would rather fight the guy who took 'em all out? Good luck with that."

Men grumbled and glared, looked angered enough to attack, but no one moved to raise a hand.

"There is more at stake here than holdings," Sebran reminded him with forced calm, "as clearly evidenced by this battle. Even you must see that."

Even me? What the fuck is that supposed to mean?

"You're right. There is more goin' on here. A whole lotta *secrets*." Eric whispered the last word. "The kind you don't want others to know about. Right?"

Sebran's jaw clenched. He chose not to reply.

"That's what I thought," Eric said. He turned and headed back toward the castle entrance. "Don't take any of my stuff on your way out."

Eric had done his best to pile the bodies once Sebran and his men left. There were so many, however, it ended up more of a long mound. He considered burning them to prevent further spread of the infection, though he would've preferred to do that outside of the castle walls. The resulting metals and ashen debris might still be contagious. If the goblins came back—

He heard horses and wheels in the distance.

When he looked out from the broken gate toward the south, he saw goblins heading his way. They led a train of wagons, carriages and merchant carts all tied together in a line and pulled in front by four horses. None of them seemed alarmed or surprised to see him as they drew closer. Some, like Bel and Bri, even raised a hand in welcome. Their caravan carried all manner of goods, from stolen wealth to sacks of grain, clothing to weapons and even small livestock in wooden crates. Their wheel tracks leading toward the castle left an obvious trail.

"It's good to see you, Master," Griz said, as he and the generals approached him with smiles.

"How'd you know it was me?"

"Scouts, Master," Stalk replied. There were spatters of blood across the front of his dark armor. "They've been keeping watch ever since we were forced to abandon the castle."

Eric scanned the goblins passing by, watched them bring in their spoils and start to unload. Only a few were wounded enough to warrant bandages and what little blood he saw could've been their own. The green general wasn't injured, though. Eric also noticed that while some seemed happy to see him back, many didn't care or were oblivious to anything but their own inane chatter. What really caught his attention were the few who glanced his way with disapproval. None had dared to directly meet his gaze, but the sentiment was there all the same.

"What happened at the keep?" Eric asked, giving Bel a meaningful look. He'd left specific orders. "Did you kill anyone?"

"There were casualties on both sides that couldn't be avoided, Master," the red general replied, no hesitation or regret in his tone, "but no deaths."

Eric gave a nod of approval. "Sebran will probably send for reinforcements and come back. He's got a lot going on here he wants to keep quiet." Eric pointed to the amassed bodies. "He's down to a few dozen after this."

Everyone had been surveying the damage done to the gate and castle wall and the courtyard grounds. There were scorch marks, tumbled rocks and crumbled stone where Eric had crushed the jutting spires. Eventually all eyes fell upon the fiend corpses.

"What happened here, Master?" Griz asked. "I can still feel the aftereffect of a terrible magic."

"That!" a green said and stepped from the caravan, pointing at the bodies. "That's what I saw, Master."

He was the scout who'd been sent west into the enclosed valley. Stalk introduced him as Duskrun.

"Apparently, this was done by just one of 'em," Eric said. "The rest are Sebran's men. A single scratch or bite, and dudes almost instantly changed into—whatever the hell they are. I call 'em fiends. I mean, even the horses changed."

Griz had moved closer to inspect one. "Some sort of infection, Master? It's definitely magical in nature. The affected flesh looks similar to star metal."

The generals went in for a closer look as well. Bitters kicked at one with his boot.

"Don't get scratched," Eric warned. "They could still be infectious, even dead. We're gonna need them carted off somewhere else, away from a water source. Burn and bury 'em. Make sure whoever does it wears a mask to cover their nose and mouth, just in case." To Dusk, he asked, "How many did you see?"

"From what little I explored, Master," the green said, nervously shifting from one foot to the other, "there were many, at least twenty near the village. I could tell they relied heavily on smell. I didn't want to venture too close and risk being scented."

"No," Eric agreed, "it was better to get back with the information. If even one of those things gets through, there'll be a hoard of 'em in no time. Send a group to guard that valley entrance for now, enough so they can take shifts. We want eyes on it at all times. Don't let anything past. If you have to, try to fight them from a distance. You don't want them in your face. Oh, they can jump really high, too, so don't bother with barricades or anything like that. Me and Griz will check it out in the morning, come up with a plan to kill them all. They're too dangerous to just ignore."

The generals started toward the castle to see it done.

Not my world, Eric mirrored the thought from earlier, *but I still have to live in it. For now. Last thing I need is my army turning into monsters.*

"Also," Eric called after them, "let's get a group going at one of those possible mining locations. The sooner we start digging, the sooner we get reinforcements."

Dusk had left with them, but Griz lingered behind. The shaman could tell Eric had something to discuss.

"No one else is asking," Eric said and started walking toward the castle steps, "but I bet you're wondering how I'm back. I'm glad you're okay, by the way. You looked like shit last time I saw you."

"I appreciate the concern, Master." Griz still looked exhausted, used his staff to help keep up as they went inside. "If I was asked to conjecture, I'd say when your human body was consumed you were returned to this one. You've managed to forge a bond." He continued to follow Eric down into the laboratory. "Very unusual, so early on, but then you're not like any other I've ever encountered."

How many freakin' golems do they have?

Eric led them toward the hidden vault. It was slow going, having to move at the shaman's pace. The secret doorway by the well seemed even smaller now. He was forced to pull away more rocks to make room for his new size.

"I can work magic now," Eric said, more than a little proud. "I want you to start teaching me right away."

"I see, Master. Was that your—" Griz fumbled for the words— "first spell I sensed outside?"

"Yeah." Eric drew the word out. "It didn't quite go like I planned. Almost killed myself with fire again. I did take a bunch of those fiends out, though."

They walked in quiet for a few minutes until they came into the burial chamber. They went past both rows of elaborate statues on either side. The door was still open, though the candlelight was gone. Griz had lit the way with an enchantment atop of his staff.

"What is all this, Master?" Griz asked of the jars once they entered the vault. He picked one up off the lower shelf, a storm of orange within it. "Are these what I think they are?"

"Souls. Every one of 'em," Eric said. Griz carefully put the jar back. "Sebran's family used to steal 'em and use 'em to cast spells." The shaman narrowed his good eye and muttered about spiritists. "Better yet, the lich was his uncle. Tragona held his own...grandniece or whatever hostage, and Sebran let him do it. Apparently nobles aren't allowed to use magic, and using souls is illegal or something. This whole mess is some kind of cover up to keep it secret."

"He told you this, Master?"

Eric pointed to the empty spot where Marina's shrine used to be.

"Turns out Sebran married a farm girl, which pissed off his father. Dude took her soul and kept it right there, to teach Sebran a lesson. I threatened to break it if he didn't tell me what the hell was going on. That's not why I brought you down here, though." Eric indicated the black jar. "There's a disease going around that looks a lot like that. When I went to get my body back at the keep, there was—"

"A stalker," Griz finished for him. "Yes, Master. I was told. Dire news, indeed. It could very well mean the Hunt is already on Faradim."

"Right," Eric said, "but what I didn't mention was that I could *see* the marks. Their veins glowed with it, like magic. Some were gold, most were black. I didn't think anything of it until I saw one *change* from gold to black. It's just like those guys outside but a different infection. Except this one makes it so the person can't use magic. The Dumbleduo thought if enough people were infected, it could corrupt the ley lines, which will cause some barrier at the main city to fail. Thing is, I think it already happened. That's why we've got fey and demons running around."

"Demons, Master?" Griz asked, alarmed.

"Didn't I mention there's a mark outside the gate?" Eric absently poked at a jar with his fingertip. "It felt to me like the magic that seeker guy used. Anyway, the point is, all of this shit going on is cuz of Tragona and his experiments.

156

What I can't figure out is *why*. I mean, what's the point of corrupting ley lines to bring down a protection spell over the planet if you're too stupid to survive to see it go it down? He's dead! What the fuck does he get out of all this?"

Griz looked like he was having difficulty following along. He still seemed to be piecing together the new information as he spoke.

"Well, Master...perhaps, er, his true goal was not the barrier construct but something else? Something...bigger." The shaman scratched at his chin, his mind at work. "The barrier may be affected, but it hasn't failed. I would have noticed a change in the world's magic. This is just a guess. We'd have to verify at an arcane library, like the one at the academy in Westorval or the conservatory on Xanaranth. It may be that Tragona wasn't attempting to let something in through to Taellus but rather—"

"Out," Eric interrupted, having put it together. "Like something badass was imprisoned. Still doesn't explain why dumbass would go to all the trouble if the end result means magic is screwed, and he ends up dead anyway."

Griz looked for a place to sit and settled on resting beside the coffer of gold coins.

"I'm sure he didn't *plan* on dying, Master. He had a working phylactery, even if it was cruel, and possibly an auxiliary. Few face a golem and live to tell the tale."

"I still don't buy it," Eric said. "He poisoned her. It's like he was planning on dying."

"Oh, dear." Griz furrowed his brow. "Sorry, Master. I was just struck by a terrible thought." Eric waved a hand in his own direction, motioning for the shaman to give up what he'd been thinking. "What if what he planned to set free was a god? A final sacrifice might have been just what he needed to prove his loyalty."

Eric laughed. "What the fuck good is loyalty if you're dead? And since when are gods real?"

"Gods have always been real, Master," Griz stated as if it

was fact, "but they don't follow the same rules as you and I. What might seem impossible to us is mundane to a god."

"We don't have gods on Earth," Eric said, "or magic."

"It has been my experience, Master, that all worlds have gods and magic and monsters, whether you want them to or not, whether you believe in them or not." Griz used his staff to help him stand. "If Tragona did plan to set something free, we should find out just what it is or complete this expedition as soon as possible."

Eric would have frowned if he could. He followed the shaman out of the vault.

"I'm more concerned with going home," he said and banged his chest, making a hollow metallic noise. "Ya know, once I turn this clunker into a human body."

Griz said, "The two aren't mutually exclusive." He sat down in the wide area between the vault and statues. "Are you ready to learn, Master?"

"Right now?" Eric took a seat a short distance away and crossed his legs, which wasn't as easy as it sounded. Griz had already started drawing runes in the earth between them. "I thought you'd be too tired."

"I am, Master," the shaman admitted and looked all too weary, "but you do not sleep. I'll teach you the runic alphabet, and you can practice it until morning." Eric watched closely as Griz kept tracing new runes. "There are seventy-two runes," he explained and traced them in neat rows, "to represent sounds, though you likely won't use them all, but there are hundreds of sigils, which are used to embody concepts. You can learn those later, once you're proficient with runes. For example," he said and he'd finished writing in earth. He began new ones in the air between them and sounded out his spell. "You could write fff-eye-err."

Griz scrawled three golden runes. He dragged the first toward the last, which formed a circle and vanished into sparkles of gold light. They quickly cascaded toward his open palm and took the shape of a green flame. He closed his hand, and the flame was gone.

"Or you could use the sigil for fire," Griz said and drew three interconnected lines in air, like a small golden mountaintop. He pushed his palm against it, and the sigil flared as the runes had done when they'd made a ward. He lowered his hand beneath the shimmer, and the flame appeared again.

Eric said, "So runes are phonetic, and sigils are like symbols. How come it doesn't work if I just use English?"

"I don't know what that is, Master."

"It's what we're speaking right now," Eric said. "It's what everyone here speaks, even the trolls."

Griz raised an eyebrow. "Master, your glyph allows you to understand and speak any language. What you say and I hear are very different. I'm speaking a common language on Xanaranth called Sperian. Trolls typically speak Volsh, and the humans here on Faradim speak Wystoran. For a golem, clear communication is essential. Language and dialect can vary greatly by locale and even social standing, so golems are enchanted to understand them all."

"Hmm," Eric said. What else did he not know about his own body? "Sounds handy, but it doesn't really answer my question. Why can't I just write what I want to say in my own language? Can the golem interpret what I want and convert it to the runic alphabet?"

The shaman shook his head. "I'm afraid not, Master. The runic alphabet isn't a true language. It's a focus. All magic is about desire, harnessing energy from a source and channeling it to a focused outcome. If you try to cast without a focus, you end up with wild magic. The results can range anywhere from mildly amusing to disastrously fatal."

Eric recalled his brush with wildfire and cringed.

"Point taken. So no shortcuts. Gotcha." Eric looked at the runes before him in the dirt. "Are these facing me or you?"

"You, Master."

Griz spent the next hour going over each and every rune, pronouncing which sounds each represented. Eric was familiar with many and used the space Griz had left between rows to write out their English counterparts. He didn't expect there to be so many. There might have only been twenty-six letters in the English language, but there were quite a few more sounds to be made with them. He was pretty sure they were called phonemes but wouldn't bet his life on it. At least a third of the sounds Griz had listed made no sense, as if they were intended for some other language. He left those blank.

"Can I cast something?" Eric asked.

The shaman smiled. "Everyone is eager to try their first spell, Master. It does make for good practice when learning runes. Alright, let's begin. It's best to start with simple illusions, so there is little chance for destruction. Picture in your mind what you want to create. Remember you're crafting an illusion, a ghostly image, and not something with substance. Perhaps start with a simple flower? Also remember that the simpler you imagine it, the easier it will be to create. If you envision too much detail, the spell may fall apart without proper focus. So picture it in your mind. Start to draw the runes. When all the runes are complete and while you still have a clear image, move the first one toward the last to form a circle."

Eric pictured a simple white flower in his mind, the one from Sebran's shrine but with far less detail. It was just a green stem and a few white petals. He looked down at the runes for reference and started to draw in air the sounds needed. He remembered to make it illusory, like a transparent photograph. Once he'd finished drawing the runes, he spent extra time making sure the image in his mind was strong and clear. With a finger, he poked at the first rune and dragged it toward the last. The line of runes snapped together into a circle and fell apart into a golden shimmer. The cascade coalesced into an illusory white flower hanging in the air between them.

"Well done, Master," Griz said. He used his staff to help climb to his feet. More than one old joint creaked in protest at the strain. "Try not to cast too much. It will drain your power, and you'll need to rest."

"Really?" Eric asked with surprise. "So I might have to actually sleep at some point?"

"Not sleep, Master, just rest. Any time spent not working magic is rest." Griz began to leave but stopped and turned back. "May I ask you something, Master?"

Eric poked at his flower until it dissipated into a rain of sparkles. The spell didn't last forever. He wasn't sure if it simply ran out, or he'd ended it with his finger.

"What's that?"

"Why haven't you claimed all those souls, Master?" the shaman asked and nodded toward the vault.

"Cuz they're people," Eric replied.

He might not have sounded as conflicted as he felt. Truthfully he wanted them but knew in his heart it was wrong. It didn't matter they were already dead. Taking their souls, *consuming* them, was worse than if he'd killed them himself. It was a forever death.

"You could set them free, Master."

Eric gave his full attention. "How?"

"When you encounter essence, Master," Griz said, "you can choose to reject it. An ordinary golem would not be able to, but you have free will. You can exert that free will and choose." The shaman bowed his head. He turned to leave. "Something to consider, perhaps."

For many hours, while he practiced, Eric did just that. He weighed his feelings against need, his sense of guilt against his conscience. He kept memorizing runes, casting the occasional spell, but the temptation to claim the souls was a constant buzzing along the back of his head. By the time he'd grown tired of staring at runes, he hadn't come

any closer to a decision.
The jars were still untouched.

– 15 –

Eric headed toward the enclosed valley early the next morning with Griz by his side. They followed behind Bel, Stalk and a small group of goblins. Another group had set off at the same time to begin work on a new mine, while the rest stayed behind to guard the castle. Eric had warned them demons might attack and to flee if they did. There was no sense in dying to a lost cause when they could fight the demons later on equal ground. Now that Eric could work magic, they'd have more goblins soon enough.

It was raining as they followed the overgrown road west toward the mountains. An hour from the castle, the trees grew more frequent with less space between. By the time they reached the entrance, they stood in a small forest. The road could barely be seen for the brush and fallen branches. A cursory look at the mountains on either side showed the valley had once been closed off. It had been forcefully opened by hand at a low point in the range. The rocks were roughhewn, chiseled by tool and many hours of hard work. While a great effort had gone into breaking into the valley, the road looked to have been abandoned for quite some time. With forest obscuring the pass on either side of the range, making it difficult to see a way in our out, it was no wonder only a single fiend had made it through in all this time.

A low rumble sounded off in the distance, a rolling boom that drew on and echoed against the rocks. A few moments later light flashed over the westernmost mountain, cast its edges in a silver glow beneath the winter gray of a coming storm.

Goblins were already guarding the pass when they arrived. A handful of greens were resting in the upper branches of a nearby tree, had secured themselves with rope to keep from falling.

Worst case scenario, Eric thought as he saw how the pass had been carved, *I can smash the rocks on both sides, collapse it all and seal them in.*

"Everyone but Griz stay here," Eric ordered. "Don't let anything get past."

While the others dispersed to join those at watch, Bel remained in the road.

"I'd like to go along, Master," the red general said. "If you run into trouble, I can help protect our shaman."

"Me too, Master," Stalk offered. The green general had brought a bow nearly as big as he was tall. "You never know when you'll need a good tracker."

"Alright," Eric said with a shrug, "but if one of those things attacks, let me deal with it. Everyone who gets infected is just another I've gotta kill."

Stalk's eyes slightly widened while Bel's somewhat narrowed. Eric motioned for them to lead the way.

"How was your practice, Master?" Griz asked as they walked.

The rain was falling a little harder, filled dips in the muddied road to growing puddles that were difficult for the shaman to traverse without his staff.

"I'm already sick of memorizing runes," Eric said with a short laugh. "It's like chemistry last semester all over again. I'm gonna keep going 'til I master it, though."

Griz nodded. He'd pulled his hood up to keep the rain from his good eye. "Soon enough, Master, you'll learn to channel sources other than your own, like the ley lines."

"Until we deal with the infection, that might not be a good idea." Eric looked down at his hand, worried about the glyph he couldn't see. "If infected people corrupted the ley lines, then using one as a source should spread that infection. I don't wanna lose my ability to cast."

"We don't know that's how it works, Master," Griz said in a thoughtful tone, "but perhaps caution would be best."

They'd continued along the road, which had all but disappeared for a short while. Stalk had found it for them again and led the way through the dense forest. The trees were slender but grown close together, each no more than one or two feet apart. They had very few branches but for the wide canopies at their top. Their bark was white as chalk with dark grooves and knots, though nothing like the black Eric had seen in the forest to the south.

It made him wonder how Taliana was doing.

"There's no large wildlife," Stalk noted as they walked in the rain. "I can hear birds, see them," he said and pointed at one nesting in the hole of a tree. He poked at the mud with one end of his bow, where worms had come up for rain. "There are insects in the ground and in the trees, signs of squirrel and wood mice and raccoons, but I don't see any tracks or markings of large animals. No bear, no wolf, no deer, not even fox."

"If they were sick," Eric said, "we'd at least see a few corpses. Maybe something else is going on."

"They could have been frightened off by those fiends, Master," Bel said. He didn't seem to share the same level of concern as Stalk. "Any sign of those?"

"Yes." The green left the road and knelt a few dozen paces off. He uncovered bones beneath a layer of dead leaves and mud. "I see signs of them everywhere." When he returned to lead them farther, he said, "Master, I think the larger animals have all been hunted. Some may have fled out of fear, but that's not what I'm seeing."

After a while, Stalk stopped pointing out all the piles of bone and signs of struggle he could spot from the road. There were plenty of tracks to follow but no fiends within sight.

When they left the forest, the valley continued on in low grassy hills sweeping north. There was a farm in the distance with three empty fields and more forest farther off to the east. They saw no animals or people as they drew closer to the first field. There was no smoke coming from the stone chimney at the wattle and daub house or any livestock in the fenced area beside it. Everything seemed abandoned.

They kept to the road when Eric sensed something strange. It was like magic but different, less of a tingle and more of a hum. It was a faint thrumming along his metal like a shiver down the spine he used to have.

"Hold on," Eric said and stopped. If it wasn't magic, what could it be? He didn't see anything in that direction but a rising hill. "There's something this way."

He led them off the road, beyond the untilled fields and toward the westernmost mountain. The grassland stretched out and rose to a bare hill up ahead. When they crested its muddy top, they found a massive crater with a large rock shattered into three pieces at its center. Shards littered the surrounding area in a halo about the strike.

"Cool," Eric said. "Never seen a meteor before. You guys might wanna stay back. What feels like magic might be radiation."

Griz had gasped when he saw it.

"It's star metal, Master," he said and worked his way down

the muddied slope.

The rocks were grayish blue with white speckles and striations, shot through with dark veins that branched out in thin lines.

Bel picked up one of the smaller rocks that had broken apart upon impact.

"The expedition's a success," he said in voice filled with shock and realization. "This one find is enough to offset cost and turn more profit than any other has ever seen. We can go home."

Griz waved Eric over. "It's safe, Master. We've found star metal twice before, though never in such quantity. It's priceless," he said and ran a hand over its surface. "This is an incredible discovery."

"It's very rare, Master," Stalk said and slid down to join the shaman, "so much so that it's only used to craft weapons for the greatest noble families. Only eight have ever been made. They're passed down as heirlooms to succeeding heads of house."

Eric still stood at the top of the crater. He didn't like what he was hearing, this talk of his goblins going home. He couldn't let Griz leave, not until Eric was human again. He needed the shaman to send him back to Earth.

You might have to infect him.

It was back, what he thought of as his rational self and speaking in his voice. It was as if it only came out when he was stressed or going insane. Eric had heard enough of it at the bottom of the lake. There wasn't room in his head for two voices.

Fuck off, Eric thought and tried to ignore it.

He can't leave, if he can't do magic, the voice stated in a sensible tone. *Make him teach you the portal spell. Then you get to decide when or if anyone goes home.* It was quiet a moment. *Look at the smaller third. It's been cut at already.*

Eric grumbled and moved closer. "We're not the first to find it," he said when he reached the meteor. He knelt over the piece and ran a finger across the edges where someone had used a tool. "Tragona maybe? Pretty sure I saw a star metal rod in his lab."

Griz took a closer look as well. "Could be, Master, that's what he used in his experiments, why the fiends look like their flesh had been fused with it. This may not be happenstance but proof the lich was working with a god."

"A god?" Bel asked, clearly annoyed this was the first he was hearing of it. "We should notify the conservatory at once."

Eric said, "Rocks fall from the sky all the time. It doesn't mean it's a god."

"We should send for others, Master," Griz said, "to gather this all right away."

This is where they betray you, the voice said in a matter of fact tone, *where their interests don't align with your own.*

Shut the fuck up! You don't know that. But didn't he? Eric was, after all, talking to himself. *I just need a way to make them stay.*

Gather the metal, refine it, the voice suggested, *and use it to make goblins.*

Eric nodded to Stalk and Bel. "You two go. Get all of it to the castle and start refining it. I'll decide what to do with it when I get back."

The red general frowned and asked, "What else could we possibly do with it, Master? It's a prized possession on Xanaranth, more than any other item of wealth or esteem. Ours will be the most successful expedition in history, able to ask any boon of the council we want."

You're made of star metal, the voice reminded him. *What's to stop the goblins from taking it from you once you're there?*

Eric reiterated, "I'll decide what to do with it."

The two goblins bowed their heads and left without another word, though Bel had looked back in discontent as he climbed.

Best keep an eye on that one, the voice warned.

Eric headed out of the crater and north back toward the road. The shaman followed after with a small piece of meteor in his hand. The rain had begun to let up, and they were passed the farm before Eric spoke.

"I wanna use it to make more goblins."

There was steel in his tone, one that said his mind was already made up. Eric had quickened his pace, left the shaman with barely enough breath to follow after let alone any to argue.

"Master," Griz said with caution, "the metal is too rare. It's never been used that way before." He took in a few long, deep breaths. "We don't even know if it can be or what mineral to mix it with if we tried. It's too valuable to waste."

"Disagree," Eric said. He could see a village in the distance, though most of it was obscured by fog off a lake to its south. "I think the power I felt coming off it would make goblins able to work magic. That would make your expedition stronger, able to make even *more* goblins. You could gather enough treasure that it'd be worth even more than a pile of rocks. I thought the whole point of you guys coming here was to conquer."

The village buildings were much the same as the farmhouse, single story wood and hardened mud with thatch roofs and shuttered windows. It was fairly large, with the single road running through. There were farms scattered across the hillsides, numerous fields and pens for livestock. There was still no sign of people, though, no smoke in the chimneys.

"I—I think that would be a mistake, Master." Griz was careful with his words. "The best course of action is to return the star metal to Xanaranth. It would appease the council, and we could ask them to send you home."

"Except I'm not human yet," Eric said, "and they might say no."

He saw the bodies then, one half into the lake edge and others scattered on the road inside the village. None of them moved and were too far away to tell if they'd been infected.

"I can't do the ritual on my own, Master."

Eric headed for the one that had clearly drowned. "That's why you're gonna teach it to me. So I can help."

While the buildings mostly appeared to be houses, he could see a tavern at the village center, a blacksmith at the other end and what looked to be a tannery. There was an empty pasture to the north, just across from the lake.

When Eric got closer, he could see the stitches in the bloated legs of the man at the water's edge.

"Are they dead, Master?" Griz asked of the fiends face down in the village.

"Just this one," Eric replied.

He could see the essence of each fiend. They looked starved near to death, too weak to even move. The body in the lake was like the man at Cledford, torn apart and sewn together. Whatever Tragona had done to him, his presence was affecting the water. The lake was frozen except for a few feet around the body. The water and soil beneath him was black.

"Don't," Eric warned as Griz moved closer to check the body. "Looks like another experiment. Probably died in the water and infected everyone."

"He isn't changed, though, Master."

"Neither was the other one," Eric said. "They could be carriers." At the shaman's puzzled look, Eric added, "Where I come from, you can have a disease that doesn't affect you. We call people like that carriers because they can still pass it on to others."

Griz said, "They should not have left it in the lake like this, Master. Even dwarves know not to foul their only water supply."

"Maybe they tried, and that's what started it all."

Eric headed into the village and stopped beside the closest fiend. He nudged it with a foot. It made a sound but didn't move. Like the others, it seemed barely alive. A quick look around revealed more, inside buildings with smashed and broken furniture and bloodstains all over.

"I think they're starving," Eric said back outside on the road. "They can hardly move."

"One was well enough to make it outside the valley, Master," Griz warned. "There could be others."

"Is there a way to bind them with magic?"

Griz replied, "The easiest way, Master, would be to tie them up with rope and enchant it. Aren't we here to kill them?"

"Not just yet," Eric said. He had another plan in mind. "We'll need them for the ritual."

He could have claimed all the dying fiends. He was close enough to another change, but using them to make star metal goblins was a better use. It kept Griz from leaving before Eric was ready, and put more goblins at his command.

"These souls are infected, Master." Griz eyed one from a safe distance. "Using them could have unforeseen consequences. As I said earlier, it might not even work. Whatever star metal we use will have been wasted." The shaman tried to be convincing. "It's not the best course of action to serve."

"The best way to serve," Eric said with emphasis on the last, "is to make more goblins and keep going. There are other expeditions here, right? What happens if the ley lines get corrupted? The barrier thing falls, some god gets loose and the whole world goes to shit. All those other expeditions will die."

"We could return to Xanaranth, Master," Griz said, "deliver the star metal to the conservatory and charter a new expedition to save Taellus."

Eric sighed. He was getting a little tired of the back and forth and started searching for more fiends.

"I'll think about it."

He started thinking about the corruption. The one from Cledford took away the ability to use magic. He'd taken essence from the fiends in the valley but was still able to cast. It was like there were different kinds of diseases, either by design or accident. He wondered how many experiments Tragona had conducted and how long the lich had been at it.

Or when the hell did he become a lich? Some shit must've gone down for him to pull that trigger. Eric found more dying fiends at the other end of the village. *Why didn't Dusk report seeing them like this?*

"Let's take a look farther north," Eric said and led the way. "Either that scout saw fiends still able to move, or something's happened to them since."

It was getting late in the day when they passed the outlying farms and kept going toward the northernmost mountains. They crested a large hill and stopped. In the distance were fiends searching a forest to the northwest, while others tried to climb out of the valley on the east side. There were at least fifteen, maybe more he couldn't see. They were spread out and moving sluggish. The six trying to climb kept slipping downward or falling from heights that would have killed a normal person. The ones in the forest were chasing smaller animals. They were too slow in their weakened state to be effective.

"Stalk was right," Eric said. They'd hunted the entire valley bare from south to north. There was nothing left for them to feed on. "Pretty soon these guys will be too weak to stand, too. We can tie them up then."

"It might be a good idea, Master," Griz suggested, "to keep one for study, to find out how exactly they've been changed. It might lead to understanding how they're corrupting the ley lines and possibly undo the damage."

"Maybe," Eric said, doubtful, "but that's a horror movie waiting to happen. If it gets loose, everyone's gonna die."

Griz leaned upon his staff. "Then we shall have to make certain, Master, it doesn't get loose."

16

Eric was practicing runes in the courtyard later that night when the first load of star metal arrived. All four horses pulled a wagon half full of the white rock, which apparently weighed more than it looked. The wheels had dug deep tracks in the mud and creaked from the strain. The storm hadn't let up but continued as a steady fall with the occasional crack of thunder. The horses were having a difficult time but persisted with not-so-gentle prodding from two reds riding atop the rocks.

Surprised they haven't eaten 'em, Eric thought as they went past. The smell of wet horse was a little overpowering. *I guess they stole enough food to last a little longer, but it wouldn't shock me to see horse on the menu pretty soon.*

A crowd had gathered to see the rocks that would become star metal. There were excited murmurings at the thought of going home. A few whispers later, that excitement turned to quiet resentment and more than a few unhappy glances toward Eric.

He could feel his leadership in question. It was like the butterflies in his stomach when he'd pass a group at school, saw them look and heard their whispers, *knew* they were talking about him. He'd tried not to care then and did the same now. He didn't need friends any more than he needed goblins.

Having an army made things easier, but Griz was the only one he really needed—not as a friend but for what he could do. Loneliness sucked, but Eric had found ways to deal with it in the past.

Eric quieted the goblins by giving them his attention. They quickly dispersed without a word and went back to their assigned tasks. Once he and Griz started creating new goblins, Eric could make sure they were loyal only to him. He'd had enough of the pirate booty expedition for the goblin home world. He had his own plans to worry about. He went back to practicing runes but kept a close eye on the meteor rocks.

A scout arrived hours later, his dark leathers soaked and muddied. He was from the mining group and needed to speak with Griz. Eric had the green sit with him by the fire while a red went to fetch the shaman. Another guard brought over something hot to drink. The scout nodded in thanks, took the clay mug and nearly finished it in one pull. He covered the rest with a hand to keep the rain out. Griz soon made his way down the steps and joined them. A red brought over a wooden crate for the shaman to sit on and left them to talk.

"What happened?" Eric asked the scout, certain it was bad news.

"We found a mine, Master," the green replied, and finished his drink. He wiped his mouth with a forearm and looked to Griz. "A dwarven mine." The reaction was immediate, as goblins who should've been minding their own business began to curse and spit. "We need you to open the door. It's been sealed with magic."

The cursing continued. Even Griz seemed to share the sentiment.

"Fuck dwarves," the shaman said bitterly. When Eric laughed, Griz looked up from beneath his hood with a bit of a sheepish grin. "Did I say that right, Master?"

"Yeah, you did," Eric said and chuckled more. "Why do you guys hate them so much anyway?"

Griz dismissed the scout with a nod. The green gave a slight bow of his head and left for more drink.

"Dwarves created the first goblins, Master," Griz said and pulled tight the cloak over his robe. "We were slaves in their mines."

"No shit? I've never heard anything like that before." Eric mulled over the idea. He'd already known goblins were created and not born. He'd just never given any thought as to why. "So dwarves can create life?"

"Transmute life, Master," Griz corrected. "Goblins are formed of metals and minerals then transmuted to life by magic and the essence of other living creatures."

"Like a golem," Eric said.

Eric had continued drawing runes in the air as it rained. The last one he'd scrawled was starting to falter. Griz used one end of his staff to correct it.

"Yes and no, Master. Golems were never intended to be conscious, to have intellect." Griz turned his gaze toward the fire, and his voice grew somber. "Goblins were. Dwarves *enslaved* us, treated us as property, as things like a piece of jewelry or fancy clothing. Except we were made to serve, to work their mines, cook their food, bring them drink, fight and die for their amusement." He took in and let out a deep breath, as if breathing out all his contempt. "Now we serve each other. We would never knowingly or willingly create a slave." He looked at Eric with a furrowed brow, one weighed by shame. "You were never meant to be aware, Master."

"Guess I'm just lucky that way."

Griz gave a nod and stood. "Enjoy the rest of your evening,

Master."

About as much apology as I'll ever get, Eric thought and watched the shaman head back to bed.

Not that he needed or even wanted one. Nothing was going to change what had already been done. All he could do now was move forward—like always.

The next morning he and Griz brought a small group back to the mine, in case they encountered dwarves. The storm hadn't passed, but the rain was little more than a drizzle as sunlight breached the horizon.

The mine was built into one of the larger mountains to the north, but passage to it was hidden by elaborately crafted rocks. The outer rock looked solid, from far away and up close. It was an illusion of craftsmanship and not magic, impressive and ingenious. The carved wall ahead matched perfectly with the two preceding it, creating an invisible T-junction. What looked to be a small mountain at the base of a much larger one was actually a well-constructed passageway. The secret entry was crafted into a deep enough depression that no sunlight reached through. Holding up a torch threw shadows across the rock, but the illusion still held.

"How the hell did you guys find this?" Eric asked as he carefully walked through with an arm out front to feel his way. It looked to him like he was about to walk right into a solid wall.

"By accident, Master," Mudbutt replied. The brown general went on to explain, "Scuffles are common on long outings. Two came in here to relieve themselves. One was shoved through the illusion ahead."

Typical, Eric thought. *All this work to hide a tunnel and it gets ruined by some jackass messing with someone trying to take a piss.*

It wasn't even a tight fit, as Eric moved beyond the center rock. The wide passage had plenty of room to accommodate his size. It went on for fifty or so of his paces and ended with a solid metal wall. Within it was a round door twice as tall as Eric. It looked similar to silver but with tints of gold and blue in broad streaks when light struck its surface. Griz called it mithrinum, the only naturally occurring metal with magical properties. There was dwarven writing and elaborate circles all over the door's surface and the surrounding wall.

The glyph protecting it flared to life at the shaman's touch. Eric watched Griz study it carefully, saw him turn its wards, poke at specific runes. Griz took hold of one and pulled it free, shattering it into gold shimmer. Its ward fell apart within the glyph. He then spun the glyph to its other side and did the same to another ward. The whole glyph fell apart into a cascade of sunlight sparkle. Griz pointed to one of the circles on the lower right of the door.

"Could you open the door, Master?"

Eric leaned over and put his hand against the circle. It was cold to the touch with a numbing tingle, like he'd put his hand into a bucket of ice. He pushed it inward and heard a click. The circle bent at the top and bottom, revealing hinges, and became a handle. It only turned to the right and made another click when complete. A series of rotating gears and sliding rods sounded out from within the door. It then slid free an inch from the frame and was easily pulled outward.

The door had the look of a bank vault, with wide pins receded within and facing every direction. It would have been easier to tunnel through the mountain than try to cut through its three feet of solid mithrinum. Despite the obvious weight, it took very little effort to swing the door wide open.

The tunnel beyond was just as massive, as wide and tall. Its walls were cleanly cut and smoothed by hand and tool. It was supported by stone columns and wooden beams reinforced with thick iron bands. Each column was illuminated by a torch with enchanted flame. They cast a green radius of light on either side every twenty feet.

It was a mithrinum mine, the dark walls interlaced with the heavy veins of a rich deposit. It gave off a faint silver glow, even in its unrefined state. The soft bloom of it mingled with the emerald light of each torch, lit the rails in a semblance of beryl moonlight. Metal tracks ran up from the tunnel ahead all the way to the door, but no carts could be seen in the immediate area.

Eric led the way.

The mine didn't look abandoned, was fairly clean and maintained. It felt as if they could run into dwarves at any moment, though he didn't sense anyone ahead. He'd never been in a mine before. This one seemed impressive. He couldn't imagine the amount of manpower and hours it had taken to carve the walls so smooth or to create such a perfectly straight tunnel. He could feel it sloping downward, but it was barely noticeable with each step.

They eventually reached a separate tunnel that branched off toward the right. It had support columns with lit torches, but its walls were roughhewn still. The mithrinum veins were sparse here but interspersed with bright gold. Eric had never seen gold in its natural state. He had to admit it looked pretty. He couldn't help but wonder how much it would've been worth back home.

"Master?" Griz asked.

Eric shook his head once. No matter how much he tried not to think about home, or to care, it crept up on him sometimes.

Light from the torches didn't seem to go on for very far but ended a few hundred feet in the distance.

"It's nothing," Eric said. "Keep going."

He led them farther down the main tunnel. They passed three more, branching to either side, before entering a wide chamber. The tunnel had been much the same, dead ends where mithrinum grew scarce but had mingled with gold. There were three large tunnels leading out in cardinal directions from the chamber. It was an enormous circular room where iron carts were amassed. It was a sort of switching station, where rail directions could be changed with tall handles, and carts could be added or removed from the tracks.

It wasn't long before entering when Eric caught the stench of strong alcohol and unwashed bodies coming from the eastern tunnel. He began to follow it and soon after the goblins could smell it too. They cursed and spat, called dwarves names like filthy animals and scum.

"Quiet!" Bel ordered with a harsh whisper. "And stay alert."

If there were dwarves ahead, a fight was inevitable.

There were rooms occasionally carved on both sides of the tunnel, with wide open wooden doors that led to a barracks, a dining hall, tool storage, a kitchen and eventually the source of increasingly foul odor.

It was a large room to the north, twice the size of the barracks that had housed two rows of ten beds. It was filled with wooden barrels and small casks along every wall. They were stacked two deep and layered one upon the other. They ran the length of the room from one wall to the other, held fast by the limited space between. Even in here, the faint silver of mithrinum cast its glow over the room.

In the center were at least forty dwarves, all of them barely conscious, soaked in alcohol and piss. They were taller than goblins by a hand but far stockier—or at least they had been. Beneath leather aprons and sturdy cloth, they looked emaciated from lack of food, so starved every bone showed. They were pale, their flesh a milky pallor, with hair and beards gone to an unnatural white. Blackened veins stood out in their pasty skin, though none had the metallic scales or black eyes of a fiend. They'd been changed, for certain, but not into feral animals.

By the debris all around them, shattered clay mugs and broken casks, they looked to have drank themselves near to death. Even still, while starving, some tried to weakly reach for more drink. Like fiends hungered for flesh, these seemed to suffer an insatiable thirst.

Bel cursed and grabbed a torch from off the wall in the corridor. Before Eric could stop him, the red general tossed it at the dwarves.

"No!" Eric said. "Don't!"

It was too late. Fire spread from the first until the pile of them was engulfed. They let out weak shrieks but lacked the strength to move. White hair blackened and curled as skin melted in the inferno. The fire quickly spread to the surrounding casks in a halo of orange blue.

"Shit, run!" Eric shouted and headed back down the tunnel.

Goblins scattered in sudden fear, tried to get as far away as they could. It took only moments for the barrels to catch fire and explode. Flames, large chunks of stone and a barrage of bloody bits shot out of the doorway—along with the wall. The entire room had been exposed in a thunderous instant. The whole tunnel shook but luckily didn't collapse on their heads.

Eric was about to unleash his anger when all their essence rushed toward him. He was suddenly afraid he might lose the ability to work magic. He tried to refuse them, like Griz had said, to *choose* not to absorb them. He shook his head in defiance, said no over and over in his mind, but the souls came to him nonetheless. They entered his body, flared his runes within. He tried to imagine a wall around him, a sort of force field or barrier to protect himself from their corruption. The burning of a change overcame him, threw his concentration into ruin. Rather than push the last few souls away, he was forced to deal with the rush rising inside him, threatening to burn him from within.

Transformations had been more difficult to come by. If he had no choice but to take their souls, he at least wanted to put them to good use. His main concern was losing Griz and the ability to get home. Eric needed to get better at working magic. He wanted to be proficient at casting, but if he was forced to memorize every rune, it would take forever. He needed a faster way, a shortcut or a kind of exploit. His choice made, the magic spent, the burning fell away.

Nothing happened.

Disappointment became anger. He whirled on the red general with a growl.

"What the *fuck* was that?" Eric demanded. "Not only did you almost kill everyone, you just wasted souls we coulda used to make more goblins."

Bel spat despite his imminent danger. "Never would we dirty our people with dwarf spirits."

"*Master,*" Eric said and loomed over him.

Bel gritted his teeth and made a fist, looked so angry and disgusted Eric thought he was going to have to make an example of him. Bel let out a breath, eased his grip and hung his head.

"Apologies, Master," he said with what sounded like sincerity. "I overstepped my authority."

Other goblins were grumbling, clearly siding with Bel and his initial reaction. Eric didn't care for their feelings or how much they hated dwarves. He didn't need people acting out of turn. For all he knew, Bel had done it on purpose, to prevent Eric from using the star metal.

Wait...For a moment he wasn't sure if that was his thought or the voice's. *God dammit. It doesn't matter. I still have the fiends.* There was a lingering doubt in the back of his mind that seemed to say, *Do you?*

"Master," Griz said to fill the silence, "as I explained earlier, our hatred for dwarves runs deep. They were our slave masters for generations. To birth a goblin from their foul spirits would be a grave insult to all that have come before us, who toiled so hard to set us free." Others nodded and quietly agreed with the shaman. "And again, these were contaminated spirits. It would be unwise to use them

181

in the creation ritual."

Eric was still fighting the tunnel vision of anger. He hadn't moved his gaze from the red general.

You'll have to find a way to deal with him, the voice echoed his own thought, *before he starts some kind of rebellion.*

"Clean up this mess," Eric told them all, "and start mining." To Griz, he said, "Let's get back to the castle. We've got work to do."

17

Eric spent the next two days learning the creation ritual. He sat in the courtyard by a fire and held a hand out while thinking a phrase. The runes appeared in air beneath his palm as he moved it, the result of his last transformation. He merely had to think of a word and its runes were formed by his hand without need of actually writing it out. It made for clunky, inelegant casting, as Griz had called it, but it did make Eric proficient with runes. Unfortunately, he needed to start learning sigils to be of help with the ritual.

When it came to magic, size mattered. The wards had to fit equally within a glyph. Otherwise, it was easily susceptible to tampering. If the magic wasn't also evenly spread across the glyph, it could be shorted with an influx of power. Substituting sigils when possible and filling the rest with runes made it easier to even out the wards. This was why some spells were passed down from Master to apprentice. Like perfect formulas, they were treasured and kept secret.

Additionally, the more complex a spell was the more

focus it required to cast. It didn't necessarily mean adding more wards, though that could in theory help if the caster was able to maintain concentration. It meant some wards, like those designed to increase power to a glyph, could be replaced with physical components. The magic inherent in these ingredients helped lighten the load on the caster, allowed for less attention to detail than would otherwise have been needed.

Since the goblins didn't have the various bladders and clippings from a handful of magical creatures, the ritual was going to be particularly difficult.

Eric looked out past the gate, which had yet to be fixed. It was midday with faint sunlight struggling past the winter clouds. The rain had finally ceased, but the storm was ever present. The fields south were drab and muddied. He found his thoughts drifting that direction, wondering how Taliana and her people were doing.

People, he thought with an inward laugh.

He'd never considered trolls as people—or goblins for that matter. In all the games he'd ever played, both were considered monsters. He'd killed them for experience and treasure without a second thought. None of it had been real. Here on Taellus, though? It was all too real. He'd been forced to rethink what made a living being a person.

Every fiend still alive in the valley was now face down in their old village, bound hand and foot by enchanted rope. Were they people?

Not anymore, Eric reasoned. *They're monsters.*

Letting them live was too dangerous. They could go on to infect others. They needed to be put down. He was going to use them in the ritual, so their deaths could serve a purpose. But what if they could be cured? They'd become people again, deserving of life, of their souls.

Eric looked over at the stables. There were only three horses now, but their essence was plain to see. It was more yellow than orange with tinges of red at the core. Did that mean they had souls?

What exactly was a soul, anyway? Was it a type of energy that fueled life? What happened to it when a body died? If Eric had never claimed one, what would have happened to them all? Where would they have gone? His gut instinct told him it was all tied to the ley lines, but he had no solid proof.

They're a means to an end, his rational voice said.

There were times he wished it would speak with someone else's voice, so he could tell it apart from his own. It was too confusing to hear two, made it difficult to know which thoughts were his.

Eric refused to think about it anymore, pushed it all from his mind before the voice argued it was both. He was done with waiting. It was time now for doing.

He had a wagon already prepared, kept in a corner of the courtyard with orders not to be touched. Just as he'd sent scouts to guard the fiends, he kept a close watch on the wagon himself. The iron cauldron Griz had used to summon him was loaded in back, hidden beneath a heavy cloth. The refined star metal, three bars, and the coffer of black gems from the vault were secured there as well. He had everything they needed and couldn't stand another minute of memorizing.

Eric sent for Griz and put the study scroll along with the rest in the back of the wagon. He was about to call for Bel and a group of reds, when the voice cut his thought short.

The red general can't be trusted, it warned. *None of his reds can.*

It was a problematic thought, in that Bel and his reds made up a sizeable portion of the army. Half were keeping the group at the mine safe. Without guards, he'd have to rely on others.

"Bri!" Eric called out to the blue general. She was sword training with another. "Gather your blues at the gate. We're heading into the valley."

He gave the same order to Bitters and told Stalk to pick five greens. He told the green general to stay behind. That gave him thirty goblins, the perfect number for what he had in mind.

"Master," Bel called out and approached, ten reds in tow. "Why are we being excluded? If you're going west, we're best suited for the task."

They can best serve by guarding the castle, the voice said.

"Guard the castle."

A horse was tied to the wagon, as Griz came out with the others. Most of the blues looked like they'd been asleep. Eric led them out of the gate, ignored the bitter stares and grumbling of reds left behind.

It was nightfall before they reached the village. There were two rows of twenty-three fiends face down in the mud. All of them were bound, too weak to even move let alone break free of the enchanted rope. Eric could tell at a glance they were all still alive, though their essence had faded to a dull luster.

Eric dragged the cauldron from the wagon and put it in the center of the muddy road. He ordered thirty fiends brought over as he got the star metal bars and coffer and placed them beside the cauldron.

"Thirty, Master?" Griz asked in alarm. "To use so many would be a waste of precious resources—both of life and materials."

"Line them up ten at a time right here," Eric said and indicated in front of the cauldron. "Have them kneel. I want someone behind each one with a blade."

"Master, there's no guarantee this will work," Griz continued to complain, watched on but made no move to intervene. "And the corrupted spirits might ruin the spell if it does."

It took two to three goblins to drag each one over, to position each fiend for execution.

"There's no need to use so many, Master."

Eric found it strange the shaman would plead for the lives of corrupted humans. Unless all he really cared for was the star metal. And then Eric's suspicions were confirmed.

"This has never been done before, Master," Griz said. "It's wasteful to use star metal on goblins, to use so many lives on something that might not even succeed. It goes against my very nature as a shaman."

"Just do as you're told," the voice said, and Eric was surprised to hear himself speak it aloud at the same time.

All thirty fiends were positioned before the cauldron. Goblins stood behind each one, held them on their knees with one hand on a shoulder and a blade to the throat.

"Start casting," Eric told the shaman in an ominous tone.

Griz looked troubled, conflicted but held his tongue as he dragged a wooden crate over to stand on. He climbed up and stood over the cauldron, began casting the first runes. They appeared in air with a strong shimmer of gold. Eric lent his hand to a second ward, connected to the casting and added his strength to the spell.

The cauldron began to fill with power, a thrumming swell of magic that became light. Its swirl of purple and blue brightened, took on threads of silver and became liquid. It splashed up against the iron sides, left trailers of quicksilver that ran back down into the mix.

When the first glyph was completed, Eric reached for the star metal. Griz was already into the first ward of the second glyph when Eric dropped all three bars in.

"Master!" Griz stopped casting, eyes wide with shock. "That's too much! We should only use a little, test if it's going to work."

His ward began to falter.

"If you don't keep casting," Eric said, "it'll all be gone for nothing."

He picked up the wooden coffer and emptied all the black gems in. They splashed into the mix, melted across its surface and stretched to sparkling crystals within the black of spreading star metal.

Griz set firm his jaw and fixed the last remaining rune before the ward fell apart. Even the first glyph had begun to falter. There was a time limit to be met. Too long without casting and all would be lost.

Eric continued to help Griz, working on wards they'd agreed on. Griz knew he'd be stronger in the beginning but less so as the spell went on. Eric had done his best to learn the ritual in its entirety, but he'd specifically spent the most time memorizing the final two glyphs.

He could see Griz growing tired by the time they finished the second and exhausted by end of the third. There was strain in his arms and chest, a slight pulling at his runes, but Eric felt nearly as strong as when they'd started. He didn't think it would be quite so severe, but when it happened he was ready. Before the first ward of the fourth glyph was finished, Griz collapsed and fell into a waiting hand.

Eric gently let him down to the road and returned to working the spell. He only made two or three mistakes but quickly caught them as the sigils began to fail. He finished the final ward and let out a sigh of relief. The glyph flared into place, spun back toward the first and blazed into a construct. The runes and sigils were alight with golden fire, thrumming with enough power to send a shiver up his front.

"Do it now," Eric ordered.

As one all thirty goblins drew a blade across the neck of the fiend kneeling in front of them. Dark blood spurted out, a flood at first and then a trickle. Life spent, they all fell over. The combined essence rose from them like a cloud of crimson gone to black, a storm of violet charge riding its edge with feral fervor. It came straight for Eric but was pulled down into the cauldron. The mix swirled faster yet, intensified in power, as the construct grew to a blinding light.

It fell upon the cauldron.

Eric was knocked back a step by the force of it. The goblins had gasped in awe and fear, shielded their eyes or fell to their knees. While the mix still burned bright, Eric stepped forward and put his hand in.

"You will serve only me," he said.

Silver sigils rose up from the mix along his metal, spun a circle about his wrist and formed a ward. It burned for a bright moment, sank within him and was gone. Eric could feel their spirits bind with his. Their loyalty to him would be without question.

The first goblin emerged and climbed out to grip the cauldron edge with both hands and feet. It crouched and eyed the others as if gauging their worth. It was black head to toe, a pure dark like starless night. Taller than the others by a hand, more muscular as well, it looked born to fight by tooth and nail.

The black turned its attention to Eric with a sidelong look. There was intelligence in the gaze but something more, something deadly. It was like staring into the eyes of a tiger at a zoo enclosure.

The goblin hopped down and knelt before Eric as a second climbed from the mix. It followed suit, eyeing the others and hopped down to kneel beside the first. When the third climbed out, the magic was spent. All sound within the cauldron disappeared, like air being sucked into a void. Only the scrape of nails on iron could be heard as the last black jumped down. All three knelt on one knee before Eric.

As one they bowed their heads.

* * *

When they returned to the castle courtyard, all of the goblins were gathered—even those from the mine. It was nearly morning, Griz was still asleep in the back of the wagon and Eric's newest goblins hadn't said a word since their creation. Bel stood waiting before the fire, his reds spread out behind him as if expecting confrontation. None had yet drawn a weapon, but the red general had a leather sack in one hand. He took one look at the black goblins and scowled Eric's way.

"What the hell is going on here?" Eric asked.

His loyal three took up position before him, legs apart and hands open. Eric could see them eyeing the gathered goblins, gauging where the first attack might come from.

Bel said, "I'd hoped you would change your mind about the star metal." Again, he'd purposely not called Eric Master. It seemed his rebellion was at hand. "You have put your own needs before this expedition for the last time. What you did was a selfish waste of resources." More to those gathered than to Eric, he raised his voice and said, "We could have completed our expedition with honor, gone home as celebrated heroes. Instead, we're stuck with a *human*, who cares for nothing but himself, and corrupted abominations that will *never* be welcome in Xanaranth."

The three watched Bel with perfect calm, waiting for him to make an aggressive move or for Eric to give an order.

Crush him, the voice urged. *Crush them all.*

"Big words," Eric said, "for a little man. You gonna back 'em up?"

"Belchburn," Bri said with a hand to her pommel. Her blues were already spreading out on the left side of the gathered reds. "This is not what's best for us right now. It will only make matters worse."

Bitters and his oranges had moved toward the right on their own. Stalk and Mudbutt were in back on the castle steps, well behind the reds. Either they'd chosen the wrong side or were waiting to see how things played out. All of the gobs who'd come with Eric stood quietly behind him.

"Don't do this," Bitters said in an even tone.

Bel squared his shoulders. "You think your duty is to the expedition," he told the two generals. "It isn't. It belongs to the people of Xanaranth, *our* people."

"Honestly," Eric said, "I dunno what's going through your head right now, but there's no way you're walkin' out of this."

"Perhaps not," Bel said and threw the sack against the ground. The sound of breaking glass within followed. "But neither will you."

Black essence rose up from the sack.

"You stupid fu—"

It struck Eric in the chest, sent him backward a step and took the words from his mouth with the strength of its touch. Despite all effort to refuse it, the black cloud licked along his metal in wisps of clinging smoke. It seeped inside, ran the length of his runes and gripped his spirit with the force of a storm.

Eric dropped to his knees as if violently ill. He would have wretched if he could, convulsed his every muscle to expel it from his body. It shook him from within with an implacable hold, caused both his hands and vision to tremble. Senses became dulled, as if the world had slipped beneath a blanket of noise. It blurred his eyes, rang in his ears and burned his middle with a growing cold.

I'm dying, he realized, could feel his glyph start to slowly unravel. He looked up at Bel, at the traitorous goblins beside him. *You think you won? Think again.*

"Kill them," Eric said. "Kill the reds."

None of the others made a move, not Bri nor Bitters or any of those that followed them. Whether it was out of shock at the order or loyalty to their comrades, not one of the original expedition moved to attack.

They didn't have to.

The three black goblins sprang forward like hounds loosed upon prey. They went straight for the closest red, all three on the same target. One grabbed him by the arm reaching for a sword and broke it at the elbow over a knee. A second was at his other arm, using it as leverage to drive him backward over a leg and toward the ground. The third leapt on top, punching at his face with sharp raps to the nose until he was dead. The red's sword was pulled free and chaos ensued.

One after another, all three leapt upon a target and took a new weapon with each kill. The first red had died so quickly, none of the others had time to react with anything but fearful surprise. By the time they drew their blades, another had fallen. The reds were guards and soldiers, trained to fight with sword and shield, but none of that mattered in the face of such a coordinated ferocity.

The three fought as one, blocked attacks for each other, created and took advantage of openings for one another. They were relentless in their assault, choosing the nearest target and fighting for all they were worth until it was dead. Each slash, every thrust, all their movements were deliberate and delivered with precision.

Pained screams rang out, blood spattered, and reds died one after another. Bel was last to fall, disarmed, brought to his knees and beheaded without a word.

When it was finished, the three let fall their swords and came to stand before Eric, facing the other goblins. They were covered in blood but not a drop was their own.

It happened so quickly, Eric had barely seen. His vision was blurred, shaky and playing tricks. Suddenly he was surrounded by hundreds of ghostly spirits—goblins, humans, dwarves, men and women. They were all crouched, looking away, trembling in fear.

All but one.

It was Eric, or a man that looked like him. He wasn't pale and doughy, as Eric remembered himself, but a man straight and tall. The face was Eric's though, and he carried it on a wooden stick like a mask. It spoke when he did, mimicked his expressions.

Don't leave me now, boy, the man said in Eric's voice and knelt so they were face to face. *I still have use for you.*

Griz was there beside him. "Master, are you alright?"

"No," Eric said, staring into his own eyes. "I think I'm corrupted. Can you...fix it?"

The shaman shook his head. "I know of no way to purify a spirit."

Eric recalled Sebran and his family of spiritists as the mask that was his face smiled wide with a horrific grin.

"Bring me Sebran," he said. "Whatever it takes. Just bring him here."

See? said the man with Eric's face. *Still of use.*

Eric couldn't see what was behind the mask, but he knew who it was. The fancy clothes, the boots, the gold ring with a ruby.

It was Tragona.

18

Eric struggled toward the vault. Griz and all the blues and oranges had gone to fetch Sebran. Eric knew Sebran would need the contained souls to work a spell if he agreed to help. Eric wanted to get down to the vault while he was still able, before the wrong runes unraveled and left him blind or crippled or some other horrible fate. His three loyal goblins hadn't left his side, even helped him down the stairs to the laboratory.

They were stronger than they looked.

"Do you guys talk?" he asked them, using a wall to keep himself upright. All three had their arms beneath his other hand, supporting him like a walking stick. They looked up at him but didn't answer. "No? Nothing?"

One squinted and curled his upper lip, revealing sharp teeth. All he could manage was a slow growl.

Eric nearly collapsed, smashed a table on his way to the well. His head swam in a foggy dizziness that pressed inward along his metal, sent pressure down his back. If he didn't know better, he would've thought he had the flu. There was more to it though, because he could feel it clawing at his runes, suffocating their magic. Whatever had been in the jar wasn't like Tragona's experiments. It wasn't corrupting his spirit.

It was killing him.

The hundreds of spirits had followed. He kept seeing glimpses of them flash before him, at his periphery, in a room of utter darkness. They trembled at the edge of the platform as the false Eric paced around them. He would suddenly bend to sneer or feign attacks to frighten them into submission. Silver wards on the distant walls cast their glow on the glossy floor. He could see and feel the sickness spread from rune to sigil with tendrils of black smoke. It dulled their moonlight glow, gradually doused their vibrant flame until the magic died away.

One moment Eric was stumbling, trying to break his fall, and the next Tragona was an inch from his face. In the darkness of that place, the mask's grin grew ear to ear. It was the sort of smile filled with insult, of inevitable triumph. Eric knew the look well, had worn it himself countless times in the past. When he'd been hurting the most was when he garnered the greatest pleasure from hurting others.

You should rest, the other Eric said, *let me take over for a while.*

Eric painfully climbed back to his feet. Even in a golem body made of metal, he felt at times in his old flesh. He breathed harder when he strained, felt the heat and wetness of sweat across his brow, trembled within from aching muscles. It was all an illusion, a phantom body like a missing limb. In that dark space in his mind, surrounded by his glyph, he was back in that skin. On his knees, struggling with a burning illness, scared and alone, he withered but refused to break beneath the onslaught that was Tragona.

It was difficult to tell how many hours had passed before they reached the crypts outside the vault. What he saw kept alternating between the world and his mind. It wasn't long before his reality became both.

What happened to you? The other Eric stood over him with a look of disgust and disappointment. Except it wasn't him, wasn't Tragona. It was Sebran. And the look was one of cautious fear at odds with controlled anger. Worse still, he was marked. They were both running out of time. *Can you hear me?*

"The black soul," Eric said, strained as if he'd spoken through gritted teeth. It was a struggle to stay grounded in the reality before him, too easy to believe the one in his mind. "It was—it broke. It's in me."

"And what," Sebran asked, "I'm supposed to help you now? After everything you've done to my people?"

The lord looked tired, his clothes disheveled. It made Eric wonder what promise or threat had convinced him to come. Tragona flashed between worlds, superimposed himself over Sebran. He tried to alter the meaning of his words with inflection, twist the expression on his face.

C'mon, let me play, other Eric said. *Quit hoggin' the controller.*

"I could threaten you," Eric said, "but I won't. I'm askin' for help. I'll pay you back. I'll owe you one."

"Owe me?" Sebran laughed. "Why wouldn't I just let you die and *take* what's mine once you're gone?"

The black goblins didn't move closer, but as one all their hands twitched in warning.

"Time," Eric replied, short of breath. "You don't have any." Runes kept winking out. He'd lost use of his legs and left hand, his sense of smell. His vision was blurred to a small point right in front. "You're marked. When the Hunt comes, you'll need help."

"The Hunt isn't real," Sebran said unconvincingly. *Even if it was, you're a liar. You can't be trusted.*

"I never lied to you!" Eric snapped back. A raised brow was Sebran's only response. "I was a dick, but I never lied.

The Hunt is real. It's coming. Help me, and I'll help you when it does."

Sebran shook his head. "You purposely infected my mages, stole from my people, left us to starve! How can I believe a single word you say?"

"I told you. I'm a dick, not a liar."

He lost hearing in his left ear, vision in the right eye. A deadening cold was stretching up from his legs.

Sebran looked back toward the jars in the vault.

"I don't know a spell to purify a spirit," he said, "only one to increase potency and cleanse some impurities."

Like you, other Eric said. He laughed and spun with arms wide. *C'mon! Look around you! You're dying, and I can fix it. Give me control. Go to sleep. You look awfully tired...*

The suggestion gripped his mind with the promise of needed slumber. It felt like taking cold medicine, when the comforting warmth rose up and overpowered all else.

"Anything's better than nothing," Eric said and may have slurred his words. His eyes were getting heavy.

Sebran left to take a jar from off the shelf and came back. The way he held it in his hand and looked down at its bright swirl was the way an addict might look at his favorite drug after years of being clean. There was dread and desire in that single look.

"I've never cast it on a living person," Sebran said in a somber tone. "I don't know if it will work."

It won't work. I'm your only option.

"Just do something," Eric said.

Sebran started to cast, drew bright golden runes and sigils in the air over Eric. Tragona let fall his mask, stood in the way and swept aside the runes with a broad wave of his arm. They scattered like leaves, dashed to sparkle against the walls. Candlelight died away beneath the rise of intense dark. It pulled Eric inward, back to his knees on the lustrous platform.

He looked like Sebran but older, with a full beard of snowy

chestnut and wrinkles about the eyes. His hair was oiled back, tied to a braid down past his neck. He wore a robe of crimson with black trim and gold filigree. Each finger bore a ring of different color gems, with light gleaming off their cuts. He wove a spell of his own with a wave of both hands in the form of a rainbow. A sword appeared in air. He took it down with a grin.

Let's dance, shall we?

Eric got to his feet, more out of fear than challenge. He didn't have a weapon nor did he really know how to use one. It was one thing to swing a sword with the strength and armor of a golem...

"I—I don't know how to fight," Eric said.

Long daggers appeared in both hands. The length and curve of their blades, the gold pommels and fiery red glow of enchantment. They were Sorrow and Mourn. It'd taken him fourteen runs in the Molten Carousel to get them. Leather armor covered him as well, an item set with full bonuses and fully enchanted.

Sebran unraveled the ward on the jar and broke its wax seal. Essence spilled upward in a cloud of orange, like a smoky summer sunset. It swirled and rushed for Eric but was captured in the construct. Silver runes in the far dark winked alive and glowed bright. Ghostly men and women stood, still naked and afraid but no longer sick.

"I don't understand," Sebran said. "The glyphs aren't completing. They're faltering."

Tragona gave a flourished bow, with a salute of blade to forehead, before moving forward to attack. His long sword cut the air in three whistling swipes as he closed. The fourth took Eric in the shoulder, a gash through his armor that exposed bone and muscle.

"It's as if there's more than one spirit inside you," Sebran said. He went for another jar.

It felt like being punched. Eric didn't hurt so much as get annoyed by the wetness and growing cold.

"You're gonna regret that," he said with a snarl.

Eric's perspective shifted, moved out of his body to up and just behind—like a video game. He had skills and abilities, knew their cooldowns like second nature. He disappeared into streaks of black and reappeared behind Tragona. Already facing him, Eric drove a blade into his back. Red numbers flared to life over Tragona's head as he screamed in anguish. It was a critical backstab.

Sebran loosed another jar. New runes flared, more spirits stood, but the spell wouldn't complete.

Tragona whirled about with magical flames in one hand and a crystalized frost billowing off his sword. In a frenzy of angry spellwork, he scored burns on Eric's flesh with both fire and cold. The more fury he expended, the more tired he became. He backhanded Eric, sent him sliding across the platform toward the edge.

"It isn't working," Sebran said. "It shouldn't need so many spirits to complete."

"Keep going!"

Spirit hands gripped Eric by the shoulders, halted his soaring over and into the abyss. They were hunched over in fear, faced away from Tragona, but hadn't entirely given up. They pulled Eric back, so he could stand. He'd dodged most of the attacks and used his evasion skill to avoid the worst of what he couldn't. On his feet again, Eric vanished into smoke, stealthed behind Tragona one more time and cycled through his rotation. Stun, bleed, build, build, execute! Thick green poison dripped from both wounds when Eric pulled the blades from Tragona's chest.

Runes flared, more spirits stood.

Tragona was growing tired, weaker, while Eric was gaining strength. Each opened jar eased the sickness, reinvigorated him for the fight.

You think too small.

The warrior-wizard became fire, a giant plume of blinding orange in a whirlwind blaze. He scorched the platform, marred its luster and filled the air in choking black. The air between them wavered from the heat, as embers sparked and popped. Tragona swelled to twice his size as a cyclone inferno and moved to engulf his foe.

"Break them all!" Eric ordered.

Little feet skittered to obey. Sebran shouted for them to stop.

The fire overwhelmed Eric. He had no cooldowns left, nothing to buff his resistance or defensive maneuvers to counter the attack. It licked at his leather armor, flaked away their enchantment.

"Too small, huh?"

Eric decided to change the game. He let fall both his daggers, gave up the armor and its bonuses and became a water elemental. He rose up in a splash of sea blue with sapphire eyes and came crashing back down in a frothy wave. Fire sizzled and sent up great billows of steam. Tragona was left in the flames that remained, smashed and broken against the floor. Over and again, Eric brought waves down upon him until the fires were completely out.

A roar of crackling essence caused a wave of its own, came rushing from the vault in a flurry of broken glass and exploding magic. It struck the construct first, flared all its wards to bursting flames of gold. Silver light along the walls erupted all at once, scorched and ate through darkened sickness. The construct fell, completed, but the essence carried on.

A new burning gripped Eric's middle and sent up a golden incandescence around the platform. Its intensity burned away at the smooth edges. The spirits all cried out, tried to shield their eyes and bodies from the glow. Eric shrank back down into his human shape.

He wanted protection from corruption. He couldn't let himself, his glyph and all the spirits, be compromised like that again. The first transformation felt no different, so he persisted through the others. It was only after the third, when the gold radiance abated and fell away, he felt any sort of change. It was like feeling the first rays of sun against his face after a long night of numbing cold.

He looked down at Tragona. The man was beaten but still there. Eric needed a way to handle him, to keep him in line. He wished he could lock Tragona away in a jar, like the man's family had done to so many other souls. A jar appeared in Eric's hand.

"Oh really," he said.

Sebran picked himself up off the floor. The explosion of magic from behind and in front had knocked him over.

"Did it work?" Sebran asked.

Tragona groaned, opened his eyes and became a glow of swirling orange. His essence swept up into the jar and was sealed with a glass stopper. Eric put it down on the platform.

"I think so." Eric stood in the world as well, felt all his strength returned to the metal body. "Yeah, man. You totally did it. Thank you," he said both to Sebran and the goblins.

Eric could still see inward to all the spirits around the platform. He recognized one of them as Ella. He walked over to her, was about to reach out a hand to touch her shoulder when she turned halfway to face him. She was naked, like the others. Eric wanted her to be clothed and she was. With a thought, every one of them became dressed as they were in life.

You don't have to be afraid, Eric told them. Slowly they turned his way. To Ella, he said, *Not anymore.*

19

It was strange, being able to speak with the spirits inside him at any time. They spoke with each other as well, but he could tune that out if he wanted. When he was alone, in the quiet of night, it was comforting to hear them. They had no world but what he gave them, nothing but the platform and silver glow of his glyph. So he gave them a clearing surrounded by forest and a clear stream. The day's cycle followed the real world, and by end of the first they had already started to build a community. Even Bel and the other goblins had started building out in the forest.

Why didn't I see any of you before? Eric asked Ella the next day as they walked along the stream. The sounds of chopping wood and hammering followed after. *Ya know, when I was on the platform with Jaken.*

Perhaps you weren't ready, she said. She wore a light dress more suited to summer. The days were the same there but not the season. *My great uncle controlled much as he grew stronger.* Her hair was done up in curls, and she was eating an apple, though none of them needed to eat or drink anymore. *I can tell you he won't be missed.*

It made Eric wonder if he could've saved Jaken. The memory of him drowning sometimes came to mind for no reason. They were just flashes, quickly pushed aside, but troubling all the same. Eric looked back at all the spirits living in a world within his mind. Even more worrisome was the thought he'd become their afterlife.

"Master?" Griz asked.

Eric's attention was brought back.

The construct had already completed, and the last brown climbed out of the cauldron. He'd performed the ritual by himself. Griz was still too tired from the last one.

The dwarven mine they'd found was massive, went on for miles below the surface with numerous deposits of ores and minerals. While electrum had been fairly easy to come by, there was only one pocket of topaz so far. They needed more workers and crafters, so browns had become a priority. There were sixteen fiends still bound in the valley, but Griz had insisted no corrupted spirits be used again. There was nothing particularly wrong with the black goblins, aside from their inability to speak. It was clear they could have been something greater, though, had purer spirits been used in the ritual.

Sorry, Eric told Ella, *I gotta bounce.*

He liked talking to her, enjoyed being back in his old body. It was too difficult, however, to carry on multiple conversations.

"I'm here," Eric said. "So... they turn out okay, or do we need a short bus to get 'em around?"

They'd used the last three horses instead. While using an animal spirit might have been fine ordinarily, they'd also stretched the essence a bit thin by creating twelve goblins. At least they could eat the horses—two birds and all that.

"None will be craftsmen, Master," Griz replied as he checked each one for physical maladies, "but they will all serve with honor." They weren't quite as ridiculous as the grays had been, but two had already started a laughing and shoving match that was spreading. "Speaking of which, the imperative you added was... surprising. Not that you'd want to, after Belchburn's betrayal, but that you were able. Imperatives are tricky and dangerous to accomplish. Then again, few if any casters can complete such a complex construct on their own."

"Knock it off," Eric told the browns. They quieted and stiffened to attention like a cartoon army, which would have been fine if it hadn't caused one of them to fart. Eric sighed as they all struggled to stifle laughs. "It links them to me is all. I don't want a repeat of what happened with the reds."

He looked over at the three black goblins. They stood waiting against a nearby wall in the courtyard, watching with intent. They seemed always at the ready, as if at any given moment they might leap into action. If they weren't so loyal, their severe focus might be a cause for concern.

As much as they needed browns to keep working the mines, to build a new foundry, to craft new tools, armor and weapons, Eric wanted to try using mithrinum. Griz complained much as he had with the star metal but for a different reason. It had never been done before because mining mithrinum was the very reason the first goblins had been created and enslaved. In their minds, it was a *dwarven* metal. Goblins wanted nothing to do with it. They'd been prioritizing materials for browns and reds, mostly the topaz and ruby. Still, Eric couldn't help but wonder what sort of goblin the inherently magical metal might create.

Griz gave a nod of approval to the last brown and sent them off to begin training. Crafters were smelting the last of the gold ore and would be heading back to the mine before nightfall. They looked to Eric before moving.

"It's okay," he said to them.

They were more childlike than the black goblins, looked

to Eric for orders but weren't so intense all the time. He'd told them earlier to listen to Griz, Bitters and the other crafters, to learn everything they could. It was clear they were somewhat limited by their origins. They could speak right away, though, and at least had a basic understanding of how to survive.

"They'll do fine, Master," Griz said and watched them go. "We've done far more with much less in the past."

"So do all animals have souls then?" Eric asked. He began to wonder if he absorbed a horse's essence if it would end up with the other spirits in his mind. "Like even rats and shit? What about bugs?"

Griz eased himself down onto a castle step. "I think all life is connected to a soul one way or another, Master. However strong that connection may be is a different matter. There is a reason some spells call for a virgin princess or a military leader. Some flames burn brighter than others."

"You look like you need to go back to bed," Eric said as a scout whistled a warning.

"I could always use more sleep, Master." Griz used his staff to pull himself back up. "If only the world would stop turning for a few moments."

It was a messenger from Sebran. There were no more horses at the keep, so he'd been forced to run.

"Lord Sebran is sorry to inform you," the man said between catching his breath, "that your request to access the Academy library has been denied, Milord." His eyes had been moving from one goblin to another, probably wondering if this message might be his last. Being the bearer of bad news was a dangerous job. "Furthermore, the high council sees no reason to devote resources into the matter."

"'Course not," Eric said. "They'll wait 'til the problem can't be ignored, like every other fuckin' government agency faced with a world-changing problem. I mean there's definitive proof and shit. You'd think the school of magic or whatever would be worried about a disease that makes it so people can't cast spells."

The messenger said, "Lord Sebran believes they will look into the matter, Milord. They just—they don't want to share their findings. He wanted me to assure you he will pass on any information he receives."

Griz spat into the mud. "It will be too late by then, Master. We'll have to do our own research."

"Yay," Eric said flatly. "Field trip."

"Milord," the man said and cleared his throat, "Lord Sebran also wanted me to remind you of your bargain. He has held up his end of it and done as you asked."

"We're just a few hours away," Eric said. "If you think a messenger will take too long, you can set up a beacon. Light a big ass fire, big enough for us to see it, and we'll be on our way." The man nodded, his face drawn. He looked like he'd barely eaten in days. Eric asked, "How bad is it over there?"

The man squared his shoulders, as if he'd only just remembered he was a soldier.

"Very." He gave a salute of fist to chest, turned and left.

"We should do something about that," Eric said as he watched the messenger leave the courtyard. "What good is magic, if you can't use it to feed people?"

"If you wish, Master," Griz said and headed up the steps. "I'll go get ready. We should leave at once."

While the shaman was gone, Eric went over to the smithy. He called out to the crafter in charge, a brown by the name of Mudskip.

"Hey Skip," Eric said. "When you guys go back to the mine, I want you to bring me back enough mithrinum for three bars."

Skip put down his tongs and wiped dirty hands on his leather apron. He looked up at Eric, sweat running down his head.

"What's it for, Master?"

"I'm gonna be workin' on a nunya," Eric replied and cut

Skip off before he could ask. "A nunya business. Just get it done."

Eric waited by the fire. Even though all their cooking was done in the kitchen, it'd become standard to leave the bonfire burning for the guards to warm themselves. When Griz returned minutes later, he looked refreshed but was alone. He immediately began casting a portal.

"Just us then?" Eric asked.

Griz finished the spell. "Just us, Master. Any more would draw attention."

"I'm pretty sure I'm gonna draw attention," Eric said and reached out a hand toward the beryl light between the stones.

"You should know, Master," Griz said in warning, before Eric touched the portal, "we'll be trapped once we arrive. We'll need to find a way to cross back through the barrier again."

"One of those walking sticks the white used to get here," Eric said. "Shouldn't be a problem. I hope."

They passed through to a grand chamber of white marble adorned with gold. From thick bands across the bottom and top of tall columns to an elaborate pattern inscribed into the floor like a glyph, shiny gold was used to highlight the luminous sheen of polished marble. It ran the base of each wall, swept upward through more spellwork and joined together in a single piece on the ceiling like a work of art. Magic thrummed within the metal, even stronger than the glowing white orbs that lit the room.

As tall as the ceiling was, Eric wondered why goblins would need so much room. Either it was to accommodate golems even larger, or the space was necessary to craft such an intricate spell.

There was a gasp from behind.

A white goblin was seated in a golden chair with red cushions behind a solid desk of white marble. It too was decorated in fancy goldwork, along each leg and across its surface. The goblin had been reading from a book. A golem on either side stood back against the wall. They resembled the room so much they nearly blended with the background. Pure white marble with gold filigree and wards stretched across their surface, they were barely half Eric's size at ten feet tall.

"You brought the conqueror *here*?" the white asked.

A layer of metal flaked off Eric into a swarm of black particles. They surged toward his hand and reformed into a sword. He crossed the distance as both golems began to move. The white screeched, eyes wide behind his gold-rimmed glasses. Griz began to work a spell. Eric swung clean through the first, from right shoulder to waist. Magic erupted in a shockwave of golden light. It threw the white from his seat and scorched Eric's front. The upper half of marble golem struck the floor.

Eric flung the desk aside and went after the second golem. A cloud of yellow essence took him from behind, momentarily distracting him with its charge. The golem punched him in the side strong enough to leave a dent. The second took Eric across the thigh and brought him down to one knee. The white pulled his hand from a coat pocket and threw gold dust at Eric's face. It hit against a sphere of blue light, as if the goblin was trapped within a bubble. The dust quickly spread, caused the white to choke and grasp at his eyes.

Eric drove his left fist into the golem's crotch. It didn't double over as he expected, but its marble cracked in two places. He stood up with all his strength, brought the blade's edge with him. His sword sliced through the golem's face. Its glyph was damaged but not destroyed. It continued to throw heavy punches, furthering the dents in Eric's middle. Lightning struck its right arm, broke off more marble and scorched three wards. Its arm hung useless, as it began to swing blindly with the other. Eric plunged his sword through its chest, used both hands to force it upward.

When the blade came free, the golem's glyph exploded in a golden flash. Eric slumped against the wall as he absorbed the essence and began to heal.

"You couldn't bring us directly to the library?" he asked in a pained voice. The burns were extensive but hadn't reached his glyph.

The white had choked himself unconscious within the magical bubble. Griz checked the white's pulse and found it satisfactory.

"I brought us to the conservatory, Master." Griz took the white's handkerchief and used it as a gag. "This room is a gateway." He slipped off the coat and used its sleeves to bind the white's hands in back. "As a precaution, the barrier forces all nearby portals to exit here."

"A little head's up would be nice."

"Hmm, yes, Master." Griz looked toward the golden double doors. "Perhaps I underestimated your presence. We should cloak you with illusion. It's only a matter of time before the caretakers realize I'm here without proper authority."

Eric was breathing easier with each moment. He let the sword flake away and return to his body. The worst of his burns were fading from white to dark. Even the dents had started to straighten.

"You work on my costume," Eric said. "I'm gonna sit here a minute."

By the time Griz had finished casting, Eric was fully healed. He couldn't see the illusion but felt the tingle of it on his metal. When they walked past a column toward the double doors, he caught a reflection in its gold décor. He looked like one of the marble golems, pure white with golden wards in tight circles all about him.

"Damn," Eric said. "I look fancy."

Griz said, "Master, perhaps it would be best if you behaved like a defender, as well. You'll need to remain quiet and walk a step behind me. Try to keep your eyes forward. Other golems don't look about the way you do, like a visitor from another world."

He just call me a tourist?

Eric frowned but let Griz lead the way.

Once outside the doors, he could see they were in an opened corridor. They were ten floors up, with a central courtyard to their right. The motif of white and gold went on throughout the building, whether in marble or stone, with gold decoration and spellwork. Trees and statues could be seen past the stone bannister, and the sounds of stringed instruments carried up. There were at least another ten floors above, each one same as the last. A few white petals drifted downward, where each level had a flowered balcony.

Each room and corridor they went past on the left had large double doors like the gateway. Some of them were guarded by marble golems, while others were locked with visible bars and glyphs. A multitude of whites were going about their business, talking in pairs, staring down at scrolls or merely walking with purpose. The few who had their attention drawn to Griz quickly looked away, as if a brown was beneath their notice. The corridor was wide enough for golems to pass by with plenty of room to spare. None of them seemed to pay Eric any attention at all.

Once the corridor reached its end, the only way to go was right. The next went on for the same length but at its center was a spiral staircase. They descended four floors and headed into a library directly across. Rows of bookcases on either side of the room stretched off into the distance. Long tables in between held white goblins hard at work, either writing onto or reading scrolls, their heads buried in large tomes, hidden behind stacks of books or quietly discussing an open page. There were ten to twenty at each table, with dozens of tables on each side. Their whispers were enough to cause a hushed din.

Griz motioned for Eric to wait by the door while he went toward the central hub. Behind a circular counter, whites worked a card catalogue, dispensing the location of specific books to those waiting in line. It took a few minutes for Griz to reach the front. By the perturbed look of the librarian, Griz had to do some explaining to justify his presence. The white frowned even more, left to look up the information and scrawled something down on a piece of paper. He passed it beneath the golden bars that separated them and watched Griz walk away. He kept his eyes on the shaman the entire time it took to return to Eric.

"He's gonna be trouble," Eric said quietly.

Griz nodded toward one of the doors in the side walls and kept walking. Eric followed after. They passed into a smaller room with a single table and six chairs. It looked like it was meant to be used for private study. Griz went over to the leftmost wall where there was a shelf with a large golden box and a bell. He opened the box, put in the slip of paper, closed it and rang the bell on the wall.

"This could take a while, Master."

Eric turned back to the door. It was closed but had no lock. He held out a hand and started casting a barrier spell. The runes quickly appeared, but it took far longer to imagine what it was he wanted. He saw it in his mind, encompassing the entire room. He tried to envision every conceivable way someone could try to get in or damage the barrier. It was an extremely difficult thing to visualize all at once. When he finally thought he had it, he closed the ward. The spell completed, and a barrier of blue light went up within the room.

The bell rang.

Griz opened the box. The slip of paper was gone, and in its place was a large book titled *Taellus: A History of Magic*. The book was half his size.

"That won't hold, Master," Griz said and took a seat at the table with the book. He began searching through its tall pages. "The ward is too simple to keep a practiced caster out."

"Trust me. I thought of everything."

"Did you protect the spell from tampering, Master?" Griz scanned one page with a finger, frowned and turned to the next. "Other casters can undo a spell by directly affecting its runes." He kept searching while he spoke. "The way a good barrier is cast, for example, is to create a separate ward for everything it's protecting against and turn that into a glyph. Then make a second to guard them both and link them as a construct."

Eric eyed the ward and grumbled. It looked fine to him. Thinking his effort might've been a waste of time was more than a little annoying.

"Just focus on the book."

Time dragged on in quiet. The pages were inked in elegant writing, but there were hardly any pictures.

"Wait," Griz said half an hour later. He flipped back through the pages, scanned to a passage, and hurried to where he'd left off. "Master, I think I found it. It's a bit confusing, though. I'm not sure how much of it is fact or fable. Like most human books on magic, it's written as a story and not a historical account." He went back to the previous page. "It's one of the Old Gods, Kor. It seems he was once the God of Purity, deeply in love with Lumen, the Goddess of Light. His sister Losa, the Goddess of Desire, shared his love for Lumen. To break them apart, Losa began to poison his mind with half-truths about Lumen's feelings and fidelity. One lie after another filled Kor with jealousy and rage. By the time his love had turned to hate, he'd become the God of Corruption."

"You can skip the backstory," Eric said. "Although wouldn't it make more sense for the sister to become Corruption? Whatever. So it is a god then. Just how fucked are we if he gets out? How did they beat him? What's his weakness?"

Griz skipped another page. "Here, Master. He was defeated on the astral plane in mental combat by a conclave of Master magicians. Many of them died in the process. Once Kor was weakened in mind, they were able to weaken him physically. They then parted the two and trapped them in separate, concealed prisons."

"Astral combat?" Eric asked. "How the fuck are we supposed to do that?"

"I imagine, Master," Griz said, "we would have to find him first." He turned another page. "Ah! It seems the constructs that bind him are so complex, hidden so well, no one could possibly set him free let alone find both prisons."

"Tragona didn't have to," Eric pointed out. "He used an exploit instead."

Griz closed the book and sighed. "It is quite the loophole, Master. Our only hope now is to fix the ley lines before Kor is set free."

"If he does get out," Eric asked, "what then? I don't know how to astral fight, and last I checked you were more Yoda than Professor X."

The door handle jiggled. Someone banged, and the ward flared to life.

"Open this door at once!" a voice demanded. It had the tinny high pitch of a goblin.

The runes of Eric's ward began to falter.

Griz said, "Perhaps we should discuss that later, Master." He went to the other side of the table for cover. "Once we're safely away."

Eric called his sword to hand.

He was ready when the ward failed, and the door was forced open. Eric swung his great sword with both hands toward the wall. It went clean through and beyond, over the white's head, from one end of the marble golem standing behind him to the other. The eruption of magic threw the goblin straight at Eric's leg. The white fell over unconscious, and his walking stick clattered against the floor. Eric picked it up, tossed it to Griz. The other golem hadn't moved, still looked whole. Eric poked its chest. The top half slid back and off. Its fall echoed throughout the library.

"We should probably go," Eric said.

Griz came around the table with his staff and the book in one arm and the walking stick in his other hand. Eric put a finger to the shaman's shoulder. Griz tapped the stick against the floor, and magic encompassed them.

Everything went white.

20

Eric placed three mithrinum bars on a shelf in the vault. Browns had already come through and cleaned up the broken glass. Skip planned to melt it all down and make more. Eric recalled the look of worry and disdain on the brown's face when he'd handed over the bars. It was enough to cause Eric to rethink his plan, or at least postpone it. He could always use the bars later. Besides, the remaining fiends were probably all dead. His vision blurred from the bars inward, a bird's-eye view of the village taking shape in his mind.

Griz had been studying the book they brought back from the conservatory. He'd still found no mention of a way to purify ley lines in any of the stories. Neither was there an indication of how they might've become impure. The closest to it was the tale of Kor's change of domain. The backlash of his influence over people and events that followed led to an unstable period of wild magic.

Other stories seemed to suggest the ley lines were tied

to all creatures, living and dead. They painted a picture of the ley lines as rivers of golden magic, filled by trickles flowing directly from every soul and spirit upon Taellus. It might have made for good story but sounded more fanciful than truth. If it were true, to diminish the ley lines enough to cause any magic tied to them to fail would take a catastrophic event that affected most if not every creature in the world.

If that actually happened, neither Eric nor Griz could see a way to repair the damage. All they could do was prepare.

They'd spent hours the past two nights in training for mental combat. It was a lot like when Eric had faced off against Tragona but without the advantage of fighting in his own mind. The imagined combat took place in the astral, a starry plane of existence between worlds, where the material fell away and thought took precedence. The attacks might have been imaginary, but their effects were all too real. Eric still had a headache and sore back.

It was Griz's hope when the time came, if it came, they could join forces with all of the Master magicians at the Academy. If what they might face was a god, if the story of Kor's imprisonment was true, they would need every available caster to defeat him.

That's a whole lotta ifs, Eric thought as he watched on. *Even then it's only half the problem.*

Assuming they could best a god, and it *was* a big assumption, what were they to do with him? Without ley lines to provide a constant flow of magic to new prison constructs, they had no hope of containing him. Eric was convinced killing Kor was the solution, while Griz had been taught gods were immortal and couldn't die by any means.

There was no way of knowing which was true. While Eric prepared for Kor's demise, Griz believed they needed a secondary plan. He believed the demon home world was their best option. The nexus their foundry had been built upon was ideal for powering a complex construct. A second

216

nexus of equal strength would be on the exact opposite end of Inexium. Both locations would be perfect for the prisons, so long as they could weaken Kor enough to separate his mind and body.

"How the fuck will we do that?" Eric had asked late last night.

Griz had admitted much relied on the magicians at Westorval, that such magic was beyond him. He'd also doubted any goblin would be willing to listen after what they did at the conservatory.

"The story of Taellus is not ours, Master," Griz had said. "We are not the heroes of this coming fight. All we can do is lend a hand where it's needed."

Eric glanced over at the vault he'd fashioned beyond the forest. It mirrored the one he stood in. He'd taken the time to speak to almost every spirit connected to him, even the demons and feys. They were less than willing to cooperate, so he'd put them in jars beside Tragona, with all the other monsters. The last thing he needed was a pack of wyverns terrorizing his people.

Of all those he'd spoken to, only one had a working knowledge of magic and the ley lines. He was a dwarf by the name of Korven. He'd been an enchanter most of his adult life, one who specialized in bolstering spells. He'd spent decades perfecting his wards but knew very little about what the ley lines were, why they worked or how to fix them. He was like an electrician with access to an outlet. Korven knew how to fashion wires and use them to power all sorts of things, but he had no idea where the electricity came from or how to alter it.

Eric found himself thinking it might be too late for Taellus. It wasn't his world really nor was it his fight. He considered asking Griz to send him back to Earth. It might be better to live as a golem than die trying to be human again.

There was no one left in the valley, other than the fiends. Sebran's people were in bad shape, with sickness and disease running rampant. Griz had shown Eric how to create sacks of grain. He'd then made enough to fill a wagon and sent it to the keep. Sebran was grateful but feared it might be too late. So many had fallen ill, and no help had been forthcoming from Westorval.

It made Eric think of Taliana. His attention switched back to the mithrinum bars. He'd been meaning for days to go check on her and her people. If the trolls hadn't been affected by corruption or sickness, it might offer a little hope for the future.

He turned and left the vault. The black goblins were waiting just beyond the door. They fell into step behind him, as Eric made his way up and out to the courtyard. Griz was still on the upper level of the castle poring over the book. Eric told Stalk where he was headed, stepped past the broken gate and went south toward the ruins. It smelled of rain but with the ground frosted over as it was they could very well be in for snow.

When they passed the first hill, all Eric could hear of the castle was hammering from the smithy. He looked back at the three following. They were different from the others in that they chose not to wear armor or clothes or carry a weapon. Their breath frosted the air, but none of them shivered.

"Maybe it's time you guys got names," Eric said as they walked. The ruins were in sight but at least another hour off. "How 'bout I call out some names, and if you like one let me know?"

They made no response, just watched him carefully as he spoke.

Do I just name them like dogs or something? Eric wondered.

Bel appeared beside him on a forest trail in his mind. Eric had thought there would be animosity between them when they first spoke, but the red general seemed to have left all his anger behind when he died. Eric could see Bel still felt emotions when watching him deal with other goblins, drew happiness from their interactions. When it came to the material world and the living, his priorities seemed to have shifted.

Eric had been angry at first, even thought to hurt the reds for their betrayal. Instead he left them alone, put them out of his thoughts, until one day he realized their deaths had been enough. There was no reason to hold a grudge if they didn't, to punish them for what essentially had become their afterlife. They were a part of him now. Their essence strengthened his.

Goblins are usually named for some meaningful or momentous occasion during the days that follow their making, Bel replied. He kept watch on the other goblins erecting a new home beyond the trees. *Unless there's something unusual about their appearance or the family decides a name should be inherited from one who passed away. I could suggest some,* Bel offered, and Eric spoke them as he did.

"Starless. Nightmane. Charborne." One curled his lip and growled. "Yeah? Alright, Char it is." Bel continued in his mind. "Duskbringer. Nightfall. Bloodborne." A second made two grunts and nearly looked like he'd smiled. "I guess that's okay. Not like we can be sued for copyright infringement over here. Blood it is. Okay, last one then. Pitchburn. Onyx." Eric sighed and gave a few of his own from his Warbones characters. "Stabatha. Krymor. Uhh, Pwner. Shenanigans." The last clicked his teeth and gave three quick nods. Eric laughed. "Alright, man. From now on, you're Shen."

It was midday by the time they reached the forest. It hadn't rained, but thunder occasionally rolled across the western horizon and echoed against the mountains. It felt as if a growing pressure in the air was waiting to be released.

The forest was much the same as his last visit. He even found his trail of broken and damaged trees where he'd been forced to make room. He followed it farther in, taking note of the darkened trunks. Those the feys had used for travel were eaten away, weakened by the traces left behind in their passing. The earth seemed to suffer the same ill effects, where roots had blackened, split open and spread their color into the mud.

It was quiet but for the wind, which grew strong enough to bend boughs. It whistled between the smaller trees and turned over decaying leaves into a wet tumble. The otherwise quiet reminded Eric of the valley. It was an absence of wildlife, a silence of empty cold with wind struggling to fill the void.

The smells came to him from beyond the hills before he could see the devastation. There was burnt wood and stone, the clinging sting of ash and charred detritus. He could smell and almost feel the sickly sweet mixed with copper, remnants of a battle with no one left behind. Mud buildings were caved in, collapsed and broken into pieces. The charge of magic lingered in the air and in the ground like vibrations from a distant shout. It went up the length of a fractured totem, across its bones and carved stone. Whatever ruin had visited the troll village, echoes of its passing could be seen in every corner.

Char and Blood studied monstrous tracks in the mud, cloven prints with thick talons like a horse born of nightmare. Shen pointed out others, the bare footprints of those who had fought back and lost. They were beaten down and dragged away. There was blood but no bodies. The tracks looked fresh, and at least one set reminded Eric of the collector.

Was it the Hunt? He followed the fresh tracks with his eyes. They led east. *Cledford. Fuck.*

Eric was suddenly surrounded by hundreds of spirits in his mind. Soldiers, servants, farmers, people from all walks of life urged him to help, to save their kin and keep his word to Lord Sebran. At the same time, Bel and all the goblins stressed a need to warn the others. If the Hunt was nearby, no one was safe. It was too much for him to listen and think clearly.

His vision shifted back, and he looked north.

"We'll gather everyone first," he said and began to run toward the castle, "then we'll head east to deal with the feys."

He'd had a hard enough time facing off against one. How was he going to handle a small army? He was no tracker, but even he could see there were enough prints throughout the village for at least twenty. If they were anything like the collector or the stalker, he wasn't sure he could win no matter how many helped.

Griz had magic. The blues, oranges and greens, even the browns, they may have been small but they were strong. He'd seen them fight, knew they were nothing to scoff at. They could at least be counted on to stand their ground. Sebran's mages, on the other hand, were all but useless. Unless they had more of those magic items at their disposal, the only help from Sebran would be what remained of his men.

Fiftyish soldiers, Eric thought as he ran and shoved aside the trees in his way, *fortyish goblins, not counting the crafters or new browns...*

Char, Blood and Shen were right beside him. It was the first time he'd seen them at a full run, kicking up mud with their feet, leaping forward and grabbing hold of trees by claw only to propel themselves even farther and faster ahead. It gave him a new appreciation for their strength and a little hope together they could pull this off.

If he focused, like they did, chose targets and took them down one by one, he might be able to avoid notice long enough to make a difference. It was the fear of being overwhelmed by them all at once that worried him the most. He felt confident he could face two or three without serious harm. Any more and he'd go down on his back, helpless.

Then don't let that happen, Bel said as if he'd spoken to

one of his reds. *You're outnumbered, not outmatched. Use your head. Don't worry, he said and crossed his arms. I'll be there, too.*

As will I, Korven said and replaced the image of Bel in his mind. *You have magic. Use it. I can't help with evocations, but if you forge a barrier or a containment or cast an augment, I will bolster its effects twofold.*

The enchanter faded, and Ella took his place.

You can do this, she said with a hand to his shoulder as he ran. *You're not alone anymore.*

Night was falling as they left the forest. The distant rumbles grew severe and more frequent, accompanied by the sudden crack of lightning strikes and explosive glow. Silver flashes lit the clouds, highlighted every billow and angry edge. Wind rose to a howl, buffeted against him from the east.

The storm had finally come.

Eric passed the ruins and saw the orange glow over the horizon. It bloomed like a second sunset, far brighter than any beacon. The radiance of its plea bled into the fires at its doorstep. Whatever battle raged in Cledford, sign of it was bright enough to be seen from hours out.

He felt a pit in his stomach. Eric already ran as fast as his bulky legs could carry him across the mud and between trees. He began to worry there wasn't enough time to gather the goblins. Every second he didn't turn and head east—

The sounds of battle rang out ahead.

Eric rose over the next hill and saw a small army of demons attacking the castle. Seekers had chosen hilltops to fire magic into the courtyard, lighting the night sky with volleys of purple fire. Servitors were at the fore, two packs of ten climbing up and over the wall. They tore away stone with each step, crumbled and cracked it beneath them. Greens loosed arrows down upon them but were forced to retreat.

There were others in the field Eric had never seen. Three

pairs of slender creatures on all fours spread their wings and took flight. There were spines up and along their backs from head to tail tip. With pointed maws of translucent flesh, a green glow began to emanate from their mouths. They circled the castle grounds and spat gobs in splashes of bioluminescence. Where magic fire struck it, the fluid erupted to persistent flame.

A handful of others coiled their bodies, like bristled centipedes into a ball of spikes. The flesh between thick plates of chitin began to hiss and release steam, grew so hot it reddened like an ember. Spines the size of a spear exploded outward toward the castle, sped through the air and impaled all in their path. Sections of wall collapsed from the impact, while other spines had carried over and caused the screams of dying goblins. Heat dissipated as the demons uncoiled and grew new ones.

Then came the behemoths, two massive beasts like living armaments. They stood four times Eric's height, walked on six legs that shook the ground with every step and left craters in the mud. Molten fire ran the length between heavy plates of chitin armor, dripped down and seared the earth. With a pair of wide horns, exoskeleton down the nose and a mouthful of jagged teeth, each had the appearance of a battering ram lumbering forward to deliver death.

The goblins stood no chance.

Retreat was their only hope of survival, if they hadn't already fled. Eric watched the behemoths trudge toward the castle. He felt frozen in place, uncertain what he could do against something so large, against so many. He was faced with the choice of fighting through to help the goblins, order them to get away, or trust they had they good sense to run while he left to help Sebran.

Either way, we're fucked, he thought and clenched a fist. It was stay and die by demons or run and die by feys. *Wait... Aren't they at war or some shit?*

An idea spurred him to action.

"We need to draw them east!" Eric called his sword to hand and ran for the nearest behemoth. "But first we kill the big ones. Go for the eyes, Boo!"

Shen clicked his teeth and bounded ahead. Char and Blood were a step behind. They threw themselves at a thick-skinned leg, dug in claws and started to climb in leaps and bounds.

Eric ran past for the next leg, swung his blade with both hands. It went in deep just below the knee, sent dark blood out in a spray. He'd come to a sliding stop and was pulled forward off his feet. The sword had only gone halfway through. The behemoth roared but kept on, kicked out and sent him sprawling. The sword was still embedded in its leg.

Shen scrabbled across the plates on its back when a multitude of high-pitched keens rang out from above. Blood and Char joined the fray, sending ichor and bits over the edge. Within moments tiny demons began to fall from the behemoth's back. Barely a foot tall, with claws and a barbed tail, they must have been waiting to be carried into the courtyard. By the cries and debris, there had to be at least a hundred.

As the dent in Eric's chest healed, he got back up and ran. He grabbed hold of his sword and pulled it free. He couldn't reach the unprotected underside but saw the leg was no longer able to bear the behemoth's full weight. He chopped at it again, careful to pull when the blade inevitably failed to cut clean through.

They were drawing attention. Spines struck near his feet, bounced off his back, even pierced the behemoth's leg. Purple fire flared above, and fliers were turning back. Suddenly the behemoth stopped and reared its head in an agonized cry.

Shen had reached an eye.

The third swing set it loose, like felling a fleshy tree. The behemoth bent its backmost legs and toppled over. It was all Eric could do to keep from being crushed. He rolled away and nearly fell from the nearby impact. With a stumble, he half ran and half tumbled towards its head. There were no bulky plates along the underside of its neck. While Shen completely blinded the behemoth, the other two dealt with the last of the imps. The massive demon wailed, a sonorous cry Eric could feel within his hollow. He brought his sword straight down through the knot in its neck and used his weight to push the blade down. Dark blood rushed out in spurts and hissed where it touched his metal.

Eric jumped from the growing pool and called out a warning to the goblins. They leapt from the carcass and joined him on a clear area of mud.

"Let's go," he told them. "Get everyone out and head east."

He was moving at a full run when the essence hit him from behind. Where the combined rush of a hundred imps had merely been a trickle, the behemoth was a dam breaking loose. Its burning crashed into his middle and washed over him like an inferno. More spines struck the earth nearby, bounced off his shoulder and back.

Eric needed a shield.

The fire within him abated and one formed in his left hand. It was fashioned the same as his sword, from a layer of his metal flaked away into a thousand pieces. It left his glyph more vulnerable to direct attack but gave him a way block projectiles. He used it to swipe aside a spine that would have taken Char in the back.

Servitors were all over the courtyard, fighting goblins like they were swatting at flies. Many goblins had already died. Their bodies lay bloodied and broken before the campfire. Its purple flames threw shadows across their staring faces. Eric's heart skipped a beat when he caught sight of the robes. Griz was among them, face down in the mud and forever still. Eric wanted to give in to the rage that swarmed his middle, to pay them back his pain ten times over.

Grieve later, Bel said, *when the battle is over. Your plan is a good one. You just have to see it through.*

"Retreat!" Eric shouted. "Fall back to the keep. I'll keep them busy." The wall was completely shattered in eight different places. He used his sword to point the way and headed for the eastern side. "Here! Go out this way!"

Essence rushed him from the campfire. It took him in the side as he stabbed a servitor from behind. One moment he was alone, fighting to keep grief at bay for someone he'd refused to believe was a friend, and the next Griz was beside him.

Barrier! the shaman shouted and slammed his palm against the ground. It sent demons flying in all directions as goblin spirits drew their weapons. They weren't merely in Eric's mind but stood before him as vengeful spirits. *Guard their retreat!*

Goblins ran past the magical barrier without harm. Demons who railed against it were scorched by its fiery touch. Korven materialized and strengthened it with his wards. The fiery barrier intensified to a ghostly wall of flashing sapphire.

I'm sorry we couldn't hold out longer, Master, Griz said beside Eric. *A spirit catcher was the best I could manage, so we could at least join you when you arrived.*

Eric nodded and swallowed hard. *I'm just glad you're here.* He fought back a servitor from the side, where the barrier didn't reach. *Let's just get everyone out of here. I can hold them off—*

The second behemoth crashed through the wall and into the courtyard. Only a handful of goblins were left beyond the barrier, blues who helped the others get past.

"Go with them," Eric told the black goblins. "Make sure they make it to the keep."

Eric backed away, used his shield to fend off demons on his left and swung at any who tried to rush past him for the fleeing goblins. He was careful to avoid the globs of burning mucus. The behemoth plodded on without a care.

226

Its payload of imps cried out as one and began leaping from its back. Eric looked to make sure the goblins were far enough away.

Are you sure about this, Master? Griz asked.

Oh, I'm sure. They've got this shit coming.

He waved his sword in front and imagined a barrier to protect from fire about himself. He connected the runes and waited for Korven to give it a boost. Backing away slowly, he was being overrun despite help from the spirit goblins. Eric called out another spell, without a framework, without purpose.

"Fire!"

The entire courtyard erupted in a white hot blaze of wildfire. Prolonged shrieks rang out to the pops and crackles of burning flesh. Blackened forms within the fire dwindled and became ash. His barrier flashed orange, brightened to yellow against the onslaught and broke beneath the gale. Eric was thrown back and over the tumbled remains of wall.

When the fire finally ceased, his entire front was still smoking and reddened from the heat. Eric got up with a pained groan. It felt like someone had forced his entire body against a stove. He looked out at the devastation. All the imps had been reduced to char, but the larger demons were only moderately burned. His wildfire had barely reached the behemoth's underside.

Great, Eric thought. *They've got fire resistance.*

He continued backing away, leading the demons east and fending off their attacks from the air. The servitors were about to rush him when an inverse whooshing sounded out. It was like speeding in a car with the windows down and suddenly closing them all at once. Eric instinctually swallowed to clear his ears.

When the magic settled, an army of red goblins and a dozen war golems appeared in the courtyard. A white stood in front with an opened scroll held out before him. He immediately cleared his throat upon arriving and began to speak.

"Grizzletongue Orebender," the white proclaimed in a loud voice, "you are under arrest for the unlawful entry of the conserv—"

They were swarmed by demons.

– 21 –

The unexpected arrival from Xanaranth had bought the others more time to get away. Eric thought to help, to use their distraction as an opportunity to attack from behind. There were too many demons. It was a massacre and a short-lived one at that. Eric could see even if he did lend a hand and killed a few demons, in the end he'd be left alone and overwhelmed. He turned and ran to catch up with the others.

His wounds were slowly healing. He hadn't noticed during battle, but he had numerous gouges and dents all over. The burn across his front was by far the worst. Its pain eased bit by bit as he ran against the cold wind and toward Cledford.

Within minutes he caught up, slowed his pace and turned. He walked backward with sword and shield at the ready. Char, Blood and Shen were spurring goblins on, while Griz walked beside him in his mind. The spirit goblins had lost their physical form, their fury spent, and were now resting in his forest.

How did they do that? Eric asked. He kept a close watch on the demons, both on ground and in air. It was the fliers he was most concerned about. *Better yet, how did you cast that spell without a ward?*

The rules seem different for the dead, Master, Griz said and studied his ghostly hand. *I'm able to cast much more quickly, project whole wards from thought alone. As for the others,* he said and looked beyond the trees along the trail in Eric's mind, to where goblins had built a small village, *emotion and mental state can affect spirits who linger on after death. Or perhaps they were able to manifest because you allowed it.*

Whatever had happened drained them, which was why they were resting. Eric could feel the power each spirit afforded him. The spirits who'd taken on a physical form offered so little it made him wonder if they could die—as in permanently. It felt like if he let them, they could expend their power as they saw fit. If they used it all, though, they'd be gone. It was just a feeling, a theory, and not one he was in a hurry to test.

Demons started running toward them.

We need a way to slow them down, Eric thought and looked over a shoulder. He could see the damaged wall far off in the distance, the entire keep on fire. They were still too far away. *Especially the fliers.*

There are only a handful of greens left, Master. They won't be enough.

How wide of a barrier can you make? Eric had a few other ideas, but they wouldn't work if this one didn't. Griz was still considering, when Eric said, *Nevermind. I'm giving you permission. Do whatever it takes. Just don't kill yourself. I need a barrier wide enough they won't want to run around and high enough they can't jump it. Korven, help him.*

Eric turned his attention to the vault.

You fight for me, he told them, *or you go back in the jars.*

For good. I will never give you this chance again. You don't have to kill them, but slow those fuckers down. He set them all loose—all but Tragona. *Not you, fuckface,* he said to the lone remaining jar. *I already know you can't be trusted.*

Wyverns took to the night sky in spectral form with a wild cry. Ghostly trailers of pale light traced their path toward the demon fliers. Demons and feys scrambled forth, stopped to eye one another with a feral disdain. As Griz and Korven worked a spell, the phantom feys and demons resolved to obey and charged west. Mud kicked up in their wake, and their prints smoked in pale wisps.

The barrier went up in a blaze of sapphire light. It stretched toward the stars as if the night air was on fire. Eric turned and ran, caught up to goblins and spurred them on. Many were wounded. All were tired. Yet they ran as if their lives depended on it.

Roars and cries rang out behind. Their echoed clash was drowned out beneath the crackle of bodies striking against the barrier. His spirits did as they were told, but Eric could feel the toll it was taking. His shield wavered and vanished back into a layer of metal. He no longer had the strength to call it forth.

Oh dear, Griz said and stumbled to his knees. The barrier failed, a wash of blue sparkle raining down across the mud. *I'm sorry, Master. I couldn't hold it any longer.*

It's okay, Eric said. *Go get some sleep.*

Griz disappeared from his inner sight.

Eric couldn't risk the others growing any weaker. He recalled them all and gave them new, separate areas on the outskirts of his mind. Their spectral glow faded back into the night. The demons, unhindered, continued their headlong run. Even the behemoth could be seen in the distance.

Goblins passed through the portcullis with Eric close behind. The keep from steps to tower was on fire beneath the beacon. Eric felt the magic fueling the inferno as a thrumming along his metal. It caused stones to burn and blacken, mortar to crumble and the air to fill with smoke. Sebran and a handful of men were guarding a corner of the courtyard. They stood between a group of women and children and a collector. Eric ran straight for the fey as goblins moved out of his way.

At the other end of the yard, beyond the broken wall, were hundreds of prisoners in glowing blue chains at their wrists and ankles. They were bound together by a cord of light that ran through each one at the middle and carried past to the next. Trolls and humans of all age and size were tethered together in long lines. They looked exhausted and starved, dirtied and bloodied, helpless and in despair. They were tied to fey horses that had eyes, manes and tails that burned as purple fire.

Between the prisoners and those still free stood the Hunt. Collectors were driving a final group to be chained, pushed or pulled the unwilling, dragged those unable by the collar or a leg. Stalkers walked what remained of the wall. One caught sight of a muddied girl hiding with her mother beneath an overturned wagon. It marked them with a short cry. A collector quickly grabbed them by the hair and dragged them screaming toward the others.

There were no dead, neither fey nor human. The feys who stood the courtyard with bloodied cudgels and coiled rope had no intention of killing their prey. They varied in appearance, as much as a collector from a stalker, but also looked much the same in that they were undeniably all feys. Their skin was so pale as to seem bloodless, with black talons and blacker eyes. Some had long dark hair tied back with silver chain, while others were short and fair and let their locks fly free over lengthy tapered ears. Some had sharp rows of teeth or upper and lower fangs, while others had toothless sneers. They all wore dirtied and tattered silk that billowed in the wind.

Eric struck out with his sword as the last group was put

in chains. The spell that bound them, that chained their spirits in spectral shackles and tied them to one another, sent out a sickly chill like the hollow cries of tortured ghosts. Lightning struck in a series of bright successive strikes, as if their capture had tipped the scale and let loose the looming storm. The collector's arm was cut free as the first drops of rain fell. Eric lunged forward and jabbed it in the throat to prevent it from becoming smoke. He and Sebran stabbed at its middle at the same time.

Demons entered the portcullis.

"I ask you for help," Sebran snapped and pulled his sword free, "and you bring demons to my doorstep!"

Eric kicked the de*ad collec*tor from his blade. "Yeah," he said as the demons rushed past to attack the feys. "You're welcome."

The rain was black. Its downpour was like a living shadow. Eric held out a hand to catch some, saw the black swirl within each drop. It reminded him of the corruption.

Oh shit, he thought. *Kor's free.*

As if he needed further proof, he could feel his power weaken. A piece of him had been stolen. A look inward to his vault revealed the jar had been taken.

Tragona was gone.

The rain had an immediate effect on all it touched. Some dropped to all fours and howled in pain as the darkness spread through their veins. Some growled and grew feral, enraged to the point of blindly attacking the nearest to them. Others fell over and lay still, either dead or unconscious. Those who physically changed became monstrous caricatures of themselves, with exaggerated features of face and body. The mentally affected seemed to suffer the worst, fought imaginary foes, tormented by hallucinations, harangued by voices no one else could hear.

Only Eric and the black goblins seemed unaffected. They were already corrupted, had been created that way, and Eric was protected from its touch. He could feel its magic against his metal like whispers in the dark. They sought to reach him, to break through but couldn't pierce the veil around his spirit.

Chaos ensued as feys and demons killed each other, as prisoners collapsed in agony or fought to tear one another apart. Even Sebran clutched his head, let fall his sword and screamed at visions only he could see. The goblins were at each other's throats. The grotesquely changed died first, either victim to the masses or from alterations life was never meant to sustain. Exposed organs, unwieldy bodies, flesh and bones stretched to breaking, they fell to violence and corruption in equal measure.

Eric had no way to help those who were suffering, but he could take advantage of the turmoil. He gripped his sword and eyed a fey. Lumbering stomps outside the wall drew his attention to the behemoth. Its mouth was agape and biting at delusions. It swung wildly from side to side but kept on for the keep.

"We have to stop it," Eric told the black goblins and headed for the gate, "before it gets in here and crushes everyone."

A woman leapt at his leg and tried to bite through his metal. All she managed was to break her teeth. Eric pulled her off by the waist and tossed her gently into a corner. He had a much more pressing problem, like how to deal with a crazed behemoth before it reached the wall.

Essence took him from behind, the combined rush of the resulting onslaught. By claw and magic, sword and fist, the corrupted sought to end one another by any means. The burning of a transformation overcame him as he ran. It was difficult to think clearly, with so much magic and mayhem, the mingled clamor of combat and madness.

He recalled the weakness of losing Tragona. It made him wonder if his transformations could be undone. If that was possible, he'd need protection from it happening again.

No one's gonna nerf me. Choice made, power spent, he wasn't all that surprised when nothing changed. *Typical.*

Char and Blood went for the eyes, while Eric ran for a front leg. Shen was close behind and carried with him a stolen pike. Eric swung at the tree-like leg. Shen ran up the wounded limb and toward the behemoth's mouth. It roared as Eric pulled the blade free, kicked out at him and missed. It began to stomp its front legs and snap at a hallucination.

Two more swings cut the leg free, as claws tore at its eyes. Shen jabbed the pike into its upper palate behind the teeth and leapt down toward Eric. Rather than catch him, Eric eased the goblin's fall with a palm and let the momentum carry through. Shen rolled into a tumble and slid across mud to a stop. Char and Blood held on for dear life as the behemoth tried to shake them loose, bit down and impaled itself upon the pike. It stiffened and fell forward, crashed through wall and the portcullis. Char and Blood jumped away as it fell, before joining the bloody collapse.

His next transformation did nothing as well.

Eric climbed the rubble into the courtyard. Those feral or driven mad were laying waste to everyone else, to those too weak to fight back, even the unconscious. Rain fell without relent, the storm driving them on. Pools of blood drenched the mud, swirled in the black of Kor's corruption.

Though demons had outnumbered the feys, it was clear they were going to lose. Eric jumped in and fought beside them, drove back the remaining feys until only a handful remained. Essence continued to rush him from the prisoners. The goblins were mostly gone, as were the humans. Only Sebran and a few others were left to deal with their madness.

Eric felt the third transformation take hold like a firm grip. It strengthened the bond between his spirits and his own. Not only did he feel each one more keenly, he could see glimpses of their lives when he focused on any one.

When the last fey fell, Eric held his sword out toward a seeker and four servitors. They were all that was left of the demons.

"Truce?" Eric asked.

The seeker paused. He seemed to be considering it, though his eyes twitched and darted from one end of the courtyard to the other. The servitors visibly shook as they fought against whatever magic held them in check.

"Why?" The seeker looked from the decimated goblins to Eric and the three blacks at his side. "Why now?"

"This rain," Eric said. "You can feel its magic, right?" The seeker gave a single nod. "It's from a god named Kor. He was just set free. He won't stop with just destroying this world. He'll come for yours too. A truce now means maybe we fight him together, before he kills us both."

The seeker was bleeding from a number of wounds. He put a hand to the biggest cut at his side. At his nod, the servitors turned and left south out of the courtyard.

"I will carry your proposal back to Karron," he said and began to limp away. He didn't stop but added, "You fight well."

With the feys all dead, the magic chains had fallen away into nothing. Maddened trolls and humans rushed to attack the others, leaping on those nearest.

"Kill the crazy ones," Eric told the black goblins.

As they picked up weapons to follow his orders, Eric went about doing the same. It didn't matter in the end. He could see the essence of all those who'd survived, the ones driven mad or in a coma. There were barely twenty left, and he had no means of curing them.

"Goddamn it," Eric said as he looked down at the body of Taliana. She'd been strangled by another troll, stomped into the mud in the chaos.

A column of black and purple fire erupted in the distance, bright enough to burn away clouds and light the night from days away. He didn't need to be told that it came from Westorval or who caused it. Anger roiled in his middle with a desire to kill.

"Kor," Eric said.

Though he seethed with grief and hatred, he didn't know what to do. A part of him wanted to go back to the castle, gather all the spirits from the catcher and make mithrinum goblins with the last of the fiends.

There isn't time for any of that, Ella said.

Rain steamed off Eric's shoulders. *I know.*

Another part of him simply wanted to go home. What good was he against a god? What good would it do if after all he'd endured if he died for nothing?

It's not nothing, she said. Others had gathered in the village in his mind, circled him with their unspoken desire to save their world. *It's everything. It's you and I and every life he plans to take.*

Why should I care? Eric asked bitterly. *What has this world ever done for me?*

You do care, Ella said. *I can feel it, as clearly as I feel the love for my father and my family and my people who need your help. We do right because it needs doing.*

Griz appeared and said, *Master, we serve the greater good and in so doing serve ourselves.*

Eric looked out at the column of fire, tried to imagine the sort of power it would take to create it, to corrupt an entire world with a single storm.

I'm afraid, was all he said.

Ella put a hand to his heart. *It takes wisdom to know your fears and courage to conquer them. If you go, you will not do so alone.*

"Courage, huh? Well, waddya say," Eric asked the black goblins, "wanna go kill a god?"

Char cocked his head to the side, Blood followed Eric's gaze to the northeast and Shen clicked his teeth. As one, all three turned and started walking toward the column of fire.

22

Eric laughed and said, "Hold on! There's gotta be a faster way than walkin' there." *Can we make a portal?* he asked Griz.

The shaman shook his head. *I've never been there. I need to see a destination to create a portal to it.*

I have, Ella said. She put a hand to the shaman's forehead. *Here, I'll show you.*

After a few moments he nodded and smiled at her. *Thank you. That should be enough.* He began casting a portal but frowned soon after. *There's too much magical disturbance. I'll need to create it outside the city.*

A portal appeared in the courtyard.

What about the survivors? Eric asked and looked at those still alive.

Griz said, *I can't undo what's been done to them.*

There is nothing you can do for them here, Ella said.

She'd put a slight emphasis on the last. It wasn't an overt statement meant to hurry him but a reminder how much he was needed elsewhere.

"Alright," Eric said. "Let's do this."

He touched the beryl light between the portal stones and shifted into chaos. The rain had settled to a light drizzle but encompassed all in its shadow. Stones in the road, the city wall, the flickering lanterns on either side were all slick with its touch. Screams rang out in the distance, the echoed cries of pain and loss, tormented shouts and maddened shrieks. Fire glowed across the city, lit buildings and inner walls up toward the castle. Great billows of black smoke roiled skyward from the east, where the pillar of magic fire burned.

Bodies were strewn everywhere, their blood upon the stones. From farmer to merchant, guardsman to noble, the corruption held no discrimination. It struck equally with malediction, twisted body and mind into unnatural shapes. Those who survived its touch either hid with their madness or hunted with a bloodthirsty fervor.

It's this way, Ella said.

She led him through the streets, where buildings had fallen over into dust and debris. It didn't look like fire had been the cause. There were no scorch marks upon the remains of wooden beam or stone blocks. They were simply eroded away, as if time had sped up and wrought its ravages within moments.

The mad quickly fled when Eric came into view. Each step he took joined the choir of pandemonium. Fresh cries filled the air the closer they drew toward the fire. The few crazed who tried their hand, who railed at his legs with makeshift weapons, were easily swept aside. They posed no threat but to each other. Char and Blood quickly dealt with those who persisted, while Shen had gone ahead to scout for danger.

Eric followed Ella up a cobbled hill, where shops had been half decayed. It looked as if walls, doorways and shuttered windows had been corroded by tendrils, eaten away in large swaths but left whole in others. Fire had spread farther down the street, where a haunted victim waved a torch at his delusions.

They continued north around a corner and into a large courtyard with white trees and tall, manicured bushes. Ella passed through the gated entry and stopped, her eyes locked upon the pillar of black and purple fire. It was the size of a football field across, so dense it couldn't be seen through and rippled outward with enough heat to melt stones at its base. Earth, stones and debris rose slowly into the vortex of flame.

It's gone, she said with eyes wide. *The academy, it's destroyed.*

They followed the sound of chanting to the other side of the pillar. Forty men and women in long robes clasped hands in a circle with eyes closed, chanting into the storm of magic fire and corruption. They were protected from the rain and flames by a barrier of light, but there were bodies among and between them. Another collapsed from the strain, her aura snuffed out. Those beside her closed the circle and kept chanting.

Laughter drew Eric's attention to a man in leather breeches and a white tunic. He had long black hair and eyes a luminous blue. Arms wide, he danced in the rain like a child. Magic trailed from his extended fingers, slender lengths of black that rotted all they touched. Trees, bushes, iron fence and stones, decomposed in an instant and flaked away where they were touched.

Another figure worked against the mages, toyed with their glyph from a distance. He spun wards and poked at sigils, trying to undo the barrier. Eric recognized him in the same moment as Ella.

Uncle! she said, but Tragona couldn't hear her.

"Kill him," Eric told Char and Blood.

As they moved to deal with the resurrected lich, Eric headed for Kor. Essence struck him from the side, a considerable amount but so far from a transformation he barely felt it beneath his anger. He called his sword to hand and threw it, a wide arc to the right. There wasn't much need for accuracy when throwing a twenty-five foot blade. It sliced through Tragona's protection spell and his middle, as the goblins leapt upon him. They clawed at his eyes and throat, tore away his magic jewelry. He fell to the ground in pieces, gurgling a cry for help.

The sword stuck into and through a distant building. Eric sent the blade away into a swarm of particles and called it back to his hand. He absorbed Tragona once more, forced him into the empty jar and back into the vault. Then he locked it for good measure.

Kor stopped dancing long enough to look perplexed. He glanced over at Tragona's pieces and raised a brow in mild amusement. He made a motion with one hand as if to raise the fallen man a second time. Eric felt a tug at his middle, but the vault held. The god looked Eric's way and clucked his tongue.

"It would seem you have something of mine," Kor said. He was older than Eric, possibly late twenties, with a golden sheen to his skin. His eyes were unsettling, with both irises a bright blue light. "I don't suppose you'd be willing to just give it back?"

"Maybe," Eric said, "if you'd just pack your shit and go home. Wherever that is."

Kor smiled wide. "That really is the most interesting outfit." He peered at Eric's chest, as if he could see past the golem. "Rather large armor for such a scared little boy."

Eric shrugged. "I don't deny it. I'd be stupid to not be scared. I'm still gonna kick your ass, though. Unless you wanted to shit talk some more?" Char and Blood came up behind him. "Like, what's with the glitter? You look like a stripper tripped and fell into a Ren Faire. I mean, you're not shiny vampire stupid-looking but pretty damn close." Kor's smile began to fade. "Aww, it's not all bad. I'm sure there's plenty of dudes out there into whatever it is you call this,"

Eric said and indicated Kor's outfit. "And is there a reason you're killin' *everyone*? Seriously, what's the fuckin' point in that? Oh boohoo, your sister stole your girl. Get over it already. The whole world's gotta die cuz you can't get laid? You're a god, for fuck's sake. Just make yourself a new piece—"

Kor yelled and thrust an open hand forward. Had it been a punch, Eric would've tried to avoid it. Apparently gods didn't need to physically touch someone to land a hit. The telekinetic force struck Eric in the middle, bent his metal and doubled him over. His feet dug up cobbles and made trenches in the earth as Eric was thrown a hundred feet backward. He tore trees from the ground in an attempt to slow himself and crashed into the iron gate surrounding the courtyard.

Eric sat there for a moment while the world rang in his ears. When his vision finally settled on a single image, he climbed back to his feet. The hand-sized crater in his middle was slowly bending itself back into shape. He let go and called his sword, had lost it somewhere during the flight.

Char and Blood had been thrown clear but were still alive. A clicking of teeth drew Eric's attention to Shen. He was clinging to a second story window of a half-building across the way. He pointed down toward a figure hiding in the shadows of an alley. It was confusing at first, because the figure had no aura.

"No more quips?" the god asked and stalked forward with arms wide. "You were quite the merrymaker just a moment ago."

Neither did Kor.

They're linked? Eric thought. *Or what? What the fuck am I seeing?*

Eric didn't wait for the next punch but threw his sword. It clanged against Kor and bounced aside, the blade bent where it had struck him.

Now that's some bullshit! Eric looked closer at the god. *Is he invulnerable or some kind of illusion?*

Eric rolled to the right but not before Kor attacked. The force took him in the side and sent him sprawling toward the building Shen was perched on. He smashed into and went through the iron gate, clawing at the ground to slow his beeline into stone. He slammed into both floors of the building and collapsed the roof onto his head.

Shen leapt free in time and landed beside the alley. He picked up a rock and threw it at the figure. The man groaned in annoyance when it struck him in the head. He flicked a hand toward Shen like swatting a fly and sent the goblin careening away.

It's a projection! Griz said with sudden realization. *Not mental but physical. The only way to stop it is to find where Kor really is.*

Shen already had.

Eric pushed at the nearest wall, toppled it over into the alley. The man cried out as he was buried beneath a pile of stones and mortar. The fake Kor glared and began running toward the alley.

"Stop him!" Eric said and loosed every fey and demon he could into a tangible form.

Each one a spectral image of their former selves, they leapt upon the projection, grabbed hold of every limb. It was slowed but kept on, dragging spirits along.

The figure that crawled out bloody and dirty from the pile of stones was a dwarf. Not the mythical sort but a half-sized human of odd proportion. His arms and legs were too small for his torso, with a bend in the bones that would've made it incredibly difficult to walk. His face was marred as well, with a forehead too large and jutting forward. He had a squat nose, thin lips and a cleft like an axe wound. His skin was mottled and pocked and had only splotches of beard. With a sneer, face reddened by anger, he kicked at the stones in his way.

243

If this was the god Kor, he looked as if hatred had twisted his body just as much as it had his mind.

Eric reached down for the little man, wrapped a hand around his torso. The metal began to whiten and flake where it touched him.

"You may have been protected from my rain," the god said, his mouth filled with crooked and rotten teeth and too large a tongue, "but you cannot resist my touch."

"Yeah, that's not at all creepy," Eric said, "but that's gonna be a hard pass." His metal eroded faster, and he wasn't able to pull away. Eric grunted from the pain. "No means no, asshole."

Eric called the sword to his hand. It swarmed toward his palm, pierced through Kor's chest and the ground underneath, pinned him beneath the pommel. He let go the blade and pulled free of the god's withering touch. The projection was nearly on him.

"Call that thing off," Eric said and raised a foot over Kor's head. Blood spilled from both sides of the god's twisted mouth. "You can bullshit all you want, but blood means you ain't immortal. Fucked up teeth or not, I will curb-stomp your ass."

Kor coughed up a gob of blood and spat it to the side. He waved away the projection. It vanished in a spray of gold dust and blue light. Eric recalled his spirits and relaxed his foot. He flicked the sword pommel, which sent a vibration down the blade. Kor grimaced.

"Now," Eric said, "let's talk about what you can do for me."

Kor put a stubby hand on Eric's foot. "Come join the fun, why don't you?"

The world shifted to starry blue upon a plane of pure white. Eric was vaguely aware of his golem body where his mind had left it, but here he was back to his human self. He recognized it as the astral, and he wasn't alone.

Twentyish mages faced off against Kor. Not the dwarf with

jacked teeth but the gold-skinned version from the cover of a bad romance novel. They had each summoned illusory creatures to fight, from giants to elementals, dragons to wyverns and all sorts of mystical monsters. Kor faced them as himself—or rather his projection. It could've been how he once looked before hatred poisoned his mind, or perhaps it was merely how he wished to be perceived. Either way, he took on all their creations with magic and bare hands.

While the mages seemed of a mind that bigger was better, Eric could see their tactic wasn't working. Each time Kor bested a projection it killed the mage. One by one they were falling and fading away.

A woman appeared to be faring better than those around her. She'd conjured an ogre with a giant club, and Kor was dodging its attacks. Hers was the only one getting close enough to strike. Eric moved to join her.

"Make it smaller," he told her. "Strength won't matter if it can't hit. And use a lighter weapon, like a sword or an axe. Stop going for the kill every time. Wear him down with small wounds, bleed him. Keep him busy with jabs instead of taking big swings."

She was straining to maintain the conjure, brow scrunched and sweating, her fists balled at both sides. Every punch or slap her projection endured weakened her resolve and the connection to her body. If her spirit was killed here, her body would soon follow.

Kor danced away from a gout of fire from a dragon and the end of a massive ivory column from a titan. The other conjurers were so big and clumsy they were more likely to get in each other's way than land a strike.

"Now!" Eric said. "While he's distracted."

The woman whirled on Eric and shouted, "Shut up!"

A sword appeared in Kor's hand. He lopped off the ogre's head, did a fanciful spin as part of his ongoing dance, and kicked the head away. The woman grunted and faded from the astral.

Pain burned Eric's left foot. He looked down and saw nothing wrong. His vision shifted to the physical, a brief glimpse of his golem foot, and saw Kor's little fingers still upon it.

I can't stay here, he realized but neither could he move his foot away. *Fuck this.*

Eric conjured Sorrow and Mourn to each hand and his full set of enchanted leathers. He may have been a griefer, who loved stalking and killing new players, who relished killing others on the battlegrounds and rubbing their faces in it, but he was also a dedicated raider. He put in the time, the dedication, the perseverance it took to have every item best in slot. If Kor wanted a one-on-one, he could have it.

No one beat Eric in a duel.

Well, except that one guy. He entered stealth and headed for Kor. *Fuck him, though, he cheated. Speed hacks and exploits don't count.*

Another mage faded away. Only three remained, and they didn't look like they'd last long. Eric admired their determination but couldn't help thinking they were stupid for not adapting to the fight. They all chose brute force over countering the attack style.

Eric drove a poisoned blade into Kor's back.

His body blinked and vanished then reappeared feet away and facing Eric. He waggled a finger and clucked his tongue, as if chastising a child.

"Who is the cheater now?" Kor asked.

"What? *You* are," Eric said. "You just teleported out of an attack!"

Kor looked over his shoulder, as if he could see the wound. "You still landed the blow," he said, "but sneak attacks are underhanded, not very honorable. What are we without honor, without rules?"

"Rules? There are no *rules* here," Eric said, "and I am *not* a cheater."

"As you wish."

Kor turned and threw kinetic attacks at the three remaining conjurers. Bones broke, skin and muscle tore free, and the last of the mages faded.

Of course he was toying with them. Eric inwardly sighed and couldn't help but wonder, *What the fuck am I doing here?*

Kor turned, now with a silver longsword in each hand. "Shall we?"

Eric gripped each dagger. "Let's dance, asshole."

He used every skill with perfect timing, from endless hours of practice. He vanished, reappeared and struck, evaded and dodged. After a solid minute of combat, he'd landed three bleeds and two stabs. He'd suffered a cut to his side, right thigh and forearms as well. He could feel them healing albeit slowly.

Kor had a sheen of sweat on his exposed chest that made his golden sparkles glitter all the more. He didn't seem to be healing, but neither was he slowing down.

"Why do you do that?" Eric asked, caught a blade in his left pommel and stabbed out with the right dagger.

Kor dodged to one side, pulled free his sword and danced away. "Do what?"

"That!" Eric said. "Dance like a cokehead. And why are you still wearing that Fabio-wannabe projection? We both know you're a butt ugly runt. Why hide it here? No one gives a shit what you look like. I certainly don't."

Kor stopped his prancing and narrowed his eyes. "I should have noticed sooner," he said and peered closer. "You're not alone." He waved an arm in a wide circle, and every spirit connected to Eric appeared around them in the distance. "How curious. Is this what gives you your strength?"

Kor spun and threw a sword. It sped through the air and struck one of Sebran's men through the chest. His name was Aldren Konah. He was a guardsman, a loyal husband and father of two boys. Eric had seen memories of the man's entire life and now felt them slip away like waking from a soon forgotten dream.

"You killed him," Eric said, voice quiet and filled with loss.

"Dear boy," Kor said and smiled wide, "I'm going to kill them all."

Eric gritted his teeth. "The fuck you are."

Listen up! he said to everyone. *This is now a raid! You have free rein. Pick a class, suit up and take this fucker down! Warriors to the front. Rangers and healers in the back. Mages in the middle.* Eric grinned. *Rogues, you're with me.*

One by one, nearly a thousand souls chose a class and donned their respective armor. Warriors in full plate or chain rushed forward to form a circle with sword and shield in hand. Mages in fiery and frosted robes took up their wands and closed toward the middle rank. Healers bloomed into white or gold robes, brandished staves and began casting protection spells. Rangers decked in full leathers or furs brought bows to bear and pulled magic arrows from their quivers.

The rogues appeared around Kor, stepped from wisps of black smoke. In dark leathers and face masks, dual blades in hand, they stood ready to strike as one.

All the feys, every demon, any creature that didn't quite fit the mold of a Warbones class, was given the freedom to fight for their lives however they wished.

Kor laughed in the face of it all. His body stretched, grew tall, elongated to a tail. In the span of a breath, he became a gold dragon. His metal scales glinted off the light of molten spittle dripping down from his maw. He swung his tail, and rogues vanished to avoid it.

"Let us begin!" the god roared and loosed his breath in a wide arc.

The fire struck against a protective barrier. Warriors rushed in with shield to fore, taunting and attacking to draw the god's attention. Rogues worked together with them, weaving their attacks between the heavy shields. Healers set to work, renewed their protections, mended burns and wounds, struck out with magic when they could. The mages and rangers sent out one volley after another, from enchanted arrows to bolts of fire and jagged shards of ice.

Kor was beset on all sides, barraged by unrelenting magic and steel. His scales bent and broke loose from a hundred different wounds. He swiped out with his tail, clawed the ground, even tried to take flight. Arrows and icy bolts tore at the membrane of each wing. Grounded, overrun, he lashed out in fiery anger.

Eric felt each one fade away, like losing a piece of himself. Whether human or dwarf, troll or goblin, their memories were slowly taken from him forever. He fought hard not to give in, not to anger or loss or even despair. They could win, he knew, no matter the cost. Too many lives were at stake and not just those connected to him.

Kor shrunk inward, collapsed, and became an earth elemental fifty feet tall. His wounds, however, carried over. Chunks of stone across his back were broken open and cracked. He bled molten rock along the ridges of his craggy armor and down the front of his earthen body. He brought a stony fist down, broke through a barrier and killed a handful of healers.

Ella was among them.

"No!" Eric screamed and dropped to his knees. It felt like he'd been kicked in the gut. He took in long ragged breaths, seethed as he eyed the god. He climbed to his feet, gripped hard both blades and returned to the fight.

Water! he called out. *We need water attacks!*

The raid persisted despite heavy loss and mounting wounds. They were growing weary with each attack. The longer the fight continued the less chance they had at winning. If they didn't fight smart, the god would win by attrition.

Kor had grown sluggish and given to fits of rage. Each injury spurred another wild attack that left him open but also cost the raid in lives. Ice and water struck him from all sides, eroded his body and ate away at his armor. His open wounds cooled to hard stone and slowed him further. It wasn't long before he relinquished the broken form.

He became an ice demon and faced fire, then a giant met by poisoned arrows and blades, a massive wraith against holy light, a bone devil opposed by hammers. Whatever new form Kor chose to take, Eric ordered a way to counter it.

Years of gaming had finally paid off.

"Hold!" Kor shouted and regressed to his dwarven body. Bleeding from countless wounds, from small cuts to large gashes, his twisted limbs broken and crushed, he breathed heavy and coughed up blood as he tried to speak. "Hold. Please."

Eric saw fear in his eyes. *You* can *die.*

"You give up?" Eric asked and closed the distance. He knelt over the little god, put a blade to his chest and fought the urge to drive it through. This fight had cost him hundreds of lives, people he would miss. Like Ella. Eric's eyes burned. "Please say no."

"I offer you," Kor said, struggled to get the words out, "a truce. I will give you what you *truly* desire...to be human, to return home."

"Then what?" Eric asked. "You're free to kill everyone on Taellus? Twist them into monsters like you?"

Kor gave a short laugh. "That is the trade."

"How the fuck is that any different from me killing them myself?"

The god looked at him in genuine confusion. "Only a fool would think inaction *causes* action."

Eric frowned. "Then I guess I'm a dumbass."

He drove the blade into Kor's heart. The god tried to reach for it, to pull it free. His arms were all but useless. The astral bled away. Eric was back in his golem body, standing over Kor.

"You fool," the god said and gasped for air.

Eric raised a foot and brought it down on Kor's head. "Yeah, you keep sayin' that." He ground his foot into the cobbles. "But I'm the one who's still alive."

His other foot was badly damaged from Kor's touch. It started to heal as the rain stopped, as the god's essence overcame him. The burning was so intense, so sudden, that the metal across his middle reddened and began to melt. Runes exposed, wards broken, Eric fell over to one side and onto his back in silent darkness.

Human! he shouted in his mind. *I wanna be human. Me. I wanna be me again.*

He kept repeating the thought through a multitude of transformations. Vision returned as his body began to change. The star metal faded in color to shades of silver, became stone, faded to shades of white, became clay, faded to shades of gray and finally became flesh. Over two dozen transformations, in various stage of alteration and hue, he could at last see skin. They continued to adjust, to shape him as he used to be.

Oh, he thought, *and gimme back what I lost.* With so many spirits taken from him, some transformations had been undone. *And healing,* he added, as if allocating skill points to a character. *Gimme better healing.*

With the essence fully spent, he climbed back to his feet. The spirit of Kor was there to greet him.

You fool! he said. *You've bound us for the rest of your life!*

Keep that shit up, Eric said, *and you can sit in a jar next to Tragona.*

He was suddenly cold and realized he was naked. He wanted clothes and suddenly had them, a black tee and blue jeans, socks and sneakers, a warm gray hoodie.

Do you honestly believe you can contain me? The little god crossed bent arms and gave a look of challenge.

I've got a better idea. Eric fixed Kor's arms and legs with a thought, made them straight. He did the same for the god's skin, teeth and beard. Eric made him into a perfectly normal looking dwarf. In the end, the god could even be called handsome. Eric conjured a laptop and opened it. The game was already loaded when he handed it to Kor. *Allow me to introduce you to Warbones.*

The god took it and sat in the alley, began to play with the computer in his lap and mouse against his thigh.

It looks like a caricature of life, he said and after a minute added, *The play is rather repetitive.*

Eric said, *Whatever, dude. Give it back then.*

Kor put an arm protectively around the laptop. *I did not say I didn't like it.*

Eric rolled his eyes.

"Oh yeah," he said. "I can do that now." He looked down at his hands, his fleshy arms and doughy stomach. "I should've asked for muscles or something."

Griz appeared beside him. *You look just as you were, Master.*

"I suppose," Eric said, "but not fully human. I can still see you guys, have all those abilities. I'm still a golem. Like a flesh golem or something."

Good enough to go home, Master?

"Yeah." Eric nodded, as if he was as close to getting what he wanted as he ever would. "I guess it is."

252

23

Eric was still cold.

He clenched his right hand and opened it, studied the lines in his palm, the faint blue of veins beneath, the striation of muscles when he extended the fingers. He could feel temperature again, pressure against his skin, the slight pain of digging nails into his palm. It felt like flesh but something more.

He called his sword to hand. It flaked away from his skin and became a long sword of silver-blue metal, with a black pommel in leather and golden sigils blazing across the blade. He called his shield to the other hand, and it appeared much the same, a heater of bright cobalt with faint argent streaks and flecks all throughout. Its sigils formed a circle of golden fire.

Eric pushed the sword into a section of broken wall. It slipped easily through, cut past solid stone in bright sparks and left the edges molten.

His suspicion was confirmed. It wasn't actually flesh he

was made of. His golem body had continued to evolve, grow stronger and only appeared to be human.

He pulled the sword free and sent the shield away. The sword shrank to a dagger by thought alone. He put the tip against the palm of his left hand and pushed. It didn't break the skin. He pushed harder, enough to grit his teeth. He still felt the pain of it pushing against him, but only a pinprick of blood appeared. It vanished in the same instant he pulled the blade away, healed closed with only a tingling of warmth.

He sent the sword away and picked up a rock. With the same effort it might've taken him to crush an apple, he reduced the rock to rubble and dust. He was stronger than he'd been as a metal golem.

There was a time he would've taken comfort in the thought, even relished it. To be powerful, unafraid, was all he'd ever wanted just five years ago. Now it made him feel isolated and alone, despite the hundreds of spirits so closely connected to him.

It made him wonder what there was to go home to.

Ready, Master? Griz asked.

Eric wiped his hand against his thigh. *Show me how to do it.*

Once Griz finished teaching him the portal spell, Eric opened one to the keep. He touched its beryl surface and stood in the courtyard. The black goblins arrived shortly after.

People were slowly waking from unconsciousness and delusion. The place was littered with bodies and blood and the debris of a way of life that once was. Fires burned, lit the night in a pale orange glow. The keep, its wall and the inner buildings were in a shambles.

So were its people.

Eric approached Sebran, offered a hand to help him stand. The lord took it and gave thanks. His eyes were still haunted, by whatever visions he'd endured and the terrible one before him. The smell of battle and death was overwhelming.

"Do I know you?" Sebran asked.

The way Eric was dressed, how clean he was, made him stand out in the carnage.

"I'm Eric. I'm—I was... the golem." Eric helped him with the others, walked them toward the steps where they could rest without sitting in blood and filth. "I went to Westorval. It's over."

"Is it?" Sebran asked. His gaze was distant, his voice too soft, his movements slower and shaky. "Good. That's good."

Eric assumed he was in shock.

"The castle is yours," he said. "I'm gonna go home."

"I see." Sebran stopped to face him. "You could stay, you know. You have magic. You could help. It would be much appreciated."

There was something off in the proposal, like he'd asked Eric to take charge. Eric did want to help. He thought it would be a good way to honor Ella. But as much as he sometimes hated it, he missed home.

He missed his family.

"I dunno." Eric shook his head. "I don't really belong here. I don't really belong there either, but we have pizza and video games, so..."

Sebran clapped him on the shoulder. "Whatever you decide, you're always welcome at my hearth." He turned to help another.

It sent a shock of warmth through Eric's chest, a tug and tingling in his middle. It was so rare to receive any sort of approval that he didn't know how to deal with it. He nodded and turned away, found a clear spot and opened a portal back home. With a hand out to its beryl surface, he paused to consider.

Eric stood there in the cold, undecided.

Acknowledgements

I'd like to thank Bob Nelson, Sharon Skinner and everyone at Brick Cave for all the time and effort they put into helping shape this story into a novel. Eric would approve. Probably.

Additionally, I'd like to thank Kyna Tek for all his hard work and attention to detail. It's always a joy to see one of my stories come alive in someone else's art.

Lastly, I'd like to thank Nelson Sperling for being my sounding board on this project and for enduring my many texts.

ABOUT THE AUTHOR

JOE GIUNTA has been writing for most of his adult life, in between bouts of serious online gaming. He continues to write fantasy novels, in both adult and young adult genres, in his selfish need to create worlds that amuse him. That others enjoy the work is a happy coincidence but one that he fully appreciates.

With a Bachelor of Arts in English from the Arizona State University, he is both an avid reader and addicted gamer. He writes novels full-time and longs for the day when those efforts pay some bills—seriously, even just one bill would be nice. For those of you who purchased copies of any of his books, he is eternally in your debt. Note: this is not a legally binding contract.

He lives with his wife, Lori—who is not only a doctor of both internal medicine and psychiatry, she's also an avid gamer! His daughter, Ada Rose, is fourteen at the time of this writing. She has yet to read a single one of his books, but at least she reads others. They all live happily ever after in the perpetual summer that is central Arizona (technically there is a winter, for about three weeks in January).

Joe attributes much of his success in life to good looks, incredible talent, luck, modesty, air conditioning, friends & family and his DVR—though not necessarily all in that order. Oh, and his computer.

He hopes you enjoyed this book immensely and will share it with a friend.

Visit him online at jagiunta.com

Made in the USA
Middletown, DE
16 August 2019